THERE WERE FIVE
THE TE...

Lhar—the gro... ...
very human ...

Syza—the healer, ...ing participant, a
woman plagued ... nightmare, and possessor
of the greatest medicine in the universe.

Nevin—the holy, a naive adventurer on his first
deep space mission, but whose knowledge was
the key to Tal-Lith's survival.

T'Mero—the guardian, master of the assassin's
craft, whose quartz knife stood between success and death.

Diri—the dancer, her silver skin electrified *any*
being's sensuality—but would she sacrifice the
lives of an entire people to her arrogance?

THEIR MISSION WAS RESURRECTION

A DEAD GOD
DANCING

A Dead God Dancing

ANN MAXWELL

AVON
PUBLISHERS OF BARD, CAMELOT AND DISCUS BOOKS

A DEAD GOD DANCING is an original publication of Avon
Books. This work has never before appeared in book form.

AVON BOOKS
A division of
The Hearst Corporation
959 Eighth Avenue
New York, New York 10019

Copyright © 1979 by Ann Maxwell
Published by arrangement with the author.
Library of Congress Catalog Card Number: 79-51843
ISBN: 0-380-44644-8

All rights reserved, which includes the right
to reproduce this book or portions thereof in
any form whatsoever. For information address
JET Literary Associates, Inc., 124 East 84th Street,
New York, New York 10028

First Avon Printing, June, 1979

AVON TRADEMARK REG. U.S. PAT. OFF. AND IN
OTHER COUNTRIES, MARCA REGISTRADA, HECHO EN
U.S.A.

Printed in the U.S.A.

A DEAD GOD DANCING

". . . extreme haste. Nonetheless, our computer selected fifteen probables, from which I chose a group of five. They have just completed intensive imprinting. They now know as much about the culture and conditions on Tal-Lith as we do."

[Scattered laughter.]

"I wish I could laugh with you. The mission has a deadline mimax. Think about that, Councillors: within a few hours I may send five hastily trained people to their deaths on an unknown planet orbiting an unstable star . . .

"I violated Contact procedure seventeen separate times in selecting this group. You are here to judge whether the violations make the mission unacceptable to the Concord. In my summation I will concentrate on the major violations. As is customary, all measurements are on a logarithmic scale of 1 to 10.

"Tov Ryth Lhar, group leader. Recent infac [psychic integration factor] is an ideal 7.316. He first worked for Contact as an integrator and has since become my most valuable field leader. Synthesist 9.15. Psi 8.798. Violation: he returned from leading a group on Saman less than eight days ago."

[Random exclamations.]

"Yes. Saman. I believe one of you personally decorated him for 'Unique Service to the Concord' . . .

1

"Nevin lo Skewml, specialist in energy-level-3b cultures. He is extremely skillful in his specialty. Negligible psi. Good infac. Violation: no prior field experience.

"T'Mero Verial Silariaoen, guardian and assassin. Extremely adept in the use of 3b weapons. Five maturities of Contact experience. Normal infac. Psi 5.613. Violation: he has not worked as a guardian for three centuries.

"Skandiri-Li, Lythen dancer. I see that some of you remember her; perhaps you were fortunate enough to see her dance the role of Keriamian. The computer determined that her skill and phenotype admirably matched Tal-Lith's god myth. Marginally acceptable infac. No psi. Violation: she is not nor has she ever been a Contact agent.

"Syza Zomal, healer. Probably the most gifted healer known to the Concord. I need not stress how valuable she could be on a no-technology Contact. She became a provisional Contact agent before she entered first maturity. We have not tested her since. We have no usable infac, no psi index; we have nothing but the certainty that she, alone, somehow preserved a Contact on Bjmsk. Violation: she refused integration after the Bjmsk assignment and was placed on inactive status. She still refuses integration; we have no reliable means of assessing her mental stability. Violation: she was coerced into accepting this assignment; the alternative choice was forced integration, which is a probable death sentence.

"No precedent for either of these two violations can be found in the history of Contact. Yet the computer would not give an acceptable mimax for Tal-Lith unless Syza Zomal was included in the group. When I questioned the computer it quoted the Concord Privacy Code. My application for override was refused."

[Exclamations.]

"Yes. Refused. Like the singer whose voice haunts

our conference, Syza Zomal is among those select galactic citizens who are exempt from official curiosity.

"There is one other violation that must be mentioned. Only agent Tov Ryth Lhar will be able to send off-planet messages. He will communicate only in an extreme emergency; or, hopefully, when the mission has been successful.

"Now, Councillors, if I may have your decision. . . ."

PROCEED WITH EMERGENCY CONTACT AND EVACUATION

1

PLATEAUS ROSE LIKE STONE WAVES FROM TROUGHS OF shadow. Crests eternally flattened by wind and scoured by sand, the plateaus forbade casual habitation. Talkyer, the natives called it, Place of the Wind. The wind stretched over black depressions, scraped cold fingernails of grit across unfeeling rock, boomed hollowly down blind canyons.

Lhar's taman moved restlessly, eager to join the others below. Lhar tightened the guide rein and spoke soothingly until the sound of the taman's gnashing teeth lapsed into silence. The wind curled around him, smelling of stone and drought and time. With narrowed eyes he watched the Contact group ride carefully through the boulder field at the base of the plateau. T'Mero was already far in the lead, scouting trails that would lead from the jumble of plateaus and canyons to the brackish marsh that showed only as a smudge across the distant horizon.

T'Mero vanished into a cleft between ochre walls; Lhar hoped it was not another blind canyon. The route that they had chosen from recent survey holocubes had proved impassable. In the tenth-cycle between survey and landing a rockfall had sealed a crucial pass. Their alternate route was still open—barely. Numerous detours had tripled the length of the journey. For three days they had been on half-rations of water; today the ration was reduced to one-third. The animals had none, but fared better; if necessary they could work without water for up to eight days. That

5

left five days for T'Mero to find a trail out of the stone maze.

Lhar watched Nevin's taman move out of sight, following T'Mero's tracks. The trail was plain; no other living thing had passed that way. Diri's taman followed a short distance behind, moving with an odd gait. When Diri had not been able to control the beast, T'Mero had snubbed its nose to its chest. It was awkward for both taman and rider, but preferable to having a famished omnivore loose among the smaller animals.

After an interval of emptiness and wind, Syza rode into view on his left. The muzzled pack taman she led were roped together in a long line. Occasionally a drifsen would lope up and encourage a lagging taman. Syza's whistle pierced the wind; with a golden blur of speed the drifsen returned to help its mate with the drifs. Unlike taman, drifs were not belligerent; two well-trained drifsen could control a large herd.

With a last clear whistle Syza and the animals moved into a shallow trough. They would be out of sight until they circled the boulder field. Lhar held his impatient taman and waited for the animals to reappear. As he waited, strange music drifted up, a sound not unlike the wind. He forced his taman to stand quietly and listened with total concentration. All he could hear was the erratic click of hooves on rock. His taman's ears flicked forward, remained in an erect fan to gather in the vagrant sound. Lhar held his breath and thought he heard a faint melody telling of loss and wind and the beauty of a cold mauve desert beneath an alien sun.

Long after the sound had died he waited quietly, hoping to hear more, not really believing he had heard anything. A sudden wind enveloped the plateau. His taman's skin rippled nervously; its long neck stretched into the cold wind. With a snort, the taman cleared its nostril hairs of dust. Lhar looked up from the boulder field to the distant horizon.

The horizon had disappeared.

Where land had been rose a film of dust. As he watched, sky and desert became a heaving ochre curtain. He sensed its distant, turgid weight, power which would flay and grind all beneath it. His taman snorted again and began a low, booming call. The hair on Lhar's skull stirred in primal response; if he had not already sensed danger, he would have known its presence by the taman's call. His mind reached out to T'Mero, urgently.

Storm coming. Bad. Any cover ahead?

We're on a long incline. Might be something at the bottom.

Run for it. I'll help Syza with the animals.

Lhar's golden taman needed no urging to slide down the plateau and race through the boulders. Every instinct in the taman demanded that it intercept the pack taman and lead them to shelter. Over the wind and the rush of his own taman, Lhar heard a continuous rumbling. Through wind-teared eyes he saw the pack taman hurtling toward him. Syza's distant but still piercing whistles punctuated the thunder of hooves.

Lhar reined his taman up sharply. There was no need to warn Syza of the danger; taman, drifs and drifsen were in full flight toward him. He prayed to childhood gods that the harnesses held. The loss of tools and clothes would be inconvenient. The loss of waterbags could be fatal. Lhar fought with his plunging taman and his eyes strained to distinguish a rider in the mass of running animals. He cursed Syza's refusal of mindtouch and the unbending will which enforced it.

A pack taman stumbled, somersaulted, fell in a tangle of harness and flailing legs. When it tried to get up the beast fell again, hobbled by a loop of harness. Behind the struggling animal loomed the frightened racing herd of drifs. The drifs did not swerve; in their panic, the downed taman did not exist. A drifsen

7

slashed razor fangs across the lead drif's shoulder in a futile attempt to turn the herd.

The taman was doomed, and with it as many of the drifs as were killed or maimed in the pile of flesh that would come as one drif after another was tripped and trampled. And Lhar could only watch. The drifs would reach the taman long before he could.

A dark shape separated from the laboring drifs. A taman fully extended, head down, ropy tail lashing. Stretched low over its driving shoulders rode Syza. In her hand a quartz knife refracted light in splintered colors. Behind her ran the golden shadow of a drifsen. A crystal arc flashed over the harness and the taman was free of its hobbling pack, but the animal was too dazed to get to its feet. The running drifsen leaped on the taman and sank its claws deep into struggling flesh. With a scream of terror the taman was on its feet and running.

Drifs poured over the pack and harness in a bellowing mass. A few went down to be trampled into shapeless smears, but the rest of the herd survived.

With a shout Lhar released his taman and raced along a diagonal that would intercept the pack taman. When he appeared in front of the running animals his taman gave a hoarse call, and repeated it until the other taman followed. Lhar eased his taman toward the cleft, slowing the pace by degrees until the animals were no longer in panic flight. Soon he heard what he had been straining to hear above the staccato of hooves—Syza's shrill commands to her drifsen. The herd was catching up.

As was the storm. Lhar felt a sudden thickening in the air, a gritty swirl heavier than the dust stirred by running animals. He looked back and saw the drifs just as the storm overtook them. He yanked on the rein, forcing his taman in a wide turn. After a few instants of confusion, the baggage taman ran ahead without their leader, spurred by their fear of the storm. After a fierce, swift battle, Lhar's golden

8

taman obeyed its rider and matched strides with Syza's mount.

Lhar shouted over the sound of wind and hooves, but Syza could not hear him. His anger blazed through her tightly held mind. He saw the instant negation which swept over her face, sensed the force of her resistance ... and felt the cold reluctance of her mind-touch.

T'Mero found shelter, 20° right.

Syza's whistled commands split the air. Drifsen deflected the herd toward the right. Then T'Mero's mind, cool and machinelike as always, told Lhar of trouble ahead. Lhar allowed his taman to overtake the pack animals as he relayed information to Syza.

Cliff before shelter. Narrow path at end of boulder field. Slow drifs or they'll be killed.

More whistles sent the drifsen ahead of the herd. Just as Lhar managed to turn the pack taman toward the cleft, the leading edge of the storm enveloped them. In an instant, ground and sky melded. Abrasive wind scoured even the thick-furred taman, driving them before its irresistible power. The pack taman turned their backs as one to the storm and slowed to a walk, bodies heaving, coughing when even their bristled nostrils failed to filter all the grit from the air.

It was no longer possible to lead the animals. Instinct decreed that they turn their rumps to the force of the storm. If their gold-coated leader wanted to expose his head to the cutting wind he would do so alone. Nor would they be driven. Lhar would force one to walk at an angle to the wind, only to have it swiftly turn back the moment he concentrated on another. He could either drift with them before the storm or tie them together and try to lead them at an angle to it.

Under normal conditions, roping the taman one to another would have taken only moments. But wind-driven sand made vision painful. Lhar counted to himself as he tied the taman one to another. He was working on the eleventh rope when a blast of wind

9

yanked it from his hands. The rope leaped and the knotted end cracked against his cheekbone. The jagged cut spilled blood which the wind spattered over his eyebrows and hair. In moments his face was matted with a mixture of blood and grit. The twelfth rope was slippery with blood.

Lhar waited for his dizziness to pass. One side of his face sent searing messages to his brain. One eye pounded with the magnified rhythm of his heart. Calmly, he began to work with the pain. His body took on the relaxed tension of mental effort. He did not deny the validity of the body's warnings. He acknowledged the pain fully, then damped down its urgency. When he resumed normal consciousness, T'Mero was patiently repeating his efforts at mindtouch.

The drifs are safe. Syza is out looking for you. Said you were hurt.

Lhar readjusted his hood and scarf. *How long ago did she leave?*

Four and one-half standard minutes.

Hold mindtouch. Lhar widened his mental awareness, letting his senses lift, float, and seek T'Mero. He felt a distinct pull toward his left. As he had suspected, the storm's direction had shifted while he was roping the taman together. *I'll find Syza. Hold mindtouch for bearing.*

The grit had thickened. During some gusts Lhar barely could see past his taman's ears.

Syza.

Here. Reluctantly.

Lhar let his awareness float again until he sensed a presence like an ice sculpture, burning with green flame. She was directly between him and T'Mero. Lhar kept contact as he urged his mount toward her—and was nearly jerked out of the saddle as the guiderope he held snapped taut. The taman, though securely roped together, still had no intention of exposing their heads to the storm. He tied the lead rope to his saddle and once again urged his taman forward. With glacial reluctance, the string of animals confronted the wind.

Go back, Syza.

No.

For the first time he sensed an emotion other than distaste in her contact. Danger.

The storm will break soon.

Lhar squinted at the pulsing waves of wind-driven rock dust, felt again the abrasive, implacable edge of the storm, rocked as a gust of wind nearly blew him off the taman.

Break! Sweet Xantha, if it gets any worse—send me your drifsen.

Then Syza appeared just in front of him. Her dark purple hood and gritscarf completely covered her face; even her eyes were muffled. She made no sound, yet the drifsen ran quickly along the line of laggard taman. On an impulse, Lhar's mind reached out to a drifsen; there was awareness, but it was as slippery as quicksilver. The taman began to trot as the drifsen moved among them like fanged shadows. The trot became a pace, then a lope. Lhar pulled his hood over his face and concentrated on T'Mero.

A choking wall of grit and small pebbles broke over them. Both riders bent low on their mounts, coaxing greater speed. Lhar coughed repeatedly, though the air he breathed was strained through both scarf and hood. For the taman it was worse. The protective hair in and around their nostrils was clogged with grit. Constant snorts gave only fleeting relief. He could hear the sound of their labored breathing even above the storm.

Lhar knew they could either stop and pray that the storm did not kill them or run and pray that the cliffs did not kill them.

Syza. Has the storm peaked?

No. We must get to shelter before it does. Soon!

For the first time Lhar struck his taman. With the will and stamina of the desert-born, the taman stretched into a labored gallop. The drifsen made sure that the others kept pace through the choking purple wind and staggering changes in air pressure. An

11

arrhythmic, blind plunge into darkness finally ended with a jarring slide down into the shelter of an ancient gully. Somehow they had avoided the cliffs.

The taman snorted and coughed, clearing their nostrils in the quieter air of the ravine. Without urging they walked forward, following the sinuous course of a long-dead river. Dust sifted over everything, but the steep walls and turns of the ravine baffled the full power of the wind. The ravine deepened into a narrow canyon, free from all but occasional shouts of wind.

Lhar lowered his hood and unwrapped his gritscarf, grimacing as the cut over his eye reopened. The eye itself was swollen shut, but he could see well enough to guide his taman beneath an overhanging ledge of rock. When he dismounted, T'Mero was waiting.

"Where—drifs?" said Lhar, coughing.

"Up canyon. There's a blind spur. The drifsen will keep them there."

"Good. Where—"

Lhar stopped as Syza rode in and pulled her gritscarf off. On her face streaks of sweat-washed skin alternated with irregular bands of dust, but most startling were the dark channels of exhaustion around her eyes. Wordlessly she dismounted and began unpacking the lead taman. Her hands shook over the knots. She reached for the pack bag, heaved it onto her shoulder and would have gone sprawling in the dirt had not Lhar and T'Mero leaped forward to catch her. Lhar took the pack.

"T'Mero, send Diri to help with the taman. They're too tired to bite even her."

Syza started to speak, coughed, then managed a hoarse whisper. "You'll have to sponge out their nostrils and mouths. A tiny drink." She saw Lhar's blood-streaked face and swollen eye, then looked away. "You require healing," she said tonelessly.

"After you rest."

Lhar felt her surprise and her acute relief. He watched narrowly as she was half led, half carried to the shelter of overhanging stone, and he wondered

12

why she radiated fear at the thought of healing. Somewhere in the Centrex files was the answer. He ran his fingers absently over the coarse fiber belt that concealed the many fine wires of his psitran. He could assemble the psitran, contact Yarle . . . and be told again about the Privacy Code.

With a feeling of unease he turned and began removing packs from the taman. By the time he finished, his mind was already immersed in other difficulties. A reluctant healer was the least of the problems he faced on Tal-Lith.

The storm thrashed and groaned and spat grit over the steep canyon walls. Occasional blasts of wind evaded the natural baffles protecting the huddled animals; the pervasive dust made breathing miserable and seeing impractical.

"How can she sleep so long?" said Nevin, looking enviously at Syza.

Lhar shook out his gritscarf and replaced it before opening his mouth. "Exhaustion. Controlling those taman and drifsen is work. Especially the drifsen. Their minds are elusive."

"Minds?"

"Syza used psi to control the drifsen. How do you think she heals if not with her mind?"

Nevin moved uneasily. "I never thought about it. All my time has been spent studying retrograde cultures."

"That's why you're here. You worry about nursing this culture through exodus intact. I'll worry about Syza."

"Glad it's your job."

Lhar let go of the tent flap and turned back toward the younger man. "Psi talents are no better or worse than a talent for singing or dancing or leather working," said Lhar slowly. "The Chanteuse was born with a special ability. Do you dislike her for that?"

13

Nevin looked shocked. "No one could dislike her for anything! The whole galaxy loves her, whoever and wherever she is."

Lhar smiled. "Psi is just another talent, no matter what your native culture taught you." He turned back toward the flap. "I have to check on the drifs."

"They'd better stay healthy. In this culture they're second only to water as the source of life."

"And prestige."

"Ugly beasts," said Nevin. "They smell like singed zarf."

"A matter of taste," said Lhar over his shoulder. "You'll acquire it."

As Lhar had expected, the drifsen had the animals under tight control. None looked sick or lame. He took his time checking them anyway. As he finished he sensed T'Mero approaching from behind.

"Everything clear?" asked Lhar.

"No large animals have moved into the canyon. No water lines anywhere on the canyon wall. N'Lith's storms are dry."

"Was Syza awake?" said Lhar, assuming that T'Mero had also checked the tent.

"No."

"Diri?"

"Coping with Nevin."

Lhar gave a last pat to the drifsen lounging at his feet. "I hope Nevin's innocence was more apparent than real. Were the waterbags secure?"

"As long as Diri is busy, yes. Her discipline goes no further than dancing."

"She'll learn."

Lhar and T'Mero walked slowly to the tent. Syza was awake, examining harness for signs of wear in the muted tent light. She glanced up at their entrance, then returned to her work without a word.

"How do you feel?" asked Lhar.

"Better."

"Your drifsen have the animals well under their fangs."

14

Syza said nothing.

"There's more to this assignment than animals and harness. We are supposed to be a native khaner, a breeding group, an extended family. Friends. Your preference for being left alone does not coincide with the reality of a native khaner."

Syza's slim, chapped fingers tightened on the harness and her mind shied from the unwanted contact. When she looked up her green eyes slid away from his unhealed cheek.

"Yes, the drifsen are very quick," she said quietly. "It's a pleasure to work with them."

Before Lhar could respond, Diri and Nevin pushed aside the flap separating the sleeping area of the tent. Nevin watched Diri with a look of stunned admiration; obviously his innocence had been real. Lhar quickly decided that this was an excellent time to test the depth of Nevin's Tal-Lith imprint.

"Nevin, what's your function within the khaner?"

Nevin looked blank, then said hastily, "I'm a miran."

Lhar waited.

"I'm mur-Lith. My life is spent pursuing the subtleties of her truth and essence."

"What is Her first command?"

"Waste nothing," said Nevin promptly, "especially not water, children, and fertile women."

"Where do you come from?"

"The place you—the natives we will meet—call n'Lith, without Lith."

"A lie," said T'Mero. "No one can live in n'Lith."

"We live on the edge of the desert, as you do," said Nevin easily, wholly into his role. "Surely your legends speak of the past when the river flowed longer and people settled on the far side of n'Lith?"

T'Mero grunted, but said no more.

"Legend," said Lhar. "You're real. How did you get here?"

"Lith was bountiful this year. The river stretched its tongue very far into the desert."

"Is that true, Syza?" said Lhar.

15

Syza looked up again. "It's true. Ask your First Khaner if the river was not larger than in past memory."

"Who leads your khaner?"

"If the question concerns Lith, that one," she said, pointing to Nevin.

"If not?" said Lhar.

"The one called Lhar rides the golden taman."

"And you?" said Lhar, turning suddenly on Diri.

"I am mur-Lith. I dance for Her."

"Why are you hidden in all those robes? We can't even see your eyes clearly. Are you n'gat?"

"I'm not deformed! When I dance at the Festival of Union, you'll see the truth."

Lhar turned on T'Mero. "You?"

"T'Mero the Hunter."

"Syza, what is the history of Tal-Lith, particularly the far side of n'Lith?"

Syza set aside the harness. Her eyes were iridescent in the dusky tent light.

"Long ago," she began, "before the time of my khaner's memory, Tal-Lith rolled green and fertile beneath the sun. But we were sinful. We turned away from Her beauty. Lith removed Herself from our wickedness and Her river no longer laughed. The land became dry, barren, empty. At last my people stopped crossing the rocks. We called them n'Lith and became isolated from others.

"Nevin mur-Lith believed we were being punished for straying from Her. He believed that if we could find Her river and the people who drank from it we would once more hear Her laughter."

"You've caught the melody of their ritual speech," Lhar said. "Excellent. Are the facts correct, Nevin?"

"Basically. The target population does have stories of a people beyond n'Lith. Apparently there was trading before the desert became impassable. This has been a good year, though. It's possible that pilgrims would try a crossing."

"Our trade items?" pressed Lhar.

16

"Gifts to Lith's people. The artifacts we have are different enough from the native wares to be unusual, but not different enough to be alien."

"What about us?" said Diri. "Even with me wrapped up we're a zarf's nightmare."

"Well within native standards," said Lhar, wondering if her imprinting had failed. "They've had an extraordinary mutation rate in the last several thousand cycles."

Diri's silver hands flashed restlessly out of her muffling robes. "This Festival of Union I'm going to dance at—what if we're late? The kerden storm is as strong as ever."

"The storm will end tomorrow," said Syza quietly.

Lhar accepted her comment without question. "We'll use the time to perfect our roles," he said, ignoring Nevin's sudden questioning look. "Once we reach the river and follow it toward the city we can expect contact within days. Diri will dance at the Festival, be worshiped as Lith's image, tell the natives we're Her messengers . . . and leave. Within one cycle, three at most, the population of the city will be prepared for exodus and resettlement on a new planet. And you will have the pleasure of knowing you helped save a race from extinction."

Diri grumbled and thrust her hands out of sight in her sleeves.

"Anything else?" asked Lhar.

"Songs or chants or both," said Nevin quickly. "They're nearly as important as the dance. I can't carry a tune in a grav net. Who is our khaner's voice?"

"Syza."

Syza drew in her breath suddenly. "I'm a healer, not a singer."

"Contact said you had a pleasing voice." Lhar looked at her with sudden intentness as his mind correlated odd facts into an improbable theory. Her eyes burned in her pale face and she stared unwaveringly at him.

"Is nothing private?" she asked bitterly.

17

"Not on a mission. Ask Nevin."

Nevin looked puzzled, then squirmed as comprehension came.

Syza ignored him. "How can the natives expect a khaner this small to have both singer and dancer?"

"We aren't just any khaner. We have Lith's image with us."

Syza said nothing.

"Is public singing taboo in your native culture?" asked Nevin curiously.

Syza picked up a piece of harness and began rubbing oil into it.

"T'Mero," said Lhar, "start Nevin and Diri on the throwing stones."

Lhar waited until the others had left before he sat across from Syza and unceremoniously took the harness from her hands.

"Agent Zomal, either you convince me that there is a very good reason why you shouldn't sing or I will trip the psi net and get a ship to pick you up."

"My songs are wordless. They aren't at all like native songs."

"Wordless . . . did you sing while you were herding drifs?" he asked suddenly.

"No."

The lie did not bother him as much as the reason behind it. He sat very quietly, recalculating Syza's relation to the whole of the mission in view of the new facts. He sensed Syza watching him covertly through the curtain of bronze hair which swung out from her downcast head. He had an odd, double sensation in which he was her, wondering what thoughts lay behind the handsome mask of his face. The sensation vanished.

Beauty is a matter of taste and culture, Syza. We must have much in common; to me you are very beautiful. And if what I suspect about you is true . . .

There was no response. He realized that she did not know she had inadvertently reached out in mindtouch.

He sighed, and when he spoke his voice echoed his inner regrets.

"I'm sorry, Syza. You'll have to go back. I can live with Bjmsk, but I can't live with a hostile team member. It's too dangerous."

"Who is Bjmsk?" she asked in a thin voice. "Is he or she dead? Was it someone I couldn't heal?"

"Bjmsk is a planet. According to Contact, you healed it very nicely."

Syza looked at him without comprehension, fear darkening her eyes.

"Kere Zomal died on Bjmsk," he said bluntly, and sensed tremors of memory swaying through her mind.

"Did he . . . ?"

"Part of you knows, Syza. Remember."

"I married Zomal on Earth," she said dully. "He had entered Decline. I healed him and healed him and healed, and then I lived on Fshamn. Alone. Alone. No one demanded my energy in healing or my soul in song. Free."

"You'll never be free until you remember," he said softly.

"You mean I'll never heal until I remember! Or didn't Contact tell you that I lost my talent when I lost that year from my life?"

"You can no more 'lose' that than you can 'lose' the color of your eyes. Was it difficult for you to heal before Bjmsk?"

"No," said Syza, brushing her hair away from her face with an impatient movement. "What was hard was ignoring the truth."

"I don't understand," said Lhar, his voice undemanding.

Syza was silent for so long that he was afraid he had lost the fragile thread of rapport. Finally she spoke in an emotionless voice.

"I was raised in an Earth commune by Uniparents. They couldn't train my talent. It was a long time before I found out that I could bypass a patient's consciousness and still heal. I was forever discovering

19

things in their minds. When I told my Uniparents they insisted I was lying. 'Dear kind brother Yirn could never lust after his Unidaughter, Syza,'" she said in a voice of grating mimicry. "'You must cleanse your mind of such thoughts, child. If you think of evil you will be evil.'"

Lhar listened quietly, intently, trying to feel what it had been like to be a sighted child in a world of the determined blind.

"They taught me to lie and called it truth. They taught me I was evil but could be redeemed by healing them. They—" Syza spread her fingers in a rigid gesture of rejection. "Zomal taught me to heal using only their bodies. He also taught me that Uniparents were not the only people in the universe. They did not know the whole of creation."

"And you loved Zomal."

"Of course."

"And he loved you . . . of course."

Syza's eyes narrowed. "You sound just like them. They didn't believe anyone could love me either. They were wrong. I'm not evil."

"You misunderstood, Syza. I know you are not evil."

"It's enough that I know."

Lhar sat unmoving, mind racing to analyze and correlate and extrapolate from her reactions and his own scant knowledge of Zomal and Bjmsk. It had been his choice to accept Syza without a recent infac. Now he had to live with it or send her back under a virtual death sentence. Or force an integration right here and probably kill her himself.

"What is singing to you that you risk forced integration rather than share your voice?"

He looked at the tight planes of her face and thought his gamble had lost. Then the hair on his body stirred as thick impossible harmony surrounded him. Wordless, yes, but gravid with despair and hopelessness, a shroud of song that sucked light out of the air, smothering, crushing, a clear melody revealing a clouded soul. The voice was one he had often listened to with pleasure. Now it was a curse.

"Enough, Chanteuse."

His eyes were unfocused as he integrated her identity into the probabilities of Tal-Lith. When he finally spoke his voice was tight.

"You will heal us?"

"Since Zomal I—"

"Will you heal us?"

"I'll try."

"You will sing if I require it?"

When she said nothing, he took her cold hand between his fingers and spoke gently within her mind.
Work with us, Syza. I don't want to order the destruction of your mind.

A chaos of painful images swept through him and vanished before he could do more than sense their presence.

I will sing.

The minute sounds of Diri's stealthy approach brought Lhar into full wakefulness. He waited until her hand touched the waterbag, then said casually, "You're early, Diri. No water until we're ready to leave."

Diri's eyes blinked in the sudden flickering light of the candle Lhar lit; she saw that he slept as naked as she did.

"I didn't come for that kind of water."

As she walked toward him the golden candlelight added to her incomparable dancer's grace. She knelt so close to him that he could feel the heat of her body through the marvelous suede texture of her silver skin/fur. Her hands moved over him deftly.

"You're an expert, Diri. But you still don't get any drinking water now."

Diri just smiled slightly and continued her work. Though Lhar read the meaning of her smile he did

21

nothing to evade her hands. Instead, he pulled her across his body in a long, sensual caress.

She smiled widely. As his breathing deepened and he became hot and heavy to her touch, she redoubled her subtle undulations, knowing that soon he would be in an agony of desire. When she judged the moment to be ripe, she collapsed and whimpered of thirst.

Lhar's laughter woke everybody in the tent.

For a moment Diri was too surprised to speak, then she cursed him vividly. When that had no effect she reminded him that she was indispensible for getting the natives off Tal-Lith.

"Give me water or I'll blow this contact all the way to Centrex. And you with it!"

The curtain parted, revealing T'Mero. In his hand a quartz knife dripped candlelight. A tremor rippled through Diri as she felt orange eyes measure her.

"I doubt that we'll need the knife," said Lhar.

T'Mero sheathed the knife with a hissing sound.

"Diri is only dangerous so long as she believes herself powerful," continued Lhar. "You're a convenience, Diri. No more. If you won't cooperate, we'll do without you."

Diri lay unmoving for a long moment, then rose to glare imperiously at them.

"I am Lith. There is no other. I am All."

"You are merely Lith's messenger," said Lhar coldly. "There are other ways of delivering a message."

Syza stepped forward into the sphere of candlelight. Behind her, Nevin watched and learned.

"You endanger us, Diri," said Syza. "Not just your pig thirst for water, but your selfishness in all things."

"You should know about selfishness, healer," said Diri sarcastically, pointing to Lhar's raw cheek. "I at least share my talents."

Syza's eyes shone like green opals against her pale face. Diri dismissed her with a contemptuous look.

"Ask your anthropologist if I'm only a convenience," she said to Lhar.

Lhar spoke before Nevin could tell the uncomfortable truth.

"I don't have to ask, Diri. I know."

"I don't."

She smiled insolently and approached the waterbag. Syza and T'Mero moved simultaneously to intercept her. Lhar signaled for T'Mero to step back.

"Tell us why we need you," said Syza. "I don't quite understand."

Though her tone was innocent of any threat, Lhar's senses leaped at a feeling of raw danger and he remembered that eight people had died mysteriously on Bjmsk.

His mind poised for attack. "Syza," he said in a low, penetrating voice.

At Lhar's quiet word, color returned to Syza's face and her eyes lost their strange sheen. Diri leaned close to Syza and spoke in a sibilant whisper.

"You need me because the natives wouldn't follow your bony ass to water if they were dying of thirst."

"Your arrogance will kill us," said Nevin. "If we can't function as a group we'll all die."

Diri's laugh shattered Nevin into silence. "But I don't need anyone," she said triumphantly. "All I have to do is take off my clothes and the natives will worship me."

Lhar weighed alternatives with the speed and precision of a computer. He could use psi to control Diri, but to enforce it he would have to break her. Physical force would be the same.

Syza.

Immense reluctance, then acquiescence to his command.

Lhar stood and walked almost lazily toward Diri. "You think you're vital because only you can inspire the natives to worship?"

Diri smiled. "I'm the one who looks like their God."

"But if you weren't the only cheap goddess on the planet, then you'd need us, wouldn't you?"

23

Diri moved her hands impatiently in the direction of the waterbag. "I'm the only goddess, so why—"

"Yes or no, Skandiri-Li."

"Yes!"

Lhar smiled, but the gesture lacked all trace of warmth or comfort. His gray-crystal eyes moved to Syza.

Give her a song she'll understand, but don't break her. She is still the most convenient goddess around.

The only thing that animal understands is sex.

Sex reflects the mind behind it. No more. No less.

Lhar purposely wrapped around his thought a nimbus of emotional imagery. He felt Syza's dismay with the subtle intimacy of emotive mindtouch. Hastily she narrowed mindtouch to a curt relay of information.

Then I'll give her what she understands. Warn T'Mero. Guard your own mind.

Syza turned slowly to face Nevin. When she spoke her voice was so soft that he could barely hear her words.

"In order to make Diri understand, I'll have to sing to the most . . . to her abundant lust. You won't hear all of my song. If you had mind training you could cope with the little you'll hear. I'm sorry, Nevin."

Abruptly Syza turned away and confronted Diri.

"Will you cooperate with us, obey Lhar as we all must?" she asked tonelessly.

Diri laughed.

Syza bowed her head momentarily. Only Lhar sensed the lash of her rebellion overriden by the primal drumroll of her voice. Lhar closed his mind to the hot tentacles of melody, to the notes that aroused and burned with lust. Nevin's breathing rasped in the still air, yet Lhar knew that Nevin was aware of only part of the song. Lhar's mind leaped across Nevin's with stunning force. Diri writhed with the same mindless lust she had sought to inspire in Lhar. Too soon. Too much. Too—

Syza!

His mental command split like lightening across the

24

turgid storm of song, but the song only deepened, became violence seething on the brink of eruption. In the instant that Lhar sent Syza spinning into unconsciousness, T'Mero's control broke. The crystal knife flashed wildly in his hand and he fell upon Diri with a hoarse cry.

Lhar's mind seared across T'Mero's for an instant, then withdrew. The knife quivered in the ground next to Diri but even Lhar was not sure whether he or T'Mero had willed it to miss her straining silver flesh.

Lhar turned his back on the violent black-silver coupling and carried Syza out into the chill night air. Returning consciousness brought shudders of revulsion to her thin body. She gagged convulsively. When he would have comforted her she lashed out at him.

He waited until she controlled her retching, then said, "Go back inside, Syza. Tomorrow will be a hard day. Or do you want to talk about what happened?"

Syza laughed bitterly.

"Talk? With you? You'd push a child into filth and then patronize it with a helping hand."

"You're not a child, Syza. Your choices are no longer a child's easy choices between pure good and pure evil. Were Diri to rule us, we, and all the natives of Tal-Lith, would die. A waste, for Diri as much as for everyone else. I could have controlled Diri, but I would have destroyed the arrogance that is essential to her dancing. Then the natives would also have been destroyed. By balancing her arrogance with humiliation—"

"—used me, just like everyone always has."

"Of course," snapped Lhar. "Would you have preferred the other alternatives? Would you?"

Syza did not conceal her loathing.

Lhar laughed humorlessly. "Not that way, Syza. That's too easy. Think! What would you have done?"

Lhar's mind bored through her defenses, compelling an answer, disturbing deeply buried memories of

loathing, hatred falling,

death-pouring discovery of

25

"Stop it! I don't want to know!"

Lhar let her scream echo before he spoke quietly, implacably. "Then know this, Agent Zomal. Group leaders are selected for their ability to make choices while others are strangling on their emotions."

He moved away abruptly and stepped back into the tent.

11

Lhar tested the belly strap on his taman. The beast looked too thin to support its own weight, much less that of a rider. The chest and barrel and buttocks which had formerly swelled with excess water were now flattened. The drifs looked as though they had been squeezed dry. The last echoes of the storm still stirred their coarse coats and made seeing painful, but the khaner could wait no longer. If water were not found today a drif would be killed and its scant fluids shared among the humans. In two days, at most, the taman would turn on the drifs, then fight among themselves for a moist scrap from the kill. In three days humans and animals alike would be dead.

Lhar jerked the belly strap tight. The taman's teeth clicked indolently near his wrist. He mounted and looked over the assembled group. T'Mero seemed impassive as always, but apparently his taman sensed otherwise; in a blur of motion it reached around to savage T'Mero's leg. T'Mero reacted just in time. The taman got a mouthful of boot delivered with enough force to be heard up and down the canyon.

Lhar let out his breath, glad to know that a night with Diri had not completely addled the guardian. Diri herself was slouched bonelessly in the saddle. She had made an effort to be cooperative in breaking camp and had refrained from more than a longing look at the slim waterbag tied onto Syza's taman.

Syza herself had not spoken to anyone. Lhar assumed she had slept with the drifsen, for when he came out of the tent before the first hint of light, the

27

drifs were rounded up and the taman roped together waiting for their burdens.

Nevin sat gingerly on his taman. Though he had saddled and mounted it without incident, he obviously did not trust it. But other than making a deliberate effort to avoid Syza, he seemed to have absorbed the night's experiences without harm.

The khaner moved slowly down the canyon under Lhar's eyes. He moved in to check the belly strap on Diri's taman, then bent to tighten it without stopping either animal.

"Keep an eye on that strap, Diri. Getting dumped on these rocks would hurt more than your dancing."

Diri smiled widely. "I didn't think you cared about my ass."

"Try me when you're not thirsty," he said as he reined his drif away. "And pull up your gritscarf or you'll be coughing rocks by the end of the day."

Diri's mobile mouth rippled into a pout, but like his taman's clicking teeth, the gesture owed more to ritual than to rebellion.

Lhar tightened his own scarf until his eyes were nearly covered. The baggage taman and drifs slowly passed by but Syza was not with them. She was on the opposite side of the canyon, as far away from him as the rocks would allow. He cut across to intercept her. As she had been during the height of the storm, Syza was completely concealed by her gritscarf. Not so much as a glimmer of green eyes showed through.

"Syza."

Either she did not hear him or she chose to ignore him.

Syza.

"What do you want?"

Lhar did not comment on the sudden rebirth of her hearing.

"You missed the morning water ration. Have you taken it yet?"

"No."

28

"Then drink it now."

Syza unwound her gritscarf and poured a small trickle of water into a stone bowl. The amount was barely two-thirds of her ration. The drifsen glided up as she swished the cold liquid in her mouth and held it before swallowing a few drops at a time. Without looking at Lhar she divided the remainder of her ration between the drifsen.

"The drifsen are desert born, Syza. You aren't."

"They also work harder for me than they would for a normal herder."

"Are they suffering from thirst more than the other animals?"

"Yes."

"Will they need extra water again tonight?"

"Yes."

"Give them a third of my evening ration. If that isn't enough, tell me. Don't give them more of your own water for two days."

When she protested, he overrode her.

"Last night you vomited what little fluid you had in your system," he said curtly. "Take one-sixth of a ration every two hours for the next twelve hours, plus your usual ration tonight. And don't share a drop with the drifsen no matter how much they whine."

By the time Lhar reached the head of the column the taman were beyond the sheltering canyon. Gusts of stinging grit buffeted them occasionally, but the taman merely snorted their displeasure. Such winds were common in n'Lith; the taman had long ago learned to endure. Their riders were less well adapted, but their motivation was equally great: survival. Though n'Lith was not hot, the wind desiccated as surely as a savage sun. The caravan groped across a landscape barren of life, barren of movement other than the ubiquitous wind.

Just before Lhar signaled for an evening halt, he sensed a flicker of thought from Syza.

Is something wrong?

I'm not sure.

Her thought carried metallic reticence. Hurried image/impressions tumbled through his mind. A drifsen's elusive mind resonating with unease. A drif's normally stolid bearing slowly changing into skin-rippling restlessness. A taman's ears fanned repeatedly to catch sounds that did not exist.

Why?

I don't know. It's not the same as before the storm. It's not thirst. It's not other animals. The drifs refuse to go near cliffs or rubble hills. That's why I'm so far behind. Remember that low pass between plateaus you crossed earlier?

Yes.

I had a zarf's own time getting them through.

You're sure you aren't being stalked by something?

Yes.

Lhar didn't question the source of her certainty.

Do you need help with the animals?

What kind of land is ahead?

Mainly flat. No more passes and no cliffs near the trail.

Rest there while I catch up.

Though Syza didn't press, he sensed that it was important to stay in the open.

I'll give the order now. Is there anything else? he thought searchingly.

I—all I know is that the drifs are being driven by a survival reflex. Since drifs normally live in canyons and forage beneath the cliffs, their fear of those very places is important.

Thank you, Syza. How are you doing?

Lhar's switch to emotive mindtouch caught Syza by surprise. His thought carried concern for her as a useful member of the group, certainly, but there was also a bright thread of affection-respect woven through. Her sudden confusion narrowed mindtouch to a curt reply.

Don't worry; I'll get the waterbags to the khaner before ration time.

That's all I can ask for, isn't it?

Syza did not answer. Lhar attempted to regain mind-touch, but T'Mero's arrival commanded his attention.

"We'll rest here in the open," said Lhar. "Have you seen anything?"

T'Mero's dark face changed almost imperceptibly. "Have I missed something?"

"Do you think you have?"

"No. But your manner tells me I did."

"And your uncertainty tells me you agree. Is it Diri?"

T'Mero's orange eyes widened into embers. "Are you ordering me to stay away from her?"

"Only if she interferes with your work."

"Nothing interferes."

"Good. Syza says the animals are nervous and she doesn't know why." Lhar sensed alertness suddenly humming through the guardian. "She says that she is not being followed nor is another storm coming. She wants us to rest in the open. Any objections?"

T'Mero was silent for a moment, then said, "None. We can't be ambushed here. Is the water safe? How far behind are the drifs?"

"They'll be here before ration time."

Lhar loosened the belly strap and hobbled his own taman. T'Mero was helping Diri; indeed, T'Mero had stayed close to Diri most of the day. Perhaps that was why he jumped at the least hint he was not doing his job. He had not made more than two reconnaissance sweeps. Not that it mattered; once the hills were passed, sweeps were a waste of energy.

"Not quite so tight, Nevin."

Nevin loosened the hobbles and was rewarded by the sound of his taman's lips batting together. Nevin snickered.

"I could almost stop hating this hag-ridden clown," he said. He loosened his gritscarf, flexing his neck muscles in obvious relief. With a covert glance at T'Mero and Diri, Nevin asked, "What happened last night? All I remember is . . ." Nevin swallowed and looked away.

"Your response was as natural as breathing," said Lhar. "But the song was too much. You passed out—with a little help from me."

"Thanks. I probably would have made a total zarf of myself. That female should be sent to the vats."

"Diri?"

"No, though I thought so for a while. But Syza—she's dangerous," said Nevin emphatically. "Anyone who can suck over your mind like that should be sent to the acid death."

"Would you condemn this planet?" said Lhar. "Didn't you recognize her voice?"

Nevin rubbed his neck wearily. "No and no." Then he dropped his hand. "She can't be. I've listened to the Chanteuse thousands of times."

"Even the best recording is a reflection of a shadow. Reality is far more potent."

Lhar watched the young man intently; a lot depended on Nevin's resilience. Lhar had neither the time nor energy to integrate Nevin right now.

"Would it help you to know that Syza was more revolted by her song than you were?"

"A little," admitted Nevin. "But."

"Go on."

"What gives her the right to manipulate us like that?"

"I do."

"You told her to?"

"Yes."

A long silence followed Lhar's blunt words. At last Nevin smiled weakly. "My mind accepts the necessity, but my emotions don't."

Lhar relaxed. "Good."

"Good?"

"Shows your survival reflexes are working. I'll bet the first time you nailed a rope up a high cliff you felt the same fear."

"I got used to it. I knew that as long as I didn't panic I would make it."

"So will we."

32

Nevin rubbed the taman's shoulder absently; his eyes were focused inward and a wry smile slightly curved his lips.

"Something else?" said Lhar.

Nevin blinked. "Just thinking. When I was on my home planet, I had three dreams: becoming part of a Contact team, finding a willing woman, and meeting the Chanteuse. Now . . ." He kneaded his fingers through the taman's rough coat.

" 'Sacred Xantha, may I never measure the consummation of my dreams with the rod of my lost innocence.' "

"Is that a prayer?"

"From my childhood. When I understood the prayer I was no longer a child."

Nevin smiled ruefully.

Lhar hesitated, then said, "If you need help, ask. I was an integrator before I talked Centrex into field assignments. We need your mind and training intact, Nevin, as much as we need Diri."

"Diri . . . yes. You'd better watch her," said Nevin thoughtfully. "She scares me almost as much as Syza. I'm scared right now."

"So are the drifs. Syza says that nothing is stalking them, nor is another storm coming. But they are tighter than a zarf's ass."

"How do they act?" said Nevin sharply. "Are they avoiding loose rock, narrow canyons, that sort of thing?"

Lhar's gray eyes flicked over Nevin appraisingly. "Yes. Do you know why?"

"Earthquake coming. If I were a real miran I would slay a drif and cast the stones from its first stomach to find out how bad the quake will be."

"Can the drifs really sense future quakes?"

"The natives say yes. And the drifs would get plenty of practice. Did you notice how many of the cliff faces showed unweathered rock? A good quake shakes rock loose along hidden joints in the plateaus. N'Lith is supposed to be the home of the quakes. Reminders

33

of Lith's displeasure. Most of the tremors are very small, more sensed than felt."

"Let's hope so," muttered Lhar. "Although the idea doesn't seem to make you nervous."

"I was raised with earthquakes. I rather miss them."

Lhar laughed shortly. "I hope this one misses us."

By the time Syza herded the drifs close to them, light had vanished from n'Lith. Hobbling the skittish drifs was nearly impossible. The taman flashed restless teeth, though they were still easier to control than the wiry drifs. When the last animal was hobbled, the drifsen immediately lay down. Syza poured out a tiny ration of water and took it to them where they lay.

"Water for them?" said Diri incredulously.

"Without the drifsen," said Lhar, "we'd have lost the drifs today."

Diri said no more, but her tongue moved futilely over cracked lips while she watched the drifsen drink. When her own water ration came, she raised it hastily to her mouth.

"Don't," said T'Mero. "Take a little at a time."

Diri's greed was stronger than her will. T'Mero took the cup from her. Strangely, she made no objection.

"Like this," he said, holding the cup so that she could take but one tiny sip at a time.

The water that they drank did little more than remind them of their thirst. They oiled their cracked lips and chewed carefully on dried drif meat. Just as Lhar was about to give the order to ride, tremors shook the rocky plains. The animals screamed and lunged but their hobbles held.

"Down!" said Lhar.

The land rolled beneath his feet, snapped, and sent him sprawling. The worst of the quake passed within a minute, but during that time the animals were in a frenzy. Lhar watched them uselessly spend their strength and knew that travel would be impossible. He stood and began giving orders before anyone else even looked up.

"Syza. Pick out the three strongest taman. T'Mero.

34

Take the taman and two drifs. Ride until the second moon rises. Kill the drifs, take their fluids and feed the rest to the taman. Then keep going until you find water. We'll follow your trail as long as we can."

"I'm lighter than T'Mero," said Syza, "and I can get more out of the animals."

"No, we need you here. The drifs will be wild during the aftershocks. They're all we have until T'Mero gets back."

Lhar looked at the drifsen for a moment, then reached for a bowl. Though their minds were difficult to control, the thought of water brought them rubbing against his knees. Deliberately he gave them a generous drink of the remaining water.

"But why?" said Nevin finally.

"We'll need them."

When Syza returned with the taman, T'Mero was struggling with the second drif. Though they reached only to mid-thigh on T'Mero, the drifs were tough; a terrified drif tested even T'Mero's strength. Eventually he hauled it away from the herd and tied it over a waiting muzzled taman.

Long after night had engulfed T'Mero, the others could hear the drifs' frantic calling. Nor was there relief in sleep. Each aftershock of the quake sent the drifs into mad plunges, taxing Lhar's and Syza's endurance as they worked with the revived drifsen to keep the herd under control. Nevin and Diri were the only ones who slept. By morning Syza was too exhausted to lift the saddle to her taman's shrunken back.

"Let me."

Syza stepped aside and let Lhar saddle the taman. Amazingly the taman had the energy to lash out, but Lhar evaded the yellow teeth.

"I wonder if they ever get too tired for that," said Syza hoarsely.

"We'll find out today," said Lhar, yanking the belly strap tight. Before she could protest he lifted her into the saddle and began to tie her in place.

"When I'm that tired, I'll die," said Syza flatly.

Lhar finished the last knot and smiled up at her. "You'd be surprised how much your body can take. I've ended more than one trip tied to the saddle of an alien riding beast."

For an eerie moment he was watching himself through her mind, measuring his own wind-burned face and quicksilver eyes with new interest. But she said only, "Keep the taman separate from the drifs. I don't have the strength to prevent them from killing the drifs. Survival surges are almost impossible to control mentally."

"I know. Do you have enough strength to give the drifsen an imperative?"

"I don't know."

"Then I'll help you."

"No. I'm strong enough."

Lhar had expected as much; Syza's dislike/fear of mindtouch had been evident from the first. It was not surprising that she should refuse the deep mesh required for unified action.

"Tell the drifsen to keep all of us on T'Mero's trail."

The implications were not lost on Syza. She looked as though she were about to speak and he felt the most tenuous of mental touches fade before he could even be sure it had happened. His gray eyes followed Syza for a moment before he led the pack taman away from the drifs.

Syza had tied the taman securely together with double ropes, a precaution Lhar was grateful for when the aftershocks continued. None were of the magnitude of the initial quake, but the animals reacted badly. As the day lengthened, both the earth tremors and the animals' strength waned. The taman merely fanned their ears at the trembling earth and continued their slow progress over the desiccated land.

When the animals had fallen into the machinelike indifference of fatigue, Lhar assumed a near comatose state in which only those functions vital to life continued, and then only at the minimum level required.

A small fraction of his mind remained alert, ready to awaken the body if the need arose.

In the brass light of late afternoon, that inner sentry aroused Lhar. He ignored the myriad knives of returning circulation and searched for whatever had brought him to full consciousness. T'Mero's trail still stretched ahead, a series of puff marks in the stone dust and pebbles which overlay the land. The pack taman still followed obediently. The riding taman still carried three slumped figures.

A drifsen's plaintive whine brought Lhar's attention back to the trail. Of course, the drifsen needed water. He poured a ration for both of them and carefully retied the shrunken waterbag. While they drank he scanned the back trail, but saw nothing unexpected. Nevin and Diri were obviously unconscious, tied to their taman as he had earlier tied Syza—and himself. They would be chafed raw and bone-sore when they awoke. If they awoke. He checked the ropes which secured him to the taman. If anything, the knots were tighter now than when he had first tied them. The knots would hold long after he was beyond needing them.

The temptation to contact T'Mero haunted him as strongly as the need for water, but the energy to call T'Mero would be wasted. T'Mero was either alive or dead. If alive, he had either found water or not found it. If he had not found water there was no point in contacting him. If he had found water, knowing it would not bring the first drink more quickly.

The drifsen whined nervously and Lhar felt tension building up in his taman. While he had sat and dreamed, the drifs had moved closer to the ravenous taman. A piece of rope cracked loudly, and the knotted end uncurled painfully along the taman's belly. The animal jumped and snapped its teeth together, but it obeyed. Tension drained from the taman as it resumed its dogged, head-low progress.

Lhar felt the emergency surge of energy fade from his body like light from the sunset sky. He cursed his

37

carelessness; a few seconds more and the taman would have been uncontrollable. He cursed the taman for their toughness. He had hoped by now that they would be too exhausted to be interested in drifs. That they were not, meant that he would have to wait to kill a few of the drifs. He could not risk a surge of bloodlust when the taman scented a moist kill.

Lhar sighed and looked at the beckoning tracks ahead. The only good thing about this justly damned desert was that its pebbledust surface held a plain trail—until the next strong wind blew.

Pain was a silent scream which penetrated every cell of his body. Light cut into his eyes and burned like phosphorus under his lids. Automatically his hand groped for the waterbag; then he remembered he had given the last drop to the drifsen yesterday . . . or was it the day before. . . .

With an effort he concentrated on the present. Something had gone wrong or he would not be conscious. Something. His eyes focused fleetingly. Midday. The trail. He blinked repeatedly, but the trail did not appear. Then he finally received the message his ears had been patiently sending; the wind was howling and scraping over the land again. How long it had blown he could only guess, and guessing would not make the trail appear.

As though in agreement, his taman stopped and lowered itself slowly to the ground. The others followed suit, lips batting loosely over folded knees. Lhar knew that the taman were finished. Indeed, it was Xantha's own miracle that they had not given up sooner. Or was it? If the taman had not lasted so long, he would have had the strength to dismount and kill a drif.

Slowly, in spite of the agony that movement caused, Lhar turned to look at the backtrail. The drifsen apparently believed the taman were still capable of attack; they had stopped the drifs a safe distance back from the taman. And from him.

Perhaps Syza . . . no. The drifsen had driven her taman away. It had walked until it caught up to its own kind, then it had quit.

For several long moments he considered dismounting, but knew it would be futile. He had no strength to walk to the drifs. He knew that as surely as he knew he would meet death astride an exhausted taman. No, not death. T'Mero. T'Mero would bring water, and water was life and Lith . . . Lith knew T'Mero . . . Death's eyes burning orange, burning orange thirst . . . T'Mero . . . T'Mero . . . T'Mero.

And through an orange veil he saw

blurred taman standing asleep and fat with their feet in water and his hand a black claw with crystal nails sawing knots, sawing, sawing until freedom came in an endless fall to water and life.

Now come to me.

Come to me!

But the veil thickened, darkened, and he felt his strength sucked dry by the sands of fatigue. He could not sustain the call and water would pour endlessly and lost over barren sand and cold until green ice melted, pouring Syza's strength like a drumroll fusing self to other in power greater than either alone.

COME TO ME
COME TO ME

Cool fall of water over his eyes and lips. He swallowed and knew it was no dream.

The others.

Lhar's thought was both question and command.

Alive, for now, answered T'Mero. *Your mind-call would have quickened mountains.*

T'Mero's thought crawled with emotions Lhar was too tired to categorize though the image of Syza was unmistakable . . . Syza somehow cutting herself free and coming to him, hand touching his mind melting in green cascade—he shook his head, hoping that pain

39

would bring order out of the chaos that was his mind.

The images stopped. He opened his eyes slowly, expecting an assault from the midday sun. But it was evening, and the light was as cool as the wet rag pressed between his teeth. He sucked the last drops from the rag and carefully dunked it in the bowl of water T'Mero had left between him and Syza.

Syza . . . Lhar's gray eyes widened as he saw the blurred trail left by her when she had crawled to him. Dream and reality coalesced while he probed deeply for some life in her too-still body. His mind found nothing, though he did not sense the total absence which signified death. He rolled painfully onto his side and pulled the gritscarf off Syza's face. Gently he squeezed water between her blood-caked lips until he found himself rigid with anticipation of the bittersweet, baffling, pouring presence which was Syza aware.

The rag paused over Syza's lips while he grappled with the intense, irrational currents of his own emotions. He tried to remember what had happened before T'Mero found them. He had called T'Mero, yes, and the call must have been general enough to bring Syza, too. But where had he found the strength to sustain such a call through the afternoon? His call had sprung from the essence of himself, from the very core of his will to live. Such a call could not be partnered by another mind unless that other mind complemented him so deeply that the result was fusion rather than mere sharing. He had heard a few other psis talk of such a joining, but had never found it himself. Even if he accepted that Syza was his complement, he could not conceive of her allowing such total intimacy.

Then what had happened? Why did he feel a tender and fierce desire to know her aware again?

Nevin is conscious. Diri will be soon.

T'Mero's information ended Lhar's questions. Whatever had happened, they now had water again. The only important thing was to get some of that water into Syza. He trickled water past her lips and finally

40

saw her throat move as she swallowed. Remembering his own discomfort, he gently washed the caked dust away from her eyes. The dark fringe of lashes stirred, then opened into compelling pools of green and he floated whole and infinite as she in him, complete—a blink, and gone—or dreamed. Lhar resumed dripping water between her silent lips, careful not to touch her with either mind or flesh, too tired to do more than accept her, once again a stranger.

Lhar stretched, grimaced as muscles reminded him that riding tied to a taman was a harsh way to travel. He rubbed his hands across gritty hair and face, then stiffened in astonishment when his fingers failed to find the crusty, swollen wound near his eye. Healed! But when, how? Syza.

He turned to look over the backtrail, ignoring the lancing pain brought on by sudden movement. Syza was there, far back as always, more mysterious than ever after their near-initiation into death. He was tempted to mindcall her but thought better of it. After they had driven the last of the animals to the river, tonight when the others were asleep, he would go to her and—with a surge of impatience he gathered his scattered thoughts and concentrated on ordering his own mind.

His golden taman snorted and fanned its ears. Its gait quickened to a smooth pace, spurred by the scent of water on the rising wind. Soon the taman breasted a small rise, giving Lhar a view of a huge swamp. Namaylith. They were close enough to the river that the water was only mildly brackish. Further into the desert the water became too salty to drink. The taman rushed eagerly forward and thrust its nose into the cool liquid. What water T'Mero had brought in several trips had only been enough to revive the animals. Now it was time to replenish the stores.

Lhar slid off his taman, laughed at the cool silver shock of water splashing his legs. He loosened the taman's belly strap and watched the animal swell with water. He hesitated, but did not interfere; Syza had said that the animals could drink enormous amounts of water without harm. He abandoned the taman to its physiology and concentrated on his own needs.

Lhar was still scrubbing at his clothes when he saw T'Mero approaching. A certain tension about the guardian brought Lhar upright with expectancy.

"Tracks?" said Lhar.

"A khaner. Maybe two. They camped further up, where the river ends. They moved out when their animals had eaten the area flat."

"How long ago?"

"Three, five days. Some of the taman droppings were still damp in the center."

Lhar debated, then called Syza over.

"How soon can the animals travel under full loads?"

Syza looked at the animals scattered along the margin of the swamp.

"Tomorrow is the soonest. The day after would be better. That would give them time to flush out their salt pockets and fill their second stomachs with fresh food."

"Not to mention us," said Lhar. "Is Diri on her feet yet?"

"No," said T'Mero, and his eyes seemed to hover over Syza demandingly.

"No healing now," said Lhar. "It would leave Syza too exhausted to handle the animals."

T'Mero's eyes flicked to Lhar's cheek, but he said nothing.

"There's more than one way to heal," Lhar pointed out. "Syza's imprinting included the herbs of Tal-Lith." He waved his hand at the flourishing plants. "Somewhere out there must be something useful."

Syza's eyes focused on a point above their heads while she reviewed what she had learned. Finally she nodded slowly.

"Yes. Yefa. Circulatory stimulant, mildly psychogenic, nonaddictive. Found near still water. Pick only blue-veined leaves or the smell will . . ." Syza moved

42

off, muttering about the harvest and uses of yefa, searching for the tiny bushes at the margin of the wetlands.

"Praise Lith that there aren't any venomous animals here," said Lhar drily. "Unless they had blue veins, Syza wouldn't see them until it was too late."

"She healed you." said T'Mero bluntly.

"Only when the alternative was death. Does Diri need healing that badly?" said Lhar, fixing T'Mero with an unflinching gaze.

T'Mero's muscles moved subtly, then smoothed.

"No. Nevin's making a litter for her now. Rest, water . . . she should be dancing in a week."

Lhar put his hand briefly on T'Mero's shoulder. He understood that T'Mero wanted his lover well again, yet he disliked having to point out that what was good for Diri was not necessarily good for the group. Even worse, a guardian of T'Mero's experience should not have to be told about the realities of a Contact mission. Lhar watched thoughtfully as T'Mero moved toward Diri's shelter. He saw T'Mero stiffen, then pounce on something just inside the tent.

Nevin.

Lhar raced to the tent. His mental commands bounced across the guardian's rage, but they had the desired effect. By the time Lhar reached the tent, T'Mero had released Nevin.

"Diri asked me to—" began Nevin.

"She's unconscious!" snarled T'Mero.

Lhar's command tone cut across their angry words.

"Guardian, what reason do you have for attacking a member of the Contact group?"

Under the lash of Lhar's voice T'Mero's body straightened from a half-crouch. "He was bathing Diri. He has no right to touch her."

"If we were on Nucki your jealousy would be a valuable asset to your role," said Lhar coldly. "But we are on Tal-Lith. We are a khaner. If Diri wishes to eat, bathe, sleep, or cope with anyone, she is free to do so. Anyone. Do you understand?"

T'Mero tipped his head stiffly.

"In the context of your native culture, your reaction is understandable. In the context of a guardian's training it is irrational. If you wish, I will help you to integrate your mind and emotions."

"That will not be required," said T'Mero formally.

"Your choice," agreed Lhar. "If it happens again you will have no choice."

Lhar waited until he sensed T'Mero's leaping readiness to kill drain away completely. Then he turned to Nevin and asked mildly, "What's that stinking mess you're bathing Diri with?"

"Boiled yefa leaves," said Nevin with a sheepish smile.

Lhar laughed. "Were they blue-veined?"

"Ah . . . not all of them. Will they hurt her?" he said anxiously.

"Not if she can't smell them."

Nevin looked at Diri's limp form and shook his head. "She was conscious for a little while and kept mumbling about water and baths. I remembered about the yefa."

"Then I'll give her a yefa bath," said Syza, breathless from running.

Lhar took the leaves from Syza's hands.

"We all will. How long do you cook yefa before you use it?"

"Until the leaves turn pale blue. I've got some cooking now. These should be crushed and tied in a bag around Diri's neck."

Lhar finished pulping the leaves just as Syza returned with a cooking skin full of yefa water.

The yefa leaves—properly selected and cooked—yielded a pleasant intoxication that was rather like floating among the flowering wetlands reeds. Even T'Mero relaxed, smiling vaguely, muscles working smoothly as he massaged the heady liquid into Diri's velvet skin. When the last drop was absorbed, Diri stirred and opened her eyes.

"More," she whispered.

44

Lhar laughed quietly. Diri smiled in return and moved her hands over his chest.

"Nice," she murmured.

Lhar smiled, though he sensed a flash of anger from T'Mero.

"You too," she whispered to Nevin, then the blue of her eyes deepened as she saw T'Mero. With a long sigh she curled up against his thigh and fell asleep.

Syza rested one hand lightly on Diri's back. "True sleep," she said quietly.

"Good," said Lhar.

"Someone should stay with her, though."

Lhar looked at Syza. "T'Mero will. Should she have any more yefa?"

"Later."

"Nevin will gather the leaves now, and cook them. You and I have animals to attend to."

Syza started to object but stopped after a look at his face. They followed Nevin out of the tent. When Syza would have spoken, a gesture from Lhar stopped her. Not until they were among the animals did Lhar turn toward her.

"Decline?" he said abruptly.

Syza's face became closed, remote. Lhar waited with outward patience.

"I'm not sure," said Syza finally. "My healing talent is . . . erratic. Were it not for your cheek, I would have said vanished. As it is," Syza's hands hovered like birds looking for a place to rest, "I can only say her rhythms remind me of Zomal. That, at least, I'm sure of."

"If we doubled her extender drugs? Gave her boosters?"

Syza's hands hesitated in the midst of a negative gesture.

"Perhaps. I'd guess she's well into her seventh maturity. Immune to the extenders now. But we can try."

"How much time does she have?"

"To live?"

"As a dancer."

Syza's lips twisted into a humorless smile.

"You would think only of that."

Lhar snuffed out the flame of his anger and waited. "Unless something else happens to drain her, she should be able to—"

"Should?" he demanded.

"I'm not a seer," snapped Syza.

"No. You're a healer. And not just an ordinary healer, but one who has reversed Decline." Lhar smiled sourly. "You're also a healer who refuses to heal. So be it. Healing can't be forced, as I'm sure T'Mero will learn to his displeasure."

"At least you accept that I can't heal."

"Won't heal," said Lhar flatly.

"Then you accept me as a nonhealer."

"I wasn't aware I had a choice."

"You don't, but not all people are so logical."

Lhar bowed sardonically. "I'll remember your praise the next time I require you to sing."

Her indrawn breath told him that he had finally reached her, but he felt more anger than pleasure. She responded only to the lash. As a leader he would far rather have willing consent. As a man he wished for much more.

"Only one thing escapes my logic," said Lhar blandly. "People who lose valuable things usually try to recover them. If recovery is impossible they at least show regret for the loss."

Syza said nothing.

"Wasn't the ability to heal valued by you?"

"It was a curse."

"Odd," said Lhar softly. "Did you think healing a curse while you prolonged your lover's life?"

Lhar used Syza's confusion to evade her natural shields. Even then only her surface thoughts were open, but it was enough to confirm his guess: she had never thought of Zomal as her lover. He was—Lhar probed discreetly, futilely, as Syza's shields locked again.

"Well?" said Lhar.

"Of course I was glad to prolong Zomal's life."

46

"Of course," he repeated. "But what happened that turned you against healing—and yourself?"

"You've read my cube. A year of my life is missing. Amnesia."

"Convenient."

"Oh?"

"Yes," said Lhar. "Convenient. You don't want to know what happened."

Syza's laughter was brittle, and she said with mocking sympathy, 'Poor Lhar, stuck with a tool he can't use."

"The idea pleases you."

"Yes. I'm tired of being used."

"Not used. Needed."

"It's the same thing."

"Is that what Zomal taught you, Zomal your lover?"

Syza's rage exploded through her mental control, and Lhar suddenly felt as though someone were forcing his brains through a white-hot sieve. He fought her invasion point on point, appalled at the relative ease with which she eluded his defenses. After the first instant of shocking contact he no longer doubted that her mind was the complement of his, however much her perceptions had been warped by experience. The discovery brought both elation and fear. They were too well matched; his greater training was countered by her greater desire to hurt. Yet in one way he had the advantage. He was not afraid to have his thoughts known. Under the guise of defending himself he outflanked her, penetrating beyond her inchoate rage to the experiences beneath

dry laughter
digging into her mind restlessly, undermining hope and trust until both collapsed, jagged-edged, lacerating, bleeding faith and future into laughing dust, betrayed diminished, degraded

Lhar poured comfort into the dry emptiness, told her of himself and what could be if she would but trust again. Abruptly he found himself staring into the green fire of her eyes, close, her body pinned

47

against his, sweat-slippery, yet remote as Tal-Lith's moons. His thought finally penetrated her cold mind.

Wouldn't our energies be better used in exploring the possibility of love?

I've tried love, came her metallic response. *I found it unconvincing.*

Like the worm that ate poisoned fruit; it was so determined not to repeat its mistake that it starved to death.

He sensed a fleeting resonance, a haunting flash of laughter, but Syza was rigid in his arms and her mind was closed to him.

"Let go of me. Or does being an agent require being handled by the team leader?"

Lhar released her so swiftly that she staggered.

"You and Zomal were well matched."

Lhar turned away and walked with quick, hard strides. He knew it was not the right time or world to reach Syza. Each time the mission required her talents she would feel abused. She was needed far too much to be ignored, yet if he wished to awaken her, he must wait until she volunteered. He could only hope there would be time to wait.

THE TAMAN WERE SPREAD ALONG THE RIVER TRAIL LIKE bright drops of blood. A clot of drifs moved slowly behind, encouraged occasionally by tawny flashes of drifsen. Even further back rode Syza, barely visible in the dust of the khaner's passage. Lhar swore and reined his taman off the river bluff. The animal turned eagerly to rejoin its kind.

"See anything?" asked Nevin as Lhar drew abreast.

Lhar shook his head in answer. "The land rolls as it climbs toward the Nine Steps of Tal-Senet. I can't even see the Ramparts, and according to my briefing the Ramparts are one huge pile of rock. T'Mero is probably hidden in one of the folds the land makes between here and the first plateau. He should overtake the native khaner soon."

"Maybe he already has," said Nevin pointedly.

Lhar smiled. "Relax, miran. T'Mero is all right."

"Tell Diri."

"She worried?"

"I think so. She's been restless ever since he left last night." Nevin's tone left no doubt that he could not understand Diri's sudden attachment to the guardian, but he accepted it without rancor.

Lhar dropped back until he rode next to Diri's litter. Her eyes were closed, then opened, startlingly blue.

"How do you feel, Diri?"

"Like I was stomped by a lary of zarfs."

Lhar chuckled quietly; Diri's voice had regained its former cutting edge and her skin/fur its former sheen.

49

"Why did you send T'Mero ahead?" she said petulantly. "I need—"

"Rest," said Lhar firmly. "T'Mero is making contact with a native khaner. He should be back by tomorrow night at the latest."

Diri mumbled and her hands moved restlessly. The litter swayed and bumped.

". . . kerden rather ride."

"Tomorrow," said Lhar. "That will give the drugs plenty of time to take hold."

"Kerden bored."

Lhar hid his smile as he guided his taman away from the litter. The smile vanished quickly when he saw that Syza had dropped even further back, as though she were afraid that she was next on his list. He debated mindtouch, then decided the drifsen would do as well. He concentrated on their mercurial awareness for a moment. It was enough. They leaped after the drifs, sending the animals into a hurried trot. The pack taman followed without urging. Lhar could barely make out Syza's taman, but from the jerkiness of its movements, it was fighting her. She gave in and her taman leaped to close the gap separating it from the rest of the group.

Before the taman came within hailing distance, Lhar turned away. He had no desire to force conversation on Syza; he merely wanted her to stay closer to the rest of the khaner. If she did not take this hint, he would make it even plainer.

The golden taman moved eagerly to the head of the line. For the rest of the day Lhar forced a good pace, leading them between river and bluffs without slowing or resting. As the sun dropped into evening the khaner climbed up and away from the river on a steep trail. Thunder rolled ceaselessly across them, yet the sky was unclouded.

"Waterfall," yelled Lhar at Nevin's puzzled look.

Nevin's face cleared. "I'd forgotten. Must be the mother of all falls."

"It is. We're half a day's ride away . . . no wonder they call it Sukalith."

Nevin drew closer, but the wind shifted, making shouts unnecessary. "Sukalith. Lith's Anger. I'd like to see it."

"No one ever has. The bluffs get steeper and crowd the river. By the time you're halfway to the fall, the air is a thick mist and you can't hear anything quieter than a falling mountain."

"All the same . . ."

"Yes, it would be something to see," agreed Lhar.

Lhar's taman plunged and snorted over the crumbling lip of the plateau. The taman's nostrils flared, and it cantered toward a broad depression carpeted by bronze plants. Lhar looked up from the plants and automatically curbed his mount. An impossible range of mountains surged in the distance, backlit by the falling sun. He could only think of a massive tidal wave of rock and ice and heights frozen at the moment of breaking.

Beside him Nevin's low, monotone oaths penetrated Lhar's trance. He glanced at Nevin curiously, then realized that Nevin was saluting the mountains in his own way.

A taman crowded close to Lhar. When he recognized its rider he made a startled sound—Syza. She did not hear him. As he looked at her rapt face he realized that she did not even know he was there. Her lips were slightly parted and her eyes never left the stunning mountains ahead. It was as though she had finally looked upon the face of a lover. Hunger twisted through him, and he forced himself to look away.

But it was many minutes before his eyes saw anything except her face lifting to the Ramparts of Lith. He drove her from his mind by concentrating on the mountains. He knew that even the foothills were at least ten days distant, yet the mountains rose in the light-drained sky as though they were closer than his breath condensing in the twilight. Even as his eyes calculated the Ramparts' mass, his mind veered away

51

from knowledge. There was no way to measure a barricade flung across eternity, and no desire to do so. The mountains simply were, crushing everything else into insignificance as they shone diffusely, coldly returning the light of rising moons in a frigid symphony of ice and deepest blue.

"A planet's water," said Lhar softly, "locked in ice, waiting. I didn't know such mountains existed . . . or such waiting."

He heard Nevin's reverent curses and Syza speaking in unconscious counterpart to his own words.

> ". . . they shall carry bright
> Seas frozen in their arms
> Carved heads silent
> In the long waiting for light
> And release."

The ancient lament swept bitter and lonely over Lhar, made more painful by the beauty of her voice so close to him.

His legs clamped around his taman and it reared against the bit. He sensed fear surging from Nevin and Syza and he caught Syza's image of himself astride a rearing taman, his face a savage mask, as forbidding as the distant peaks.

"We'll make camp ahead," said Lhar curtly, releasing his taman into a tight gallop.

Lhar's eyes opened in the darkened tent. The only sound he could hear was the breathing of the others. Surely that had not wakened him. He closed his eyes and searched with his mind. Diri, Nevin, Syza, all asleep. Taman and drifs grazing quietly. Drifsen dozing.

His search widened beyond the campsite, deftly seeking out other life. There . . . three, no four people, riding slowly across the moonlit plateau. Why had T'Mero not warned him? Unless the natives had psi.

52

With utmost care Lhar studied the energy patterns of the four people. One was a trained telepath. T'Mero. The others were untrained, with the typical erratic aura of people who use only a fraction of their minds. One of them showed real psi potential. He should have expected as much; the native language was replete with such words as luck and hunch and chance.

Are you prisoner or guest, T'Mero?

They haven't decided.

Although T'Mero added nothing further, he made it clear that Lhar was a fool for risking mindtouch.

It's safe enough. The three with you haven't the training to intercept my thoughts. Or even yours.

Good. No use letting them see the length of our knives. Is Diri better?

Complaining of an empty bed.

Lhar smiled at the distinct feeling of pleasure which T'Mero could not conceal.

I made her stay in the litter today, though she was well enough to ride. She cursed me thoroughly. And now that your mind is at ease concerning your lover . . .

Lhar felt T'Mero's vague sense of guilt before he began a crisp report. *I made contact with the khaner at midday. Thirteen people plus several thousand animals. I told them I was the hunter for a small khaner which crossed n'Lith. They didn't believe me, but they can't come up with a simpler explanation for my presence. They sent someone ahead to the city. Three of them are returning with me. The rest will go on with the animals.*

Are you under any restraint?

No.

How far away are you from the edge of the plateau?

We'll be there around dawn.

We'll be waiting. Let me know if you learn anything useful.

Lhar lay awake for a while longer, his mind busy with various plans. Yet even then Syza ringed his thoughts. He would have to do something about her. Soon. And not just for his own peace of mind. Soon the real work would begin. He smiled at the familiar feelings of anticipation and contentment as he faced a task of unknown difficulty. He would be far too busy to feel private hurts or private hopes.

With an exasperated sound Lhar rolled over and sent himself into sleep.

Dawn rose on the back of a chill wind that tugged at tent ropes and stirred stone dust into a haze. Taman snorted and the morning rang with the sound of their hooves striking pebbles. The shrill call of a drifsen greeting the day brought Syza upright inside the tent. For a moment she was oblivious to Lhar watching her. Then as though she felt his eyes she turned quickly to face him. He sensed the merest brush of her mind, and he sent to her the beauty of her face lifted to the mountains. She looked away but Lhar thought he had felt a tiny pulse of response.

"T'Mero and three natives will be here within the hour," he said quietly.

Syza began dressing.

Lhar reached out and shook the two bodies that still huddled under the warm hide blankets. Nevin yawned and reluctantly emerged. A muffled obscenity indicated that Diri would much rather sleep. Lhar casually peeled the covers off her, knowing that the chilly tent would force her to get up. When she still ignored him he smacked her bare bottom soundly.

"Up! And from now on sleep with clothes on. And never, repeat never, let anyone see you without a dust veil and gloves."

Diri muttered, then brightened. "T'Mero?" she said sleepily.

"Patience," laughed Lhar. "If we're to pass you off as Lith's messenger, we can't have you chasing T'Mero like an unpaid whore."

54

Diri chuckled and stretched with unabashed sensuality.

"Anything else, Great Master?" she said, rubbing against Lhar like a thirsty drifsen.

Lhar stroked her absently, his mind divided between Syza and the coming meeting. "Yes, there is one other thing. You can skin all the hides you like, Diri, but make kerden sure no native sees you."

"As long as my own men keep me warm, I won't rape a native. Keep me warm, Lhar," she whispered, curling against him in an unmistakable request.

Syza leaped to her feet; a blast of cold air swept the tent as she stalked out, radiating scorn. Diri's laughter was not at all pleasant to hear.

"I think the skinny ass is jealous. You been keeping her legs warm, Lhar?"

Lhar dumped Diri's clothes on top of her.

"Good as new, aren't you?" he said drily.

Diri dressed with a satisfied smile and left to prepare breakfast.

"I don't understand her," said Nevin.

"Who? Syza?"

"Diri. She—T'Mero."

Lhar began dressing. "Diri is as used to sex as you are to breathing. She'd prefer T'Mero, but sees no need to hold her breath."

"I don't blame you saying no."

With a sigh Lhar put Syza from his mind and gave Nevin his full attention.

"I didn't refuse because I wasn't first choice. I don't have such a high opinion of myself that I won't take a little time and energy to please Diri, especially as she would return the favor. And that's all it would be— a simple, small favor. The next time Diri wants you, remember that. If you're too tired, say so. If you're too proud, think twice."

"What about T'Mero?"

"His problem, not ours. As long as she wants other men he'll have to put up with it."

"I haven't noticed you exactly pursuing her."

"No," said Lhar slowly. "And you won't."

"Yet if she asks . . . ?"

"Of course."

"What about me?"

Lhar grinned. "You're as free as Diri to pursue or pass."

"I'll pass," Nevin said, then sighed wistfully.

Lhar laughed softly and followed Nevin outside. Low clouds of rock dust obscured the base of the mountains, but the peaks bloomed magenta in the early light. Lhar noted that Syza already had the pack taman lined up and waiting for their harness. He grabbed a bowl and filled it with the dark bitter ssan which was the preferred native drink. With a grimace of distaste he swallowed some. At least it was hot.

"Syza eaten yet?" he asked Diri.

"Zarfs don't eat."

Lhar grunted, then gathered a handful of camp-bread and fruit. He refilled his cup and headed for the pack taman and Syza.

"Here. The taman can wait while you eat."

"Afraid I'll be too weak to work?" said Syza coldly, reaching for the food.

The food fell unnoticed to the ground. Lhar's hands closed over hers until his knuckles showed white. Then he said in a voice that was no less chilling for its softness, "That's the last time, Syza."

"You're hurting me,"

"Why shouldn't I?" he said coolly.

Syza's face became a blank of surprise.

"No answer?" he said. "Aren't you going to tell me it's not nice to hurt other people?"

"I just want to be left alone!"

But as she said that, Lhar probed and caught an image of himself and Diri, bodies redolent of sensuality and pleasure.

"Do you?" said Lhar, returning the image, but now it was Syza who arched under his caress.

"You're disgusting!"

"How would you know? You've never made love with me or any other man."

Syza's face paled until her eyes glittered like green pools surrounded by snow. Her breathing was rapid and shallow and he could feel her pulse beat erratically in his hands. He had hurt her far more deeply than the bruises purpling beneath his hard fingers. Suddenly he felt sick and weary.

"It doesn't really matter. What does matter is our work. Nevin is afraid of you, Diri would cheerfully see you die, and T'Mero watches you like you were an assigned target . . . ."

"Go on," she said. "Finish what you really came here to tell me."

"I'm finished."

"Such restraint," she said bitterly, no longer fighting his grasp. "You should have added that you loathe me more than the rest of them together."

"You really believe that . . . . When you crawled to me over those dry rocks and poured yourself into me, you filled spaces I hadn't even known existed. For a time I was complete. I assumed you felt the same." Lhar's eyes closed and he released her hands. "My mistake," and his eyes opened, gray and impersonal.

Syza's eyes were wide and green and confused, and in their depths were black glints of fear. A taman snorted nearby; she started as though it threatened her and her eyes were nearly black as they searched his face like an animal gauging the strength of an approaching storm.

"And now you fear me," said Lhar quietly. "I probably deserve it. I'll not touch you again." Lhar felt fatigue rise like a dark tide in his body. He turned away, back toward the fire. Mechanically he gathered up more food and returned to Syza, who had not moved. "Here. The taman can wait until you eat."

Syza took the food with trembling hands.

"Thank you," she whispered.

Surprise flickered across Lhar's face as he turned back toward the fire. Diri would need help packing up the tent, and Nevin was out of sight in the rocks.

Lhar worked quickly. The repetitive rolling and tying of hide blankets was somehow soothing. Soon an ordered tent emerged from the chaos of early morning. When Nevin's excited shout came, Lhar was ready to give the upcoming contact his full attention. He stepped out of the tent. A prolonged clatter of falling pebbles marked Nevin's reckless descent from his vantage point.

"They're coming," said Nevin breathlessly.

Lhar smiled at the young man's eagerness.

"How far?"

"Oh . . . we've got enough time to finish packing up."

"Good. Take the bedding to Syza. I'll finish the tent."

Nevin heaped hides in his arms and staggered toward the waiting taman. Diri followed him with the meager cooking supplies.

"Veil, Diri," reminded Lhar.

". . . sucking zarfs," she muttered as she yanked the veil down and tied it securely. "I'm blind."

Lhar smiled briefly; he knew that Diri's race had supreme vision. She could see more in darkness than most people at midday. He resumed work on the tent. With a rustling sigh it collapsed upon itself. The supporting ropes were stiff with cold. By the time Nevin came back the tent was ready to be loaded. Lhar's muscles bunched and tightened as his body took the weight of the tent.

"Got it?" said Nevin.

"Yes."

Nevin snatched the loose ropes and pegs off the ground and hurried toward the last unloaded taman.

"Ready," said Nevin.

Lhar nodded and heaved the tent across the pack-frame.

"Look out!"

But even as Nevin shouted, Syza appeared and

yanked at the taman's bridle. The taman's teeth missed Lhar's bare neck by the width of a fingernail.

"Too close. Thanks, Syza. I was careless."

Syza twisted the bridle hard, then released the pressure slightly. The taman lunged again, wickedly, nearly tearing free from Syza. Its eyes flashed wildly and its jaws made vicious snapping sounds. Lhar added his own force to Syza's until the beast subsided, trembling.

And waiting for another chance.

"Not your fault," said Syza breathlessly. "I was waiting for help to muzzle it. If it gets any worse I'll have to kill it."

Lhar looped a noose around the taman's nose while Syza and Nevin wrestled the muzzle on. The loose end of the rope went between the taman's front legs and underneath the belly strap. Lhar jerked the rope taut, then tied it.

"Let go," he said.

They released the taman and jumped back.

Immediately the taman struck again, only to have the rope bite into its sensitive nose. A few lunges convinced the animal; it stood sullenly, chewing at the already frayed muzzle.

"That will hold him for now," said Lhar. "But don't unpack him alone."

"I won't," she said, unconsciously touching her left arm.

"Let's see it," he said.

Syza stood without protest as Lhar pushed up the wide sleeve of her robe. His eyes hesitated over the marks on her wrist, then dismissed them. They had not come from the taman. She flinched when his fingers touched the swelling on her upper arm.

"It's been a rough morning for you," said Lhar quietly, and suddenly wished to kill the taman himself. He ignored the surge of emotion for it was personal and therefore irrelevant.

Nevin gasped at the sight of the ugly knot of flesh, big as a clenched fist. Though the skin was unbroken they could plainly see the livid crescents left by the taman's teeth. Syza tensed, but said nothing as Lhar's fingers gently tested the extent of the damage.

"Badly bruised, but not fractured," he said finally. "When did it happen?"

"After we—while you were working on the tent."

"Can you ride?"

"Yes."

"Get her taman, Nevin."

When Nevin had gone, Lhar said in a low voice, "Can you heal yourself?"

"I . . . I've never had to."

Lhar cupped his hand lightly over the injury. "Try. There's been enough useless pain without this."

Syza's dazed look did nothing to ease Lhar's feeling of guilt; if he had not pressed her this morning the taman would never have caught her unaware.

"Try," he said, delicately reaching out to her mind. "Think of your arm free of injury, strong, resilient with health . . ."

Syza's eyes became unfocused beneath his lulling voice and mind and her breathing deepened, slowed.

". . . supple, muscles flexing and sliding under flawless skin, nerves a relaxed net of awareness, your blood a steady cleansing pulse . . ."

Lhar felt the swelling beneath his hand cool and diminish. He waited quietly until at last Syza stirred with a slow sigh.

"It's gone," she whispered, then her eyes widened in surprise. "You healed me!"

"You healed yourself."

He sensed her violent negation and a soundless explosion of fear. Of him, doubtless. He turned away and began methodically tying the packs onto taman. When Nevin returned with Syza's mount the khaner was ready to move.

With a single, swift motion Lhar mounted his taman. The animal pulled impatiently at the bit. He held the taman to a slow walk as he moved up the line of animals, checking knots and packs and cinches. Satisfied, he raised his hand. The drifsen leaped into motion.

Soon the khaner was walking into the morning that flowed across the plateau.

T'Mero?

Here.

We're moving toward you. Can you see us yet?

My taman smells you on the wind.

Lhar's answer was mixed with rueful laughter. *That bad?*

T'Mero's mind echoed the laughter, then became serious again. *The girl—woman—with me is a miran but she has a hunter's eyes. Be sure Diri is well wrapped.*

Done. Is she suspicious?

Not sure. But if the rest are as quick as she is, we've got a narrow trail ahead.

The two men?

They follow her.

T'Mero's thought dismissed the men as independent sources of danger. It was the woman who worried him.

Lhar broke the link with T'Mero just as the golden taman sent its call booming across the morning. He signaled Nevin to stay back, then allowed his own mount to increase its pace. The taman trotted eagerly up a low rise and stopped. Once again the taman's "ruuu-uuu-ruuu" rolled through the silence.

This time there was an answer.

Lhar's taman snorted and swung its head impatiently, trying to find a weakness in the hard grip of its rider. It reared suddenly, then came down with enough force to make Lhar's spine ache.

"Patience," said Lhar soothingly. "A broken back would serve no purpose."

The taman snapped its teeth together ringingly. Lhar hesitated, then with a curse at his own reluctance he reached out for Syza. The mindtouch was as impersonal as he could make it.

Monitor the contact, Syza, and relay it to the others. If you can, get impressions from the natives.

When Syza agreed Lhar loosened his grip on the reins and allowed the taman to canter toward the four small figures in the distance. One of the shapes broke away and began to enlarge rapidly.

She's coming.

Lhar acknowledged T'Mero's warning absently; even now the figure was close enough that he could distinguish taman and rider. The flashing gold of the animal told him that its rider was the secular head of the khaner. And, perhaps, the religious head, too. Yes. She wore the midnight blue robes of a miran. Unusual to find both functions combined in one person.

Lhar held his taman to a fast canter as the distance between himself and the woman diminished rapidly. When the animals came within three body lengths of each other, both stopped abruptly.

"Lith's blessing on your khaner," said Lhar formally.

"And yours," returned the woman.

Further formalities waited while the two golden taman snorted and whiffed over each other. Then as though at an unseen signal, both animals ignored each other in favor of the few wisps of vegetation that braved the arid rocks.

Lhar relaxed his hold on the animals' awareness. Domestic taman rarely fought each other, but when they did it was considered an omen of trouble between the two khaners.

"I am Kaffi of the First Khaner," said the woman in a clear, young voice.

Lhar took his cue from her formal tones and phrasing. He responded in kind.

"I am Lhar of the Forgotten Lands."

Kaffi reined her taman alongside his.

"We have much to talk about, Lhar. No one in living memory has crossed n'Lith."

"Lith was merciful to our need," said Lhar carefully. "Our own river ran swift and sweet for twice its normal length this year. When it dried, we prayed that Lith might guide us safely to Her fabled Ramparts, that we might learn from Her Chosen who live there."

"We are all drops in Her river."

Lhar weighed the nuances of Kaffi's tone. The

flattery of being one of Lith's Chosen had been deftly ignored; Kaffi doubted that they had risked certain death merely for the pleasure of her company.

"We are all drops," agreed Lhar. "But we of the Forgotten Lands are a practical people. We know that some drops vanish in the desert, while others remain with Her." He spread his hands in the ancient gesture of a buyer accepting a price which he knows is too high. "We would rather live than vanish."

"Yet you crossed n'Lith. Such courage is indeed rare."

"It takes small courage to run before a storm," said Lhar, permitting a trace of asperity to enter his voice.

Kaffi's face expressed interest without committing her to the truth of his story. Her whole manner was one of bland curiosity. If he were indeed a pilgrim, he would attempt to pierce her indifference with a flood of words; her technique was one he used when he wanted to question someone without appearing to do so.

"As T'Mero probably told you," he began, then paused as though for agreement.

Kaffi smiled thinly. "Your T'Mero is a man of long silences."

"Please don't think him rude or—"

"Or overawed at being among the so-called Chosen. He is a hunter, that one, with a hunter's eyes and silences. I don't think him rude."

Lhar returned Kaffi's smile. "Ours is a long story, Kaffi. You were kind to call us courageous when we were only desperate." Lhar fell silent, as though his thoughts were back in the Forgotten Lands.

"I'm sure your story is at least as strange as the desert beyond the river," said Kaffi neutrally. "And I am tired from the night's ride. If I sit very quietly will you talk about it while I rest?"

She looked so much like an engaging child begging for a treat that he grinned in spite of his certainty that she had chosen to stop here only because the hillock commanded a view of both approaching

63

khaners. He dismounted and turned toward her expectant silence.

"Nevin, our miran, will have much to add to my words. He sees the world with devout eyes."

"And you're not devout," said Kaffi as she sat on a flat rock and pulled off her scarf and veil. She had vivid yellow eyes against bronze skin. Yellow hair wisped across her taut cheeks.

Lhar's left hand turned palm up in the native equivalent of a shrug. "I see drifs and taman and food and water and storms. I don't ask why this storm or that dry river, nor do I mourn a fertile time that is only a whisper blown from mouth to mouth across the years."

Kaffi gestured agreement. "After the khaner is cared for, then there is time for legends."

"For me there is no 'after.' My home grudged every leaf and drop of water. Each year worse. Animals dying, rattling dry bones in a dirty wind. Khaners vanishing into the dust, unmarked, unmourned, for who can mourn when hunger twists his belly . . ."

Lhar made an impatient gesture, as though to wipe away the past.

"We were a river curdling in the dust."

Lhar's face tightened into planes of anger.

"T'Mero came to me after many empty weeks. He shattered his blood knife against a rock and cried, 'I am unworthy of this knife and this khaner!' We sat without fire in the darkness. I would have comforted him but I had only crumbling bones to offer.

"And no children. Was life to end with us, childless? What possible sins had earned us such extinction? It seemed that even Lith must lie gasping on the bare rock."

Lhar touched three fingers to his forehead in quick apology.

"I forget your robes, Kaffi. I meant no blasphemy."

Kaffi raised her head and Lhar could see that his story had echoed truth in Kaffi's mind. Her eyes glittered yellow and desolate. "You are not alone in your questions. Anyone with eyes knows that your past is our future."

"Here, too? I had hoped for better."

"Oh, we eat today, and drink. But soon, soon. We still bring souls into squalling life, yet for every baby ten adults die with no chance to be reborn. On windless nights you can hear their thin laments echo in the Ramparts." Kaffi closed her eyes suddenly. When they opened again they had lost their fire. "But speak with a slow tongue, Lhar of the Forgotten Lands. Not all who wear blue robes like to hear the dry truth. Many prefer to wait and pray and die in sacred silence."

Lhar lifted his fingers to his forehead again, but this time it was more a gesture of respect than apology.

"I shall remember that, Kaffi."

And indeed he would. Such a warning from such a woman was not to be dismissed.

Kaffi turned her hands palms upward. "It is little enough to give to one who has dared n'Lith. And don't dismiss the faithful waiters too quickly. In an ugly and brutal land, to be blind and numb is perhaps a mark of wisdom."

"Yes," said Lhar softly. "We had our faithful, too. If they still live they are waiting for Lith to return and lead them to Seytal-Lith, a fertile world She has prepared."

Lhar stood without seeing her, apparently immersed in his own thoughts and memories. He felt T'Mero's mind leap to full alert. If anything would rupture the contact, it would be Lhar's casual disclosure of another "world" waiting. Tal-Lith was supposed to be the only heaven; all else was hell. Syza's amusement lightened Lhar's thoughts.

Nevin nearly fell off his taman when you mentioned the new world. How's Kaffi taking it?

Lhar suspected Syza knew as much as he about Kaffi, but he responded anyway. *Not badly. The words for 'world' and 'land' are very similar. She's—*

"Another world?" said Kaffi suddenly. "What devil's tongue is this?"

65

Lhar appeared surprised, then offended. With a visible effort he made allowances for Kaffi's youth and strangeness.

"No devil's tongue. We were taught that after a period of trials Lith would give us a new world, for this one is too ridden by old sin to feed Lith's worshipers. What is it that your faithful wait for, if not another world?"

"The rebirth of this one," said Kaffi bluntly.

Lhar allowed pity to show in his face, and gentleness. "It is of no matter," he said slowly. "Neither dream will put flesh on the body of hunger, nor add one drop to the shrinking river."

Kaffi sat in brooding silence, her eyes opaque as she looked across the ravaged land. Lhar could sense her recoiling from his blasphemy, yet at the same time her basic pragmatism agreed that such differences mattered little in the face of common hunger. Suddenly her face lit with amusement, and when she spoke her voice had lost the sonorous rhythms of formal discourse.

"You're right," she said with a mischievous smile. "Let the g'mirans rumble among themselves like drifs eating gasweed. The one who farts the loudest will decide which dream we die for, and we'll bow to its pious stench."

Kaffi leaped to her feet and stripped off her long gloves.

"I would greet you as a friend," she said simply.

Lhar's gloves joined hers on the rock as Kaffi approached him. Her hands moved quickly inside his long, loose sleeves until her fingers were firm arcs across the muscles of his upper arms. Lhar returned the grip, the fingers of each hand overlapping around Kaffi's thin yet strong arms. He waited while her yellow eyes examined his face as though he were an important trail blurred by the winds.

"You're a strange man," she said softly. "As strange and yet as familiar as the Ramparts. I can't read the winds which howl from your summits, yet for all their tearing force the winds are clean and sweet with water. A rare thing in a dry land. Almost you make me believe that you crossed the wastes. Almost."

Lhar sensed the sudden flaring energy of her mind, knew that her latent psi was stirring and reaching for knowledge in ways she did not understand. Her eyes stared sightlessly for a moment, and he barely heard her voice murmuring.

". . . bring pain and sorrow and hope and change . . ."

Birth is always that way, he thought very gently, though her fingers were arcs of pain across his arms.

The flaring energy died, leaving no memory save warm reassurance. Her fingers loosened and flew to her forehead in apology. When she looked at him again it was with deference. She no longer thought herself his equal, though she did not fear him. He wondered if even such a light mindtouch had been an error.

No mistake, came Syza's thought, so deft and skillful that he felt a moment's shock. *She was becoming afraid of you. When she touched you she sensed vast distances and alien experiences. Danger— but not to her. Be careful of your thoughts when her hands are on you.*

"A smile to melt the glaciers," said Kaffi. When he protested she laughed richly. "Modest, too. A leader. And now our khaners draw near. Perhaps you would finish your story over ssan and dried fruits?"

"And my miran to help me tell it."

"Just so. Is he old, your miran?"

"He's as young as you but not so wise, I'm afraid, nor so beautiful."

Kaffi smiled. "Yes, a true leader." She raised her voice to include the two men riding with T'Mero and made a sweeping gesture of humility.

The greeting of friends—quickly!

Even before Syza's urgent thought was complete, Lhar's hands once again wrapped around Kaffi's arms. Her pleasure was both surprised and genuine.

*Thought I was supposed to keep my hands off

67

her,* returned Lhar to Syza—after he had released Kaffi.

A mixture of protest and exasperation spilled over to him followed by a crisp apology.

My error, Lhar. I didn't make myself clear.

And I'm a demon for double meanings. How are Kaffi's men taking it?

When Lhar's bland assumption that Syza was monitoring four minds simultaneously and also relaying to Nevin passed without comment, Lhar allowed himself a tiny glow of triumph. She had a rare mind when it was not strangled by the past or his own bungling.

There was a slippery moment when they saw her bowing to you. Apparently Kaffi is both well-liked and powerful within her society.

Tell Nevin to watch himself. If he measures her by his home culture we'll get badly burned.

He won't like it, coming from me.

Be tactful.

When it occurred to him to wonder why Syza was being so helpful he brushed the thought aside for another, quieter time. For now it was enough and more that she was easing the critical contact as though born to the work.

Lhar introduced Nevin and Diri to the natives; Syza had fallen back to help the drifsen hold the restive animals. One of Kaffi's men, Tokor, moved to help Syza with the loose taman. As he rode past the pack taman, Lhar called out a warning.

"Watch the last taman, Tokor. It's salt crazy."

Tokor lifted his hand in acknowledgment and gave the taman a wide berth. Even without Lhar's warning, the bloody rope which snubbed the taman's nose told its own story.

"You must have gone long without sweet water," said Kaffi.

"Too long. We lost some drifs. We thought that all the animals flushed themselves clean at the river. But it must have been too late for that one." Lhar measured the taman's sullen stance. "We'll wait as long as we can. There aren't enough people here to eat more than part, and we've no time to dry the extra meat."

Kaffi licked her lips delicately. Taman were too valuable to be used as meat animals except on rare occasions. Their flesh was a delicacy.

"My appetite says that I could eat that taman myself and leave only hide and hooves for the drifsen."

"Then I'll—"

"No, no," laughed Kaffi. "My words are bigger than my stomach. If you let me lick the bones after the feast, I'll be content."

"You'll have to do better than that."

Kaffi looked at him in puzzlement.

"Unless," said Lhar, "it's your custom that the honored feast guest eats only the leavings."

Kaffi's yellow eyes gleamed.

"It's our custom that the honored guest eats alone. All the rest eat drifcakes."

Lhar grimaced broadly. "We've been wasteful."

"Oh?"

"We burn drifcakes to heat our ssan. Maybe that's why the ssan tastes like it's already been through a drif."

Kaffi's laughter rebounded in the dry air.

"Come, my friend," she said. "I must try some of this ssan."

"You've been warned . . ."

Lhar and Kaffi walked over to the small fire that Nevin had started in the lee of a boulder. The pungent smell of dried, burning dung rose in the air. It had taken Diri some time to get used to the idea of cooking food over a dung fire, but she had learned what the Tal-Lithens already knew: without wood, the price of fastidiousness was a cold meal and colder ssan.

Diri set the oblate earthen pot in the center of a tall stone trivet. Underneath, the fire blazed hotly. Five bowls ringed the fire. Nearby a reed basket was heaped with dried meat. A smaller basket held dried fruit and the omnipresent flat circles of campbread.

"You eat well," said Kaffi.

Lhar laughed shortly. "The meat was lately drifs. We barely made it beyond the salt flats."

Lhar waited for further comments but Kaffi appeared satisfied. What meager dried fruit there was looked gritty, leathery and tired. The bread was stone hard and rubbed smooth by the relentless shaking it received no matter how carefully packed. In all, the food looked as though it had been dragged the width of n'Lith behind a frightened taman—which was exactly the impression Lhar had hoped for.

"A poor meal," said Lhar.

"I would be surprised if it were otherwise," said Kaffi serenely. "Ahhh, we must have overlooked those."

Lhar followed Kaffi's glance to the basket Nevin had just put down. It held a mixture of fresh sweetberries and reed hearts.

"You missed very few," said Nevin regretfully, "but Lith provides."

"Somehow She seems to provide more to those with keen eyes and strong backs," observed Kaffi with a sideways glance at Nevin.

Nevin smiled and offered the basket of fruit to Kaffi. "Perhaps that's because devout prayers come more often from full stomachs than empty ones."

Kaffi's hand paused over the berries and she smiled directly into Nevin's dark eyes. "A practical miran," she said distinctly, "is more valuable than extra water."

"We must indeed be among the Chosen," said Nevin, his voice resonant with subdued laughter, "when a miran is more valued than water." He sighed with exaggerated pleasure, yet his eyes lingered over Kaffi's and told her that her compliment was not unwelcome.

Kaffi laughed softly and her lips showed even redder than the sweetberry juice. Then Kaffi's man touched her sleeve lightly and his deep blue eyes stared past the standing animals where Tokor had gone.

Lhar tightened inside; what had Birol seen that was important enough to interrupt the conversation of two mirans? Lhar's eyes made a rapid search but could see only Syza and the drifsen working the herd animals.

The drifs were skittish at the smell of the three strange taman. The herd seethed and spat occasional frightened drifs, but each breaking drif immediately met either Syza or leaping, fanged drifsen.

Soon the drifs would tire of useless alarms. Then Syza would dismount and hobble the three drif leaders. The rest would disperse nearby and resume the everlastingly serious business of filling their bellies under watchful drifsen eyes.

There was a distinct beauty to the interplay of Syza, drifsen, and herd animals. Even her taman transcended its angular nature as it spun and parried drif lunges. The result was close to a stylized dance with stunning leaps and sudden curves of energy, all choreographed by Syza's clear whistles.

Then Lhar realized that Tokor was merely watching. He held his taman ready to help, if needed, but it was obvious that he was not needed. Was she too good?

Lhar reached out to the edge of Tokor's thoughts. The Tal-Lithen was watching closely, absorbed in the beauty of the dance. There was no suspicion or unease in his thoughts, only pleasure. Tokor was First Herder of the First Khaner; he knew his work, enjoyed it, was very good at it. He also knew he was watching a master and the knowledge warmed him quietly. For the first time Tokor believed that the strangers had crossed n'Lith. With such a herder a khaner could cross even the Ramparts.

Lhar wryly noted that while Tokor had resented the deference Kaffi had shown Lhar, Tokor himself had neither doubt nor resentment as he bowed to Syza's superior skill.

The lead drifs were hobbled now, and the taman were quietly nosing for food among the stones. The drifsen bounded over to Syza in an exuberant game that had become a ritual at the end of the day. Syza laughed and called out to them, pet names and praise. The drifsen leaped and twisted in tawny arcs which wove between her upraised arms and laughter.

71

Lhar knew that each leap brought a piece of dried meat to the drifsen. But the drifsen leaped as much for Syza's laughter as food; when she spread her hands to show they were empty, the drifsen still played. Only when she no longer tickled their bellies in mid-flight did the drifsen stop, their mouths wide with silent animal laughter as they sat in the dust and hoped she would change her mind.

When Syza turned to her patient mount, the drifsen trotted off to watch the herd. She loosened the belly strap with an expert yank and slipped the stone bit free from the taman's mouth. The taman stood with its head against Syza's chest, jaws working over a chunk of dried meat. When she rubbed its sensitive lips, the taman groaned in comic contentment.

Lhar found himself grinning and realized that the others' frank admiration of Syza pleased him for reasons he would rather not acknowledge. He straightened his lips, hoping no one had noticed. But Kaffi had, with her hunter's eyes. Yet her words tactfully spoke only half the truth.

"Yes," she said, too quietly for the others to hear. "One of the few joys of leading a khaner is watching such skill at work and knowing you are a part of it. A small part, true, but still a keen joy."

"I wish I had been as wise when I was young," said Lhar. And meant it.

"Were you ever young, Lhar of the Forgotten Lands?"

Lhar's surprise showed, but not his shock. Did he appear so cold and foreboding? Was it that which had made Syza afraid?

"I was born in the normal way, Kaffi, and my wraps stank as any other child's."

Nevin apparently had heard at least part of the conversation, for he laughed suddenly.

"He sometimes frightens me, too, Kaffi. But it's a silly fear. If I had to cross the black space of kylith I'd follow no leader but Lhar."

Again Lhar was surprised, but this time he concealed it; Nevin's words were sincere and the tone of affection, genuine. Lhar's hand gripped Nevin's shoulder lightly.

"And I'd ask for no other miran. Who else but you could turn rocks to water with a compliment and a prayer?"

Lhar saw that Kaffi's eyes missed nothing of Nevin's face, especially the dark curls of hair which framed his forehead. Lhar interpreted the glance immediately, but Nevin seemed unaware of it. If Nevin had forgotten that Tal-Lith's religion viewed chastity as an abomination, Kaffi would remind him.

Syza and Tokor joined the group around the tiny fire. Syza's face was relaxed and her lips curved in a smile which made even the beauty of the dance seem pale. Lhar sensed that Tokor had complimented Syza on her work and felt sharp regret that his own compliments to Syza seemed only to provoke her. He bent swiftly and refilled his bowl of ssan, offering it to Tokor.

"N'Lith was cruel to our bowls, Tokor. We have few left."

Tokor accepted the bowl, then held it out to Syza questioningly.

"I've not spent the night on the back of a stumbling taman," she said. "Take the ssan. You need it more than I do."

Tokor's fingers brushed his forehead before he drank the ssan with evident relish.

"He always did like it bitter," said Kaffi, filling her bowl and giving it to Syza. "But don't be insulted if my first gift to your khaner is a basket of fresh ssan stems."

"Insulted! Sweet Lith—the ssan alone would have driven me from my home. These last summers brought enough river to keep ssan plants alive, but not enough to flush the winter bitterness." Syza sipped and shuddered delicately.

"It's hot, though," she conceded, "and wet. After what we've known, I'm glad for even this bitterness."

73

Lhar held his hand out to her; a reed heart lay across his palm.

"Here. It smooths the bitterness."

Syza took the food without hesitation and her fingers curled against his palm in casual intimacy. His worst apprehension faded. If she had not been able to conceal her fear of him when Tal-Lithens were present, there would have been real danger. But she handled her public role as deftly as she handled her drifsen. If Diri did half so well he would feel personally blessed by the Dancing God.

Lhar watched covertly as the two groups mingled, talking and laughing with the growing ease of people who are no longer complete strangers. Even T'Mero was almost relaxed. Soon Tokor and Diri were laughingly raiding the packs for tent pegs. These they hammered into the ground at varying distances, then turned to face the two hunters expectantly. T'Mero and Birol went through the forms of mild protest, then pulled out their throwing stones and smoothed the cold leather thongs into supple lines.

Lhar watched with real interest; he knew T'Mero's expertise with weapons, but to see a guardian at work was always exciting.

The morning hummed with the sound of stone-weighted leather thongs whipping through the air. Birol held the knot joining the three thongs in his right hand, almost absently rotating his wrist. The appearance of ease was deceptive. The thongs snapped taut until they became like spokes dividing a wheel into three equal parts. Birol released the knot and the throwing stones spun through the air, revolving evenly around the common center of the knot.

With a puff of dust and a muffled clack of stones, Birol's weapon wrapped neatly around a tent peg. Yet so deft was the throw that had the peg been the legs of a young drif, the animal would have been brought down uninjured.

Lhar looked at Kaffi and gestured approvingly.

T'Mero fingered the stones idly, as though he had

not chosen a target. Then the stones leaped to the end of their thongs and wheeled through the air so rapidly that the eyes saw only a blurred disc against the bright sky. The disc arced, then swooped like a raptor on a distant peg. The throwing stones rang vividly; had the peg been an animal, the animal would now be a pile of cooling meat.

Throw followed throw, each different and more difficult than the last. What had begun as competition evolved subtly into a ritual in which each man tested the boundaries of his own skill and then surpassed those boundaries, for the morning and the other man deserved no less.

Finally Birol made an impossible throw; out of a pyramid of stones his weapon plucked just one, leaving the pyramid standing as though the thongs had never sung through the chill air. T'Mero's eyes burned orange, and he turned to Birol with a whoop of joy.

"We will hunt together!"

Birol's hands gripped T'Mero's arms and his blue eyes fairly crackled with pleasure.

"We will hunt," agreed Birol.

Lhar relaxed and glanced toward Kaffi and saw that she was looking speculatively at Diri. When Kaffi spoke her voice was quiet, almost indifferent, yet everyone heard her question. "And you, Diri. What is your special skill?"

Diri turned away from the men with a movement that made her robes flare gracefully. "My skill?" she said, as though confused.

Yet Lhar knew that Diri had put all her dancer's grace into that single turn.

"Yes," said Kaffi. "Syza communes with animals. T'Mero communes with stones. Nevin communes with Lith. Lhar . . . Lhar communes with the Ramparts. All are answered. What answers you? Are you a water-finder, or do the winds tell you of tomorrow's storms?"

Lhar waited, prayed. Diri was arrogant, and Kaffi's words were a challenge. Diri's soft, exciting laughter reassured him.

"Nothing so rare. I am mur-Lith, a dancer."

"But you must be a rare dancer if they carried you across n'Lith for your talent alone."

"Diri may be mur-Lith," said Lhar drily, "but she also works for the khaner. She isn't a stone in the campbread."

"I'll look forward to her dance at the Festival of Union," said Kaffi. "It will be Lith's Dance, of course."

"Of course? You have great faith in the skill of an unknown dancer," answered Lhar.

"Anything less would shame the khaner."

Lhar accepted Kaffi's second warning with silent thanks.

"She'll not shame us . . . or those who are our friends."

A sudden wind flexed through the group, scattering flames and food. The drifsen howled in shrill counterpoint. Lhar turned to Syza automatically, realizing as he did that he had come to depend on her weather judgment. She stood with the air of one listening and waiting, her green eyes crystalline with concentration.

"No," she said, answering his unasked question. "This wind is just playful. We're safe enough, though our tongues will soon be stiff with grit."

Kaffi, who had spent her life among the shifting moods of the plateau wind, agreed. "This edge of the plateau is too open. Further in where we meet the river again, the wind isn't so loud and thick."

"How far?" Lhar said.

"Your khaner has few animals," said Kaffi evasively. "We should arrive soon after dark."

"Shake them out, Syza," said Lhar, wrapping his scarf securely around his face.

There was an orderly spurt of activity as everyone fell to work. Very quickly the tent pegs and cooking implements were restored to their packs and the food distributed among the riders. Lhar rode swiftly up the waiting line of animals, pausing only to check the belly strap on Diri's taman. He leaned over as though to tighten it.

"Well done, Diri," he said in a low voice.

"She'll curse the day she met me," answered Diri sweetly. "That yellow-eyed zarf, asking me what—"

"Careful Diri," said Lhar. "That one has fangs like a drifsen."

Diri's answer was a hiss, but she held her tongue as he advised. All through the long ride she was the soul of charm and modesty, especially when Kaffi was near. But Kaffi was not often next to Diri. Kaffi rode most of the day with Nevin, talking when the wind permitted. Often the two blue-robed mirans bent toward each other, and then laughter could be heard above the wind and hoofbeats.

T'Mero and Birol scouted ahead, though Kaffi had assured Lhar that there was little danger. The frozen season was over, most salt-crazy animals had died by now, and the few other beasts that were dangerous were also wary of people.

Tokor spent most of the time watching Syza and the drifsen. By the end of the day the drifsen allowed him to work the herd. Drifs and taman alike had become more nervous as each gust of wind brought promise of strange animals ahead. Lhar did not doubt that Syza could have handled the animals alone, but it would have been a grinding job. Tomorrow would be worse; the dung smells would be fresher as they overtook the bigger, slower khaners ahead.

He stretched his back muscles unobtrusively and settled in for a long ride.

IV

I<small>T WAS FULLY DARK BY THE TIME THEY REACHED THE</small> river. Kaffi had pushed the band as though their lives depended on reaching the river before moonrise. Even her own men had passed from disbelief into resignation.

Lhar pulled his taman's head out of the water. The others would be straggling in soon and would probably need help. He felt as though his leg bones were permanently joined in a painful curve over the taman's barrel. His butt was blessedly numb, and had been since late afternoon. With a barely muffled groan he slid off his taman and hung onto the stirrup loop until his feet regained enough feeling to be usable.

Groans and soft curses issued from the darkness behind him. Kaffi's men had arrived. Even the rugged Tal-Lithens felt the length and pace of today's ride. Lhar smiled, then immediately wished he had not. His lips cracked and bled along new sores.

T'Mero?

Coming in now.

Is Diri all right?

I tied her on; she's been asleep.

Xantha, if I could only say the same.

And I. Did Kaffi tell you why we made at least two journeys in one day?

No. She has her reasons, I'm sure.

As Lhar broke the contact he received a distinct image of Kaffi answering questions beneath the persuasive hands of the guardian. Lhar walked slowly, but with growing strength. He led his stumbling taman away from the river under the flat white eye of a rising moon. With clumsy hands he stripped off the riding harness and bridle and bent to hobble the taman.

"Vanish," said Lhar when he was finished.

The taman whuffed in his face. Lhar laughed silently and groped in his pockets for leftovers from the long ride. Limp fruit and gritty meat appeared on his palm. The taman lipped them deftly, whuffed, and waited. Lhar rubbed its lips and gave it a push. The taman tickled Lhar's face with its bristles.

"Vanish," said Lhar firmly.

With a disgruntled rumble, the taman wandered off to forage. Lhar coiled the harness and set it on a flat rock. Darker blurs against the moonlit land resolved into taman slowly approaching the river. He moved toward Nevin's taman.

"Think you can dismount?"

"Do I have to?" muttered Nevin.

"Not if you want to sleep up there."

Nevin appeared to think it over before he painfully dismounted. Lhar caught him when he sagged suddenly.

"Don't worry," said Lhar reassuringly. "It gets worse."

Nevin laughed, then swore as his lips split.

"I can make it now. Thanks . . . I think."

Lhar waited until Nevin had worked the stiffness out of his legs before he left to see if anyone else needed help. T'Mero staggered drunkenly when his feet touched the ground, but a sheer effort of will made his legs cooperate. Lhar heard muffled obscenities as T'Mero woke Diri. At least Lhar assumed the words were obscene; the required scarf and veil effectively garbled her speech. A stifled groan caught Lhar's attention. Not far away, Kaffi was leaning against her taman.

"Why Kaffi," said Lhar solicitously, "don't you feel well?"

He sensed as much as saw the yellow flash of her eyes in the darkness.

"I feel like a drifcake that's been through the fire. And if you ask why, I'll do my best to kill you."

"Lith forbid," said Lhar with a short laugh. "I thought you'd already done your best."

"We made it, didn't we? Now shut up and help me walk."

Lhar extended his arm for her to lean on.

"How long does it usually take to come from the plateau's edge to this camp?" said Lhar mildly.

"Three hard days."

"If I asked you why you drove us?"

Kaffi looked around covertly; no one else was near.

"I don't know what your hopes are. I do know the g'mirans. Many of them are good people, but . . . narrow. Change of any kind threatens them. And why shouldn't it? The only changes we've known have been for the worse. Dry to drier. Hungry to hungrier. Few to fewer.

"We have only your word that you crossed the n'Lith. Most g'mirans won't want to believe that. But if it is known that your khaner is tough enough to travel at three times the speed of our best . . ."

"I see. And how will you explain our arrival as cripples?"

Kaffi's laugh was almost a bark. "We'll go at a slower pace from here on. I'm not a fool. Nor," she groaned as a shoulder muscle cramped, "am I made of leather and stone."

Lhar kneaded Kaffi's shoulder briskly until the knot loosened. "Why are you helping us?" he said as he worked.

"Call it twisted hope. If you bring change with you, and that change is like all other changes we've known, so be it. I'd rather die quickly in a rockfall than slowly choke on dust. "And," added Kaffi in a softer voice, "I'm also selfish."

"Selfish?"

"I'll bring no children into this hopeless world. But if hope should follow you . . ."

Lhar squeezed her arm gently, then heard footsteps behind.

"Need any help?" asked Nevin.

"Yes," said Kaffi, holding her other arm out to Nevin. "If we lean on each other Lhar can go help Syza talk to the animals. Or something."

Lhar's lips turned in a small, tight smile; Kaffii was too quick.

"Then I'll leave you two mirans to your religious discussions," said Lhar. "Or something."

A second moon had risen, huge and close, blurring shadows until the eyes squinted and adjusted to the conflicting light. Behind him he could hear the murmur of voices, then Tokor's came forth clearly.

". . . mother of all rides. Not since the Great Storm has my ass been so abused."

Lhar stood and waited for the herder to catch up. At the edge of vision the herd animals materialized slowly. Even the tough drifsen were dragging their tails in the dirt. Tokor intercepted the string of pack taman.

"Can you handle the loose ones, too?" he asked Tokor.

Tokor eyed the head-low grumbling animals. His teeth flashed. "They'll behave, even for a stranger. Too tired to do anything more than snap."

"That's plenty if you're too tired to duck," said Lhar drily. "I'll hobble the leader. The rest should follow."

Lhar eased close to the young red taman and removed a hide braid from around the animal's neck. With a few quick motions he hobbled the taman. A desultory snap of its teeth was the taman's only response.

"Shake them out."

Tokor turned to lead the animals toward the river.

"And don't get near the last pack taman unless you have help. Lots of it," added Lhar.

"Or a blood knife," said Tokor. "But I'm too tired to eat even a taman tonight."

"Maybe tomorrow."

Tokor sighed. "Maybe. If we made Kaffi walk."

"And carry a pack."

Lhar could hear Tokor chuckling as he led the animals to the river. Then came Syza's whistle, dry and rasping as a rockfall. She must have used mindtouch, too, for the drifsen immediately separated one of the herd leaders to be hobbled.

"I'll get them, Syza."

He moved quickly to the waiting drif and slipped the braid off its neck. After he had finished hobbling it he went to the second drif, then to the third. When he stood up the drifsen started driving the herd toward the river. The drifs needed little urging.

Lhar felt a warm breath on his neck; it was Syza's taman.

"Wait," said Lhar when Syza made a move to dismount. He slid her boot off and rubbed the foot until her gasp told him that circulation was returning. Lhar replaced the boot.

"Keep wiggling that foot while I work on the other one."

This time he heard not so much a gasp as smothered laughter.

"Enough," she said. "Tickles."

Lhar put the boot back on. "Sorry. Every race is different. You couldn't make my feet laugh if you had to. My neck, though . . . . Ready?"

"No other way?"

Unless you're a teleport.

Lhar's amused thought roused an echo in Syza. She dragged her leg over the taman's rump and slowly lowered herself to the ground. Lhar carefully did not touch her until he saw her knees abruptly give way. He caught and held her until her legs were solid again.

"You should have seen me a few minutes ago," said Lhar encouragingly. "If my taman had wanted me for dinner I'd have rolled over and said, 'Take me. Please.' "

Syza collapsed against him, shaking with helpless laughter at the picture his mind had sent.

"Ready?" he asked when she was quiet again.

"Too . . . nice."

Lhar looked at her more closely. The competing moons made a mystery of her face, but could not conceal her cheeks, hollow and drawn. On a sudden impulse he checked the food skin which each rider carried. Syza's was full.

"Why didn't you eat?"

"Can't ride . . . and eat."

"Was it the healing?"

Syza's hand moved in a limp, ambivalent gesture.

"Anything wrong, Lhar?"

Lhar recognized Kaffi's voice and answered without turning.

"Syza was too tired to eat. Now she's giddy. I don't know how she made it this far without being tied on."

Kaffi turned Syza's dazed face toward her. Kaffi watched her intently, then nodded. "She made it because she knew she must. And when you came she knew she could let go."

Lhar doubted Kaffi's interpretation, but he said nothing.

"Bring my sister to the fire," said Kaffi. "I'll brew something for her. We use it to end miran fasts."

He looked after the retreating Kaffi and felt more addled than Syza. Sister! Sacred Xantha's Hand. Was Kaffi always so impulsive with her trust? Then he sighed at his own churlishness; Kaffi was a psi whether trained or not. She would be accustomed to making quick, accurate judgments. Or mainly accurate. More accurate, surely, that the average, psi-blind person could even hope for. Or even . . . . With an effort Lhar gathered his random thoughts.

"Syza."

"Mmph."

"We're going to walk now."

Silence.

"You're coming with me."

When Syza neither answered nor moved, Lhar reached into her mind. It was like clutching at fog—fatigue, confusion, and an icy sense of teetering blindfolded at the edge of a chasm. The fatigue he could understand, and the confusion; they were related. But why the tension, the cold fear freezing energy out of her body? Terror rising to shriek at the

room seething
with ghastly faces gruesome death dry laughter blow-
ing from his/Zomal's/hatred's faced naked and laugh-
ing and desiccated . . . a mushroom curling and
cracking and rustling deadly dry spores spreading
> *his laughter*
> *quiet and deadly*
> *growing in me*
> *drying*
> *me*
> *and cracking*

He wrenched himself out of her internal horror and felt the steady breathing of the taman, soothing and normal and almost liquid. He leaned heavily against the animal and his arms trembled from the force with which he held Syza. He forced his reeling mind to be logical. He was an integrator. He had vicariously lived in other tangled minds. Training shivered, and assumed control of his mind. He sensed levels of his awareness becoming a one-day shield through which his energy could pass but no random energy could penetrate.

Safe.

He concentrated on sending pervasive comfort with neither images nor words, power and strength and safety pouring into her until her eyes opened no longer black with fear. Just before her nightmare slinked beneath her rising consciousness he sensed a pale apology and the knowledge that the nightmare was not new; it lived in her, oozing out when she was too tired to cage it any longer. He wondered how she had found the strength to live with the nightmare so long. And how much longer she had before she broke.

"Did I faint?" she whispered in vague surprise.

"No," he said quietly. "You were . . . dreaming. Ready to walk now? Kaffi's waiting for you by the fire. She called you sister."

"She called me . . . why?"

"Because you didn't whimper and spoil the legend she's creating."

"Legend?" Syza paused and the last splinters of mindlessness vanished from her eyes. "I see. Then Tal-Lithens don't normally travel as though fleeing Hell. And tomorrow?"

"We move normally," said Lhar.

"I can manage that." Her eyes slid away from his, returned, evaded again. "You . . ."

Lhar tried to see her eyes but they were hidden behind the curving shadows of her eyelashes. He was afraid that she would slip away again, back to that horror which would someday claim her. His arms tightened around her again.

"What is it, Syza?" he said gently.

"You. You're a healer. No, don't smile. You must be. I'm stronger now than I was."

"Perhaps I am, but not in the way you think. I'm an integrator, Syza. I—"

The sudden stiffness of her body reminded Lhar that she knew exactly what an integrator was, that she had accepted this assignment rather than be integrated. He felt her fear probe coldly at the edges of her control. Then her eyelashes lifted and he could see her eyes, flat and measuring. He felt an involuntary shiver at the death that watched him.

"Listen to me," he said urgently. "I won't integrate you unless you ask."

"Why wait for my consent?"

"Because if you didn't agree one of us would die. Our minds fit too well." His laugh was cold, heed-

85

less. "One of Xantha's better jokes, Syza. I think Her laughter must sound like Zomal's. Oh yes, Syza. I've heard his vicious laugh in your nightmares. You're well rid of him. Too bad the cost was so high."

"What do you mean?" she said, fear replacing death in her eyes.

"You, maimed. And me. But we can't fairly count me. Random casualty in a forgotten war."

"Don't. I don't want—"

He barely heard her voice, imploring.

"No. This time you'll listen. You won't let me help you, so you'll have to do the integration alone. You'll need information. I don't give one cold turd for the dead on Bjmsk. They were a cruel lot. Like Zomal."

"No!"

"He was insane," said Lhar savagely, guessing but feeling certain. "You saved his flesh but not his mind. How could you? You would have become as mad as he if you had probed his slinking malevolence. And his mad cunning. He arranged not to die alone. Not him. Not Zomal the Wise. Never. You and the Contact team and a planet—an entire planet seething with life—all would die with him.

"He blew the contact deliberately. He knew that Bjmsk was at a crucial stage, that his revelations would detonate a shockwave of panic and destruction across the planet.

"But somehow you stopped him. Cleanly, quietly, tracelessly. I don't know how you even knew he had to be stopped. You're strong, Syza, incredibly strong. You did what had to be done. Then you ran. You're still running."

Lhar stopped suddenly, aware that Syza was no longer whispering denials. She had shut him out again. His fingers closed around her arms and he entered her mind with reckless force.

"I won't let Zomal win, Syza. Not here. You will not break. Not yet. Not until Tal-Lith is safe. Afterwards we can crawl and whimper and kiss our separate wounds. Then you can take your rope of lies and evasions and hang yourself with it. I won't stop you. I promise that. But if you ever want help unraveling that rope, I am here."

Lhar waited in the stretching silence for Syza to respond. She stood as though carved from the conflicting moons, remote and desolate. The quiet hummed until he wanted to batter at her stillness.

Syza's taman clicked its teeth, impatient to be turned loose. Syza drew a deep, ragged breath, then turned to the taman and stripped it of its harness. Lhar felt as though he were dreaming; her hands and body were graceful and sure as she worked over the grumbling taman. No hesitation, no fumbling. The grueling ride might never have happened. Until she turned toward him. Her tears distilled the essence of moons and solitude.

"Syza . . ."

"No more," she said wearily. "You've won. What you said must be true. I accept it, though I remember nothing. I will do what I can to defeat Zomal here."

Syza's capitulation disturbed Lhar more deeply than her nightmares; she reminded him of wire which hums as it's drawn tight, hums, and then just before it breaks the humming stops.

"Let me help you, Syza."

When Lhar's fingers touched the glistening warmth of her tears she flinched away.

"You've done enough. You've told me that I was first a fool, and last a coward. I believe you."

"That's not what—"

But her detached, unemotional words continued as though he had never spoken. She nodded her head slowly, her face an eerie blur of changing shadows. "Yes, I believe. I've been loved like this before."

For long moments Lhar could not move, could not think, could not speak as she walked away from him toward the fire. Then a single stroke of anguish broke free from his mind. He thought he heard her cry out but the darkness had congealed deafeningly, and he could not be sure.

Lhar watched his enlarged khaner move out. Syza radiated energy and strength. She had eaten enough for six people after Kaffi's salith had pumped through her exhausted body. He had expected Syza to throw up the food as quickly as she ate it, but salith kept the food inside.

With a barely masked groan Lhar shifted his weight in the saddle. Futile. There was no way his body was going to be comfortable riding today. He sighed and urged his taman into the lead. After a short time, Kaffi joined him.

"What did you give Syza? She's never looked livelier."

Kaffi's lips curved in a sensual smile. "Just looked? Salith heightens all appetites, and gives the body energy to sate them."

Lhar forced a regretful sigh. "Syza's appetites were for food and sleep."

Kaffi laughed. "Then she must have truly been at the end of her strength. Tonight will be better, my friend. And if it's your strength that needs assistance?"

Lhar's thin smile told Kaffi more than he had intended. Her playful expression vanished.

"I thought so," she murmured. "What hunts my sister, Lhar?"

Lhar spread one hand, palm up; Kaffi's face became expressionless.

"Forgive the inquiry. The error was mine."

"Wait," said Lhar as Kaffi's taman began to move away. He checked quickly but, as always, Syza was not using her psi to eavesdrop. He could sense Kaffi, though, an untrained yet acute perception, poised and concerned. Rapidly his mind sorted out alternatives before he settled on telling the truth, but not all of it.

"You spoke of your g'mirans as good but limited

people," said Lhar in a voice which carried no further than Kaffi's ears.

"Yes?"

"Syza is like them in some ways. Before she came to this khaner," Lhar hesitated, choosing his mental and verbal innuendos carefully, "she discovered that all people cannot be trusted. Especially those people who profess love but give only destruction."

Lhar glanced at Kaffi; her face showed only interest, but he could feel her awareness weighing the possibilities in his words.

"All of us," he said, "eventually learn to be selective about those we trust. Or we die. Syza was unlucky. She was even more perceptive than you, Kaffi, and far more naive. When the crisis came she was too young. She chose survival but assumed that survival meant never trusting anyone, ever. At that," he added, "she barely survived."

Lhar looked again at Kaffi but she did not notice. They rode together silently for a while before Kaffi turned toward him. Lhar waited, waited, and still Kaffi didn't speak.

"Go ahead, Kaffi."

"Being with a khaner should have comforted her. It should have allowed her to examine old questions and old answers."

"If the khaner was formed on the basis of human attachment, yes. Ours wasn't. We joined each other for physical survival. Each one of us has one or more superior abilities. This combination of abilities allowed us to cross n'Lith."

Kaffi closed her eyes, then opened them slowly. "A harsh bargain against death. Can I help her, and you?"

Lhar smothered his ironic laughter. The only thing that might help Syza was to get her off-planet, back home and alone before she fractured into deadly pieces.

"Give her what love she'll allow," said Lhar finally.

"From me, that's been very little. And pray, Kaffi. Pray that the pressures—" Lhar stopped abruptly.

"You have more to tell. But, like Syza, you cannot trust. No matter; there is time to learn."

"You're half right," said Lhar. "In time, you'll know which half."

"I'll hold you to that," said Kaffi. Her smile flashed, and she pulled her taman out of line to wait for Nevin.

Lhar urged his taman to a faster pace, letting his body relax into the animal's rhythm. The day passed to the soft sound of hooves on damp land. To the left the river ran milky and wide and deep beside the amber fieldgrass and ochre rocks which lined the bank. The Ramparts rose in the distance, changing from lavender to indigo as the day's light washed over them. As far as Lhar could see, amber and orange and gold and green plants breathed freshness into the slanting afternoon light. A fertile land when water touched it, a vast floodplain for the river which drained the icefields of the Ramparts, gathering meltwater until the river roared forth each spring and made large shallow lakes over the plateaus.

As the flood subsided, plants grew at the margins of the lakes and flourished in the wet soil. When the First Khaner left Tal-Senet for the plateaus' grasslands, a band of plants lined the retreating lakes. Throughout the season the lakes shrank, and with each withdrawal plants reclaimed former lake bottoms. At the end of the shrinking season the First Khaner grazed its way homeward along the banks of a swift deep river.

Each khaner timed its movements both with the others and with the shrinking lakes. The result was a complex, essentially diagonal advance across the plateaus, with the First Khaner taking the lead and the others following at ten-day intervals. The last khaner never went far from the city. When the lakes shrank by half, the last khaner headed back, followed at five-day intervals by the other khaners.

In normal years each khaner fattened on fresh forage and no one had to risk a lake/river crossing for the forage on the other side. In bad years the First Khaner would attempt a crossing. Even when unrelenting cold brought a drought of meltwater, the river was still formidable; many khaners had died trying to cross the swift icy waters.

A surge of fear from Syza swept through Lhar's mind. He spun his taman on its heels, and lifted it into a full run within six strides. The khaner scattered like dust as Lhar swept through. Though Syza was not consciously sending, he could easily pick up and relay the details of her fear to T'Mero.

Salt-crazy taman has gone berserk. It was unharnessed, except for the nose rope. The rope broke. You can't help. Too far away. Don't tell Diri or Birol.

Lhar snapped the contact and concentrated on the job at hand. The drifsen were defending the drifs; Syza and Tokor were defending the pack taman.

Lhar's taman was running its fastest without encouragement. Its golden hide flashed over bunching muscles and its mouth opened around gleaming teeth. Lhar judged the distances. Too far. The berserk taman had knocked Tokor's taman down. Syza cut in to protect Tokor, but her taman was no match for the crazed animal. Nor could Lhar reach its mind.

Lhar pulled his clothes over his head and threw them aside. A flintknife appeared in his hand, curved and deadly. Three quick slashes and all harness fell away from the golden taman. Lhar ducked and rolled to the ground, landing on his feet, running. Freed from harness and rider, the taman nearly doubled its speed, goaded by instinct to protect its herd.

Syza's taman went down. She rolled free, but the salt-crazy taman was close. Too close!

Lhar's mental command electrified the drifsen. They abandoned the drifs and raced to Syza, two golden blurs of teeth and savagery. One leaped onto the berserk animal's back, sank fangs and claws deep into its neck, hung on even when the taman rolled over on top of it.

RUN!

The incisive command lifted Syza into a stumbling run away from the maddened taman lunging back to its feet. The second drifsen leaped in, drawing the taman away from its injured mate. But the drifsen feint was not necessary; the high screams of the golden taman brought the salt-crazed animal swinging around to face the new threat. Tokor, still stunned by his fall, tried to reach the injured drifsen but Syza swept in ahead of him and lifted the drifsen out of danger.

"Get back!" Lhar reinforced his yell with an unsubtle mental pull.

The screams of the golden taman climbed unendurably as the two animals rushed together. The other taman scattered, closely followed by humans and the uninjured drifsen, leaving the field to the two battling taman.

Lhar ran swiftly, closer, breath deep and steady, eyes measuring, mind reaching lightly for the golden taman until he knew what his taman would do, which way to move, and when. Then the golden taman went down.

With a long leap, Lhar landed on the salt-crazy taman's back. His legs clamped down at the same moment that his knife sank into the taman's neck just behind the ears. But the taman's back was slick with blood drawn by the drifsen and Lhar slipped back, deflecting the knife's aim. Though badly wounded, the taman was far from finished.

While Lhar fought to stay astride it, the taman dropped to the ground, trying to crush him as it had the drifsen. Lhar kicked free, rolling to his hands and knees. But not entirely free. One of the taman's hooves lashed against his shoulder and the knife went spinning away. He lunged for the taman before it could regain its feet. With one knee pinning down the taman's neck, he wrapped his hands around its muz-

92

zle and twisted the animal's head toward him. The taman kicked and struggled but could not shake off the hands that were inexorably forcing, straining, twisting, until with rending snap the taman's neck broke.

Only when Lhar was certain that the animal was dead did he let go. The golden taman approached, whuffed over the dead animal, and sent a booming call over the plateau. The call echoed through Lhar, and he felt his body slipping sideways. He was barely aware of Syza kneeling close to him, still holding the injured drifsen.

"Where are you hurt? Your shoulder?"

Lhar took a few measured breaths and shook his head against the last of the eerie echoes. He flexed his back and shoulder tentatively. Sore, but no serious damage.

"Just a glancing blow. Lucky."

He moved carefully away from the dead taman and sat down. Syza sat next to him.

"What about the drifsen?" he asked.

When Syza did not answer, Lhar ran his fingers lightly yet probingly over the limp drifsen.

"Two choices, Syza."

"I know. Heal or release. Help me."

"I—of course. How?"

Syza's hand covered his, then she gently guided his hands over the drifsen's broken body. The drifsen whined once, then lay quietly. Soon its breathing smoothed and deepened. It opened its eyes and nuzzled their hands. From its throat came a low humming sound of contentment.

Lhar smiled, then realized that his own body was no longer aching. He watched the drifsen stretch and bound away to its worried mate. When he looked back to Syza her eyes were closed and her lips smiling and relaxed. She lifted his hands to her smile.

"Thank you," she whispered against his palm.

Lhar was too amazed by her touch and his own healed body to reply.

Syza watched the healed drifsen leaping and nuzzling its mate. "It's been long . . . long . . . since healing felt good."

Small sounds told him that Kaffi, Nevin, and Tokor were near. He wondered how long they had been there. When Tokor raised three fingers against his forehead and bowed deeply, Lhar had his answer.

"Not necessary, Tokor," said Lhar. "Or is healing otherwise in your khaner?"

Tokor looked swiftly at Kaffi.

"There are many ways of healing," said Kaffi. "To heal with hands is rare. And respected."

"I told you this morning, Kaffi; my khaner is made up of people with survival talents."

Kaffi looked at him intently, plainly wondering what other, perhaps less benign, talents might yet be discovered. But she would ask privately, if at all. Then her expression softened as her eyes took in Syza's subtle radiance.

"More than just survival," said Kaffi.

"We are all drops in Her river," Nevin said quietly.

Kaffi smiled at Syza and Lhar. "Drops? These two are more like meltwater under a warm sun. That was quite a dismount, Lhar. Clothes and harness are scattered all over the trail."

"A mess," agreed Lhar. "I'll spend tonight mending the harness."

"That would be a waste," said Kaffi, her eyes frankly appreciating his unclothed body.

Lhar laughed easily, though his mind licked outward to smother any antagonistic reaction from Syza. But there was no antagonism, merely . . . agreement. His blood quickened at the implications of Syza's response.

"I'm going to collect the harness and other unimportant things," said Kaffi. "Nevin and Tokor are going to help me."

"Yes," said Nevin and Tokor together. They looked at each other and laughed.

Lhar waited for them to leave before he looked at

Syza. She returned his look for a moment, then her eyes slid to his shoulder.

"I saw the taman kick you," she said, touching the shoulder. "You're sure it's all right?"

Lhar savored the feel of her fingers on his skin, but he had to admit that the shoulder was uninjured. "You—we took care of that, too. But that doesn't mean you have to take your hand away so quickly."

Lhar waited, then caught the fragments of her thought: it wouldn't be fair to touch skin awakened by Kaffi's eyes. Kaffi should have that pleasure.

"I'd rather have you touching me," said Lhar.

She searched his eyes for a long moment, did not draw back as his lips brushed hers. Because he did not want to frighten her back into her nightmare, he contented himself with the brief kiss and with holding her very gently. But when her fingers rubbed over his chest and shoulders and back, touching and enjoying each muscle, he found it hard to sit quietly. For all of Syza's obvious sensual pleasure in him, her touch was oddly innocent. She was not trying to arouse him; she was simply enjoying the feel of his body, barely aware of the effect her touch was having. And when she became aware, she apologized.

"I didn't mean—I'm sorry."

"I'm not. I'm enjoying."

"But . . ."

He waited until he was sure that she was not going to say any more. "But you want nothing further," he said. "That's your choice. As long as simply touching me brings you pleasure, I'll sit quietly and enjoy, too."

"That's unfair to you."

"If your pleasure came from frustrating me, that would be unfair. But it doesn't, and I enjoy being touched. To me, that's fair." When she still looked uncertain, he added, "If you don't believe my words, try mindtouch."

Lhar felt filaments of discreet mindtouch. After a short time he sensed her surprise.

"You really mean it," she said. "Even though you're . . ."

"Hard as wood," agreed Lhar. "But it's not a fatal condition."

"Or a comfortable one," said Syza with a quick smile. She stood up. "I won't add to the problem."

Lhar laughed and stood up too, holding out his hands to her. "You couldn't add to it if you tried."

"Is that a challenge?"

"Do you want it to be?" he said, studying her eyes, watching fear flicker in their green depths.

"N-no. Zomal . . . Zomal used to make it a contest. I never won."

"Neither did he."

Her eyes deepened but the fear was subsiding. "What do you mean?"

"Nobody wins sexual contests. Nobody. Not only do you lose body pleasure; you also lose mind pleasure. And without that, sex is more trouble than it's worth."

"I can believe that without mindtouch," said Syza, her voice haunted, bitter. Then he felt the gentle pressure of her fingers curling around his hands in response to his touch. "You're a strange man, Lhar. You make me want to believe that you'd care about me even if I were useless as an agent."

"But you aren't useless; I have to ask as much of you as I ask of myself."

"Not quite the same. You enjoy your work."

"Not this time," he said softly. "Not when each thing I must do for Tal-Lith makes you distrust me."

"But you'll do them anyway."

"Wouldn't you?"

"I don't know. I don't value other lives as much as you do."

"Then you don't value your own."

"Why should I?" she said coolly. "I'm a fool and a coward."

"No you're not, Syza. And I'm not Zomal. Don't try to make me into him."

When Syza's fingers stiffened he released them, saying, "Sometimes it seems safer to live with old pain than to risk changes which could bring pleasure— or greater pain."

Syza's lips twisted into a grim smile and he remembered her ugly nightmares.

"I doubt if there is greater pain," she said.

"Then there's no risk in changing, is there?"

"I might be wrong. I've fought very hard for what small peace I have. That makes peace too valuable to gamble with."

"Then I won't tempt you to gamble," he said, stepping back. "Too many lives depend on yours."

"And if they didn't?"

"But they do."

Syza's hand moved in a cutting gesture of impatience. "I didn't ask for anyone to depend on me. I don't want anyone to depend on me. I want to be free."

"Dead."

"Free!"

"No living person is free from past choices, Syza."

"That's not what I meant."

"Then what did you mean?" he asked calmly.

"I don't know. I don't know what I want. I only know what I don't want."

Lhar smiled slightly. "That's half the war. If I can help you find the things you want, tell me."

"Because Tal-Lith needs me?" she said, curious and wary.

"I will help you because it's part of my work. I want to help you because your mind completes mine in ways I can only guess. And your beauty haunts my dreams."

"I'm afraid to believe you," she whispered, closing her eyes.

"Don't be. I'm not demanding that you change."

Syza's eyes opened wide and dark with shadow memories.

"But I want to. Sometimes. And sometimes I think it would be better to die and never dream again. It's getting worse," she said tonelessly. "The dreams come more often and sometimes I can't tell what's real and what's nightmare. Different, though. I used to wake up screaming, back on the island in the night and the wind. I haven't done that here; something stops it."

At her look of sudden understanding, Lhar said, "Yes, I've held you, Syza, in the night when your mind and body were cold with fear. You were never fully aware. I didn't think you would remember, or want to."

Syza pressed her fingertips against her forehead, reminding Lhar of himself when he tried to collect his own scattered thoughts.

"You need time to think, alone."

He stepped back from her. "I'll send a drifsen after T'Mero. There's no need to go any further today."

"What about Kaffi?"

"Her legend? The three ahead can make camp. We'll catch up in the morning."

In the distance both of them heard the sound of Kaffi's laughter. Lhar smiled. "Here come my clothes. Go sit somewhere with the healed drifsen on your lap. I'll tell the others that you're finishing the job."

He watched Syza walk toward the drifsen before he reluctantly turned to face the others. While they all worked to unharness the taman, Lhar relayed to T'Mero, telling him to expect a drifsen.

Drifsen? Why?

How else will you explain your knowledge? Tell Birol that the drifsen is a signal meaning that we're fine and we'll catch up with you tomorrow.

As Lhar broke contact he remembered that the dead taman should be butchered; to waste it would be an appalling breach of native custom. He walked over to Nevin and whispered, "Do you have to mumble over the carcass before I cut it up?"

"No," said Nevin softly. "We can't eat or cure all of it, though. I'll make a ritual apology to Lith for wasting one of Her creatures. Tomorrow will be soon enough."

"Get the fire going, then. And remember. No matter how awful the meat tastes, it's delicious."

Nevin made a muffled sound of disgust. He had no illusions about how salt-ridden, underfed, unbled taman carcass would taste.

Both Lhar and Nevin were pleasantly surprised: the taman meat was tough, but it had an elusive flavor which kept them eating until their jaws ached. Tokor and Kaffi did not say a word; just chewed and licked their fingers happily. Syza ate well, although she had declined another bowl of Kaffi's salith.

The drifsen gorged themselves until they could only lie by the fire, panting and rumbling and humming contentment all at once. Lhar was slightly in awe of them, especially the one that had run after T'Mero, run back, and then eaten its own weight in taman.

Tokor groaned and motioned to the drifsen. "I know how they feel. Where are my hides, Kaffi?"

"Right behind you. I knew you would be too lazy to move after you stuffed yourself."

Tokor laughed and pulled Kaffi backwards with him onto the pile of sleeping skins. "Apologize or eat dirty hides."

When Kaffi's muffled protests were ignored by Nevin, she hooked her leg around him and dumped him next to Tokor.

"There. Right where I want both of you." She looked over her shoulder. "Syza? Lhar?"

Lhar laughed. "Not tonight, Kaffi. Wrestling one salt-crazy animal a day is my limit. Be grateful; I smell worse than Tokor's hides."

"Impossible," said Kaffi flatly.

Lhar laughed and peeled off his robe. Then he bunched it and threw it across the fire so that it wrapped around her face.

"Ugh. You win. Can I burn it?"

"Think of the stench," said Nevin hastily, snatching the robe and firing it back at Lhar.

Lhar draped the robe over his shoulders, chuckling, then he leaned forward and lightly touched the stones which he had earlier chosen and placed carefully around the fire. Using his robe, he rolled the stones onto a ragged hide.

"Are you planning what I think you're planning?" said Kaffi as he heaved the hide full of hot rocks over his shoulder.

"Old khaner custom," said Lhar solemnly. "A bath."

"Better you than me."

Kaffi pulled the hides over her head. Lhar called her a coward and settled the bag and stones into place.

"Anyone else interested?" he said.

"In what?" said Nevin and Tokor.

"A bath."

The two men hastily joined Kaffi under the pile of warm hides.

"You'll freeze," said Syza. "That river is little more than fast ice."

"I found a small pool that was cut off from the main river when it shrank. I'll just drop in the stones and enjoy a warm bath. Big enough for at least two," he said, then added a mental reassurance. *The pool is far enough away so that no one will know if we bathe separately.*

"I'll get the soap and meet you there."

"Don't take too long. These rocks aren't big enough to keep the water warm for long."

The rocks felt warm against his back as he walked to the river. Away from the fire, the night was filled with silver and shadow shapes and the sense of water flowing. A third moon rose, quietly shifting rocks anchored in the shadow sea.

Lhar stood for a few moments to let everything sift through his awareness, seeking other life. But there was none. He shifted the sack to his other shoulder; the rocks were becoming uncomfortably hot. Gravel underfoot rattled as he hurried along dry river margins to the pool. After he had emptied the rocks into the pool, Syza arrived breathlessly.

"Here," she said, throwing him a ball of sand-colored soap. "You first."

Lhar caught the soap, tested the water, sighed, and stripped. He submerged, then stepped out and rubbed the soap briskly all over his body.

"How is it?"

"Chilly, but better than the rinse water will be."

"Rinse water?"

"That," said Lhar, indicating the river.

"Oh, no."

Lhar grinned and tossed the soap at her. "Your turn. And be quick about it—I plan on warming up again in the pool."

The icy river brought a smothered yelp from Lhar, but he set his teeth and rinsed himself anyway. As he emerged, one of the drifsen came to investigate the source of all the yelling and splashing. Lhar did not stop to explain. He called a warning to Syza and raced for the pool. The drifsen loped behind, puzzled but not worried.

"Ahhh," said Lhar as he lay down in the pool. "Feels much better the second time. What's so funny?"

"Sand," said Syza.

"Sand?"

"The drifsen. He thinks you're crazy."

"Smart drifsen. What do you call the other one?"

"Grit. On Earth those words also describe life forms with courage and stamina."

"They've got plenty of both. Not that it matters what I think—they're your animals."

"They belong to themselves. They just happen to enjoy working with me. And you. They respond quickly when you call."

"Kerden good thing," he muttered, remembering the salt-crazy taman, "or I'd make rugs out of them."

Syza did not answer; she was sprinting toward the river. Her involuntary shriek told Lhar she had made it. He started counting. When he got to five, a silver shape splashed into the pool beside him and a stream of fiery images poured into his mind. When he stopped laughing she was glaring at him.

"Never again," she said, "will I join you for a bath."

"The bath is all right," said Lhar innocently. "It's the rinsing that's painful. I'll make it up to you, though. After I finish I'll take your sleeping hides and warm them by the fire."

"I was thinking about sleeping right here," grumbled Syza.

Lhar fell to work lathering his hair and beard.

"You aren't going to rinse again!"

Lhar chuckled behind the soap. "Not in the river. Here."

When Lhar submerged himself, Sand trotted off disdainfully.

Lhar lathered and rinsed his clothes in the river twice before he was satisfied. He left Syza working over her own clothes. When he returned to the fire, Sand refused to acknowledge him. He laughed quietly while he built up the fire. The increased light illuminated the pile of hides across the fire, but nothing stirred. The only sounds were muffled snores and the subdued hiss of the flames.

As he had promised, Lhar lined up Syza's hides and left them toasting nicely. Then he dried his hair and burrowed into his own hides. It took all of his discipline to suppress the image of Syza's body shining with moonlight and water, but he succeeded. He was asleep before she came back to the fire.

A dream condensed slowly, changing and growing until it triggered Lhar's mental alarm. He woke instantly. Nearby, Syza twitched and shuddered in the grip of her nightmare. He slid between the hides and held her, carefully changing her nightmare until it lost its horror and became only a dream. When her body finally relaxed into untroubled sleep, he gently disentangled himself and eased back toward his own bed.

Lhar?

102

°Sorry. I didn't mean to wake you. Clumsy, I guess.°

°Not clumsy. I told myself to wake up the next...°

He could not keep the amusement out of his thought. °The next time I came sneaking between your hides? Well, I was just sneaking out when you woke up.°

°Would you . . . stay?°

Lhar weighed the ambivalence that flickered around her thought; she was not entirely pleased that simply touching him reassured her. She felt rather like a child clutching her parent's hand at the first hint of fear.

°I've never liked sleeping alone, either,° he thought, moving all the way under her hides again. °Want to curl up?°

She hesitated, then rolled onto her side and put her head on his shoulder. He felt her stiffen as their bodies touched and warmed. She withdrew and lay without leaning against him. It was an uncomfortable position for her. He waited, hoping that she would get used to the feel of being close and unclothed. He had just decided to get up and put on his skin drape when she relaxed against him. Her hand rested on his chest and her fingers rubbed lightly against his skin. He let her know that he enjoyed it by relaying his sensations back to her mind. Her laughter felt warm against his neck.

°That's nice.°

°Useful, too,° he replied. °Lets you know how deep the water is getting.°

Syza's fingers hesitated, then resumed tracing random patterns on his skin. After a time she asked, °You mean you're not promising to sit still this time?°

°I'll be still. Within reason.°

°And without reason?° she asked, her hand sliding down his body.

Intense pleasure flashed from Lhar to Syza in the instant before he caught her wandering hand. He heard her draw a swift, ragged breath, then silence.

He cursed inside himself. The relay had been a mistake. He had misjudged Syza, and himself. He had reacted like a starved zarf. Then her hand moved underneath his and he heard her laughing softly.

You surprised me, Lhar. She snuggled against his chest and this time the relay was hers, telling him of her pleasure. *I was afraid you were patronizing me, like Zomal used to do. He rarely wanted me—and never so much as you did.*

Do.

I can't promise the kind of pleasure Diri gives.

Diri gives limited pleasures. When Syza still hesitated, he rolled onto his side. *Don't decide yet. Don't push yourself. Just lie still and be touched.*

Do I have to lie still?

It would be easier on me if you did. Especially when you decide to wait and think some more.

Can we make the relay two ways? she asked as his fingers stroked the curve of her lips.

After you decide.

The relay reinforces, then?

At an exponential rate. Wouldn't be fair to you, until you decide.

You call this fair? returned Syza as his hand stroked her neck and the soft inner skin of her arm.

Lhar smiled at her responsiveness. He knew where she would be most sensitive; that varied little from race to race. But he wanted to discover all of her pleasure thresholds, small and great and in between.

His hand moved over her neck and shoulders and breasts, pleasure increasing at each touch. The relay deepened until Lhar felt almost as though it were his own body being touched, and he knew what he had only hoped before. Syza was a richly sensual person, capable of completing his body as she had once completed his mind. But not now. Perhaps not ever.

Yet his hand still moved, awakening, for touching her was a pleasure so intense that he would accept as much as she could give, and try to have few regrets for what she could not give. His deepest regret was that he could not tell her of her own beauty.

He brushed his lips over her shoulder, tasted the freshness of her skin, and he heard himself murmuring her name and her beauty, her flesh alive beneath his tongue. He felt her shiver, sensed her hand seeking, finding, warm fingers holding him and delighted laughter.

"Syza," he whispered, afraid to trust himself with even the lightest mindtouch, "you're forgetting our bargain."

Oh . . . did I hurt you?

She withdrew her hand but her scattered, pulsing thoughts left fire in his mind.

Does this hurt? he countered, laughing, his hand sliding down until she drew in her breath suddenly.

Only when you stop.

She turned onto her side and caressed him again.

Syza . . . this isn't fair to either one of us.

Then don't stop and I won't. I want you and your body wants me. You can't deny it. I'm holding the proof. Unless you don't . . .

His mind opened to her, dissolving her doubts and his. He moved slowly, deeply, sharing unhurried pleasure until he felt her release in waves and he rode the waves with her, climbing until his own passion could not be contained any longer. Then they lay close, touching and sharing quiet laughter as hunger rose again and again and they explored ecstasy while moons rose and set unnoticed. Finally, reluctantly, they slept.

V

Lhar woke slowly, and reached for Syza, but he was alone. His mind called to her and was answered by a mindshield's elusive silence. With a muffled exclamation he sat upright. The air was a cold knife across his bare shoulders; another dawn outlined the chiseled Ramparts. The thin scent of ssan and toasting bread curled in his nostrils. Nearby a muffled figure moved toward him, carrying a steaming bowl.

"You wake loudly," said Kaffi, handing him the bowl. "Syza was much more silent."

"Thank you," he said, measuring her face and yellow eyes, wanting to force out of her how Syza had looked, what she had said, anything that would tell him whether he had taken from Syza what small hold she had had on inner peace. Kaffi returned his scrutiny, yellow eyes lambent in the rising sun.

"What is it, Kaffi? Was she unhappy?"

Kaffi's eyes lingered, then she sat next to him to discuss khaner relationships with all the concern of a leader and the candor of a miran.

"She was inexperienced," said Kaffi, pausing for his agreement, knowing her words were correct. "You gave her pleasure that many experienced women haven't known."

"She more than returned the pleasure."

Kaffi looked at him, laughter and appreciation in her eyes. "I doubt if she believes that." At his questioning look, she said slowly, "You are the Ramparts . . . and you don't even know it."

106

"I'm not rock and ice and silence," he said impatiently.

"Nor are the Ramparts. Give her time, Lhar. The change you offered her is as stunning as going to sleep in the rock desert and waking in the fertile fields of a miran's dreams. She cannot be the same person if she stays in the fields. She must change, and change requires strength. Be as patient with her as you will have to be with my people."

Something in Kaffi's tone moved, pulled at Lhar's mind. He wondered what unconscious knowledge had been processed in Kaffi's mind that she spoke as though she knew his true origin and purpose. With an effort he put his personal feelings aside.

"You've been candid with me, Kaffi. May I be candid with you?"

"We are leaders."

Lhar took that as assent. "What do you sense about my khaner?"

"Sense?"

"Yes."

"You are liars. Yet I would trust my life to three of you without hesitation. As for Diri and T'Mero . . . somehow I feel they live only in the dry past you spoke about so movingly. I cannot trust the past; it has betrayed me and my people." She stood up gracefully. "Now I must roll out your lazy miran."

"Kaffi."

"Yes?"

"Be gentle with Nevin."

Kaffi's lips formed a fleeting half-smile. "We learned last night that your khaner does not play like ours. He enjoyed himself, though, in spite of his reluctance. Truly, your khaner came from a dry land."

"Perhaps after we drink from Her River, we will have the strength to change."

Kaffi laughed softly. "Perhaps, but Her River is born in the Ramparts. In you. A burdensome paradox: is reality the Ramparts or the River; are you strange or are my people?"

Lhar smiled. "A paradox worthy of a g'miran."

"Remember your promise, Lhar?" She smiled at his puzzled look. "You said that someday I would know the truth about you and your khaner. Is this the day?" When he did not answer she said, "In your heights is frozen tomorrow's water. All right, Lhar, I'll wait for your melting season."

Lhar watched her leave until he realized he was shivering with cold. He found a dry skindrape and robe and pulled them on hurriedly. They were not enough; only work would warm him. He gulped ssan with a repressed shudder and started rolling up the sleeping hides.

The pack taman were lined up patiently in the translucent dawn. Far in the distance he sensed the arid stirring of the wind. The taman snorted, and their ears flicked up as the animals spotted Lhar. Syza moved down the line checking the harness for twists or wear; she looked up as the taman snorted. He dumped the sleeping hides on the ground and held both of his hands out to her. She touched them with a mixture of pleasure and reticence which told him much about her unsettled mind.

"In this much, at least, we haven't lost our gamble," he said softly. "I can see you and touch you without you hating me."

"I never hated you. After we called T'Mero, I was afraid. I'm still afraid. My past," she said raggedly, "my past betrays, and poisons. I know you might integrate me, free me, but whatever I know is slave to that gap in my memory. I am slave to it."

"And the possibility of freedom terrifies you."

Syza closed her eyes. When they opened, they were green stones. "Yes."

"I can't free you unless you want it."

"And to want freedom I must want knowledge. I must want to know what I was and can be. But if I know, if I risk and lose, if I find," her hands tightened around his fingers, bruising him as he had once bruised her, "if I find that I am what I fear . . . ." Though her

108

voice was thick, her eyes were as dry as the dawn. "I thought if I once held you, that it would be like those other times when my hunger drove me to Zomal, that the hunger would turn to ashes and nausea and I would no longer want you." The wind rose around her sudden laughter. "I was wrong. For a time with you I was as strong and clean as the Ramparts lifting on a bright tide of light. I—" Her voice broke, steadied, then became neutral. "Do you understand what I'm trying to say?"

Lhar ached to use the unique intimacy of mindtouch, but knew that if she had wanted it she would not have made language crawl where mindtouch would have soared.

"You were that to me, and more," he said. "I would tell you if I could."

"Then you know why I can't come to you again."

"No."

Syza withdrew her hands, stepped back from him. "Yes. Or I'll break."

"I won't let you."

"You'll have to," she said, her voice a blend of pain and certainty. "I don't know how long I can balance on the past and present; I do know I can't balance at all on my past and our future. And you, even you can't balance Tal-Lith's demanding present with mine. You would break. So you must choose, and you must choose Tal-Lith or you are not what I thought, and last night was a lie."

"There are other choices."

"Not for us. Not here. I will give as much to Tal-Lith as I can, though don't expect healing of me. I tried this morning, a simple harness sore."

"Let me—"

"I can't!"

The pain in her voice seeped beyond her tightly held mind, became a river of turmoil and longing and fear, a cataract pouring over him, deafening, engulfing him beyond his training's ability to aid, drowning until she pushed him out of her mind to the hard shores of sanity. He swayed slightly as he came back to himself and knew a growing horror at what it had cost Syza to be near him.

"Today—now—this instant you're right," he whispered. "After Tal-Lith."

Though she said nothing more Lhar suddenly knew that she expected her work on Tal-Lith to be both gift and epitaph to what might have been.

"Syza . . . why?"

Sorrow and fear brushed his mind in a haunting duet, a lingering lament to lost tomorrows. And then he was alone.

He sat down abruptly and pressed his fingertips hard against his forehead. Long minutes passed as he tried to integrate facts and emotions and hopes and duties, tried to order his mind that he would not fight against himself and thereby lose not only Syza but a planet as well. As he had done with the pain of his injured face, he acknowledged this new agony, and its source.

If only . . . No. Yes. Measure the ifs and might-have-beens, measure the boundaries of self and other. To retreat is to be forever afraid and weak, cut off from mind and body in the solitary horror that Syza knew, paralyzing. But confronted, it could be lived with. It must be lived with. A fact, like death. Her loss would always be there; in time, it would be just another part of him, like fingers and hands and face, accepted unthinkingly. Yes, a fact like death.

Lhar flexed his stiff fingers. Even as he saw Nevin's worried face, he knew that Nevin had been calling his name.

"You're sick. I'll get Syza."

"No!" As he heard his own voice Lhar softened the word with a smile. "I'm merely tired, Nevin. We all are."

Nevin looked so doubtful that Lhar knew his own face must appear drained and drawn. He regulated his pulse and breathing, sending color back into his face. When Nevin still hesitated, Lhar probed the

110

younger man's thoughts and for an instant saw himself as Nevin had

> *muscles bunched with surprising strength, bowed yet more powerful than T'Mero and more terrifying, Lhar with eyes like glacier ice, hard and clear and burning with a horrible cold blaze and so strong— help me my mountain gods I am alone and he is carved out of your naked heights of rock and ice and power.*

Lhar absorbed Nevin's tumbling images/thoughts with surprise and ironic silent laughter that Nevin should see him as strong at the very moment he was weakest. Deftly he reassured Nevin until the images faded into a man, tired and thoughtful. Just a man.

Nevin's dark eyes closed, then opened wide and watchful. "Syza loaded the last taman. We're ready to ride, if you—whenever you are."

"You mean if I'll get off my lazy ass," said Lhar, his laugh sounding strange to his own ears. But Nevin laughed in return. Lhar stretched, monitoring each reflex, each movement, so his inner hollowness would not show. It was an effort now . . . tomorrow it would be a little less . . . then less and less until his act and time merged to create a new reality. In time. Miserable crawling time.

Lhar mounted his taman, tired before the day's ride had begun. As the khaner strung out, Kaffi moved up to ride beside him. Lhar presented her with a smile and a carefully shielded mind.

"A dry dawn."

"All Tal-Lith's dawns are dry," said Lhar evenly.

"Someday, perhaps, we will see the rain that our sacred books speak of," she said, searching his face with intent yellow eyes.

"Your people deserve at least that."

"And yours?" she asked softly.

"Mine are survivors. They endure."

Kaffi's answer was a sigh that might have been Syza's name. They rode silently for a long time, each with

111

separate thoughts, until Lhar became once again a leader.

"Tell me about your people, Kaffi. Tell me about their memories and ceremonies and silences."

"Our history is yours."

"Our history is separated by n'Lith."

Kaffi frowned, then made a sweeping gesture of agreement.

"Shall I begin with my miran learning?" she said. "And end with a leader's practical knowledge?"

Lhar smiled slightly through lips that burned with dryness; his haunted eyes looked to the silent flowing river. He took a piece of taman from his food bag and chewed slowly as Kaffi began to talk in the eerie shifting tones of a miran chant:

In the beginning earth and sky were lovers,
And their ecstacy flowed
And Lith was born.
And her water quickened stones to people
And we knew each other, man and woman
And knew Lith and love and liquid flowing.
Sweet water in a dry land.
And we grew powerful and many
And heedless of Her.
And Her waters poured without praise
And Her life drained with no return.
And we did not notice
And we forgot that life is balance,
Those who take must also give,
No river is infinite.
Cold waters of despair
And love condensed into human form.
She came to us.
And She danced.
And we knew beauty.
But seasons cannot balance centuries.
We had weakened Her.
No longer could Her waters quench the dry stars
And She told us of Her need and weakness.

112

And we were afraid.
And empty.
And the stars claimed Her hostage.
And Her anger was blinding light and storm and
  bitter ice.
And Tal-Lith shuddered
And Her Ramparts rose.
And the Black Wind lived.
And we died.
We were few.
And fewer.
And the land was sterile
And sand was choking us.
N'Lith.
Hear us Lith!
Hear our agony and regret.
Hear us die in the dust of our neglect.
Pity us as we worship You.
Pity our unborn dying children.
And Lith wept over Her Ramparts
And Her river flowed.
And we filled our thirst with sweet water.
And forgot our promises.
And Her tears froze.
And we wept.
And we died.
And Lith spoke in a flow of melting ice.
My River shall be as long as your memories
As sweet as your worship
As deep as your love.
Drink of Me
That you may live.
Dance with Me
That you may rejoice.
Love for Me
That I may be reborn.

Kaffi's voice faded to a dry whisper. She coughed
and reached for her waterskin. She sipped a little
water. "The history of my sad and stupid people," she

said, retying the bag. "We are too weak to bring Her rebirth, too strong to relinquish Her."

"Do all your people accept the chant as truth?"

"Truth? You mean as the truth that stones are hard and taman have four legs?"

"Yes."

"Some do," she said slowly. "I cannot, not completely."

"A leader's pragmatism?"

Kaffi stood in her stirrup loop before settling back with a tired sigh. "Stones don't give birth to people. As for water falling from the sky . . ." Her hands moved ambiguously. "It is possible. We know of old ruins, vast ruins. All of my people could fit into one tiny corner of the smallest of them but there were no canals. If water did not fall from the sky, how could that many people drink?"

"Agreed," said Lhar. "But we—my own people— had not been taught that Lith was 'hostage to the stars.' Could you explain it to me?"

"Ahhhh, the Fifth Enigma. G'mirans have debated for centuries, and we have no truth to equal the number of a taman's legs. There are some ancient stones, crudely carved, that tell a tangled story of Lith's appearance here. They are also the first description of the horror that winks around us at night. The horror that took Lith's body from us. Kylith."

"'In blinding light and storm and bitter ice,'" murmured Lhar.

Kaffi smiled wryly. "Perhaps Her anger took that form. I wrestled with the carved stones for many years. Some parts of their story feel like truth. Those parts are the most baffling. Other parts . . . shall I just say that they seem more wish than truth? Or is it that I lack the faith to make stones quicken, as my people lack the faith to bring Lith's rebirth?" Kaffi closed her eyes and her face looked drawn and old. "A miran's maunderings, Lhar. Hope and nightmare. Neither one slakes thirst nor fills bellies. Enough. I am also a leader and have a leader's practical concerns."

"As a leader, what do you think of Tal-Lith's history?"

Kaffi turned toward him and her eyes were as bleak as the dawn. "There is only one truth worth knowing about my people: we are fewer than yesterday, more than tomorrow."

They rode on in silence. When Kaffi began to talk again her voice was matter-of-fact.

"By evening we should overtake the rest of my khaner. If you agree, we'll join your animals with ours, except for the drifsen and extra taman. A khaner without those would make a poor showing."

"It won't burden your khaner?"

Kaffi smiled, the first real smile Lhar had seen from her since dawn. "They will welcome new rumps to watch. When we reach the Tal-Senet you may use my khaner's compound and leave your animals in our fields."

"We're honored."

"The mirans would have it no other way," said Kaffi dryly. "The First Khaner's land is closest to the city. It will be easiest to watch you there."

"How much trouble do you expect?"

"Why are you here?" she answered tartly, but before he could frame a careful reply she waved him into silence. "Listen well, Lhar of the Forgotten Lands. I am one of many khaner mirans. Other mirans are more powerful than I. And there are the g'mirans. Those who oversee the souls of the great guilds, in particular. It was not always so. In the past, the khaners had precedence. In law, we still do. But I must be practical," she said bitterly. "The perfumed and curried luxury crafts are better loved than the dirty and tired khaners who merely feed Tal-Senet. Was it so in your land?"

"We had too few people for a city or a guild."

"Our future . . . nearer every dawn. Do you know why our guilds are so popular?"

"Full bellies hunger for luxuries."

"It's worse than that. My poor, stupid, frightened

115

people. In their bowels they know the truth of extinction. Some bury their fear under a torrent of prayer and penance. They are led by g'miran Urari; he is very powerful among the idle, the violent, the poor. Others hide behind masks of luxury. Peace of mind hangs upon the rarest foods, robes woven of threads thinner than hope, jewels found only under the deadly ice caves of the high Ramparts. They are led by g'miran Loreft, a man who claims to know his ancestors unto the First Dawn."

Kaffi laughed silently, sadly.

"Then there is g'miran Rik. Her followers are the most pathetic. They permit no talk of numbers, no comparisons between past and present, no shadow of coming death. They comb the city for abandoned houses; they destroy the houses and grind up the pieces and scatter them over the land. When anyone dies, even a day-old baby, Rik's guild takes the corpse. You'll find no graves, no fire pits, not even a jumbled cairn of water-polished stones to mark the deaths. No one knows what Rik does with the corpses, but I've heard stories of pitiful, malformed babies that I wish I could forget."

Kaffi fell silent and her eyes were glazed by ugly memories. Then they cleared and she said crisply, "Though our population has halved in two generations, you'll find neither empty houses nor full cemeteries. No reminders that Rik's dogma of changelessness is a steaming shitpile of lies."

Kaffi turned toward him abruptly.

"Aren't you going to ask how I hide from the future?" she said. When he did not answer, she continued in her brittle voice. "I gulp down raw facts garnished with a few withered leaves of hope. I have a fever to know everything, as though knowledge could make a difference. I—"

"Kaffi." The pain in his voice startled both of them.

"I'm sorry," she said, leaning over and touching his hand. "I forgot that you lived my life years ago."

"Did I?" said Lhar softly, neither knowing nor caring if Kaffi heard him. "Kaffi, there's one piece of knowledge you must have. If," he hesitated, choosing words carefully, "if my khaner could offer your people . . . their dreams . . ." Lhar sighed and began again, cursing necessary half-truths and innuendos, wishing he could risk full truth. "Many of my people could have made the journey across n'Lith. But they chose to stay and die, preferring the comfort of despair to the hard edges of hope. Are your people any stronger? If necessary, could they walk away from their dogmas? Could you?"

Kaffi withdrew her hand and her eyes looked inward. Lhar had to lean forward to hear her low answer.

"I don't know, Lhar. I can only hope."

"Who is your g'miran?"

"Firn. She is khaner born, raised in dust and storms and grazing cycles. She is the most powerful of the g'mirans, but only because the guild g'mirans feud incessantly."

"Is she as practical as you?"

"In khaner matters. In others, she is very impractical. She still hopes for a better future."

"Is she your friend as well as your leader?"

"She is my physical mother, as well as my chosen mother."

"I look forward to telling her how much I enjoy her daughter."

Kaffi smiled slyly. "If you say that, she'll assume you're skinning hides with me. That would please her; she lay with many men before she found one who could give her a child."

"Tonight?" said Lhar, with a lightness that went no further than his lips.

"Done—were it not for Syza." Kaffi sighed. "I sense she's as strange as Nevin in that way. He'll learn not to horde Lith's gifts. But even among khaners there are times when two people must share exclusively

117

before they are ready to share with their khaner."
She paused, eyes opaque with a memory, then added,
"We all have our favorites and our resentments, I
suppose. As for you and me . . . not yet."

Lhar leaned forward and lifted Kaffi's hand to his
forehead.

"You are as wise as you are beautiful."

"And you're making me regret my wisdom."

Kaffi suddenly stood in her stirrups, peering into
the distance. Lhar followed the direction of her glance
but saw nothing except a thin shadow of dust lifting
off the land.

"We'll be up with them soon. T'Mero comes to
greet us."

Lhar made a neutral sound and watched until he
finally saw a hint of movement. It became a cantering
taman with T'Mero as its rider.

Anything wrong? Lhar asked quickly.

*Birol's impatient to rejoin his khaner. He hinted
that if you hurried we would have time to eat with
them before we had to leave.*

"I'll see what T'Mero wants," said Lhar to Kaffi.
"Why don't you see if Nevin's taman is capable of
more than an injured crawl?"

Without waiting for an answer, Lhar kicked his
taman into a canter and went to receive a message he
already knew.

Under Kaffi's encouragement, the khaner caught
up with Birol and Diri at a point where the river
narrowed and the land became more hills than plains.
The climbing sun filled the air with a cold brass light.
The trail narrowed and the hills became steeper, and
everywhere there were signs of recent earthquakes.
Under the shadow of a steep escarpment Kaffi
signaled Lhar to join her.

"We'll reach my khaner soon," she called over the
echoing hooves. "I want my people to see two golden
taman moving together."

Lhar lifted his hand in agreement and concentrated

on lightly touching both taman's minds to ensure their cooperation. It was difficult; in spite of yesterday's long ride, both animals were eager to race. But when the two taman swept over the final rise they moved with matched strides, as though they had been born for this moment of unity. In a clatter of pebbles and pouring dust, both taman slid to a stop before the waiting khaner. Though Lhar could feel the intense curiosity of Kaffi's people, they looked only at her.

"Greet your brother, Lhar of the Forgotten Lands," said Kaffi into the silence. "He has ridden through n'Lith's own rockfalls to be among his family."

In response to Kaffi's formal exhortation, the eleven people gave a high ululation of approval and surged forward. Lhar dismounted and stripped off his gloves, greeting them as friends. The process would be repeated as each new member of Lhar's khaner appeared—except for Diri. It was too soon to reveal her silver-velvet skin.

"She would greet you as a friend," said Lhar carefully, "but in our land the mur-Lith touch no one's skin during the shrinking season."

As Kaffi's khaner murmured uncertainly, Kaffi said, "Yes, it's a strange custom, but sensible. They had so little food and water that their dancers had to choose between giving their energies to Lith or to their khaner. After the Festival, their mur-Lith live as the rest of us." Kaffi turned toward Lhar and said very softly, "Is that enough, or do you want to add jewels?"

"Kaffi," he murmured, "some day I'll tell you about a way of life that you were born for. You covered it perfectly."

"Some day this. Some day that. You owe me several somedays, my friend."

Lhar's answer was lost in the noise of the crowd greeting Syza and Nevin. When Birol returned from overseeing the mixing of the herd animals, Lhar saw why he had wanted to hurry back. A small child

119

emerged from the milling adults and scrambled up Birol's robes with shrill cries of delight. Birol laughed with equal pleasure as his arms engulfed the child.

"His?" asked Lhar.

Kaffi lifted her hands in an ambivalent gesture. "The child's mother and Birol have light eyes. Feyl's eyes are brown. But Birol is Feyl's chosen father. He howled like a dust storm when Birol told him he had to stay."

Lhar wanted to ask if there were other children in the khaner but something in Kaffi's tone stopped him; that and the sparks of desolation-desperation that flared out of her mind. When he felt Kaffi watching him he met her eyes silently.

"Feyl is our khaner's only future," she said, looking away from Lhar. "Feylin, his mother, is pregnant again. Each year but one she has given birth to dead children. She nearly died with the last. When I saw you and Syza heal, I knew I was right to help you. I shouldn't ask, but Feylin is my mother's daughter."

Lhar soothed the flaring sparks with a gentle mind-touch and said slowly, "If we can help, we will. But Syza's gift is . . . erratic."

"I know," said Kaffi, smiling in spite of the sadness in her golden eyes. "Thank you, from all of my khaner."

As Lhar touched Kaffi's shoulder, Syza's query rang in his mind.

Why does Kaffi radiate grief? What's wrong?

Lhar relayed the conversation, careful to strain out all emotion and avoid all hint of demand. Her response was streaked with uneasy fear.

Where is Feylin? How much time before the birth? Is she well?

"Kaffi, where is Feylin?"

"At our compound on the city's highest edge."

"When is the child expected?"

"Before Festival."

"Is she well now?"

"She was very tired when we left. "Why?"

Tell her I'll look at Feylin, but. . . .

No promises?

I can't promise!

Syza's thought was a mixture of anger and regret and fear threatening to overwhelm her control, but Lhar made no attempt to aid her. He knew that he might only make it worse.

"Syza will look at Feylin when we get to the compound."

"Are you sure? Syza is brittle now. I don't want to hurt the woman I have chosen as sister."

"If Syza can help Feylin, she will."

"Then I can hope," said Kaffi, pressing Lhar's hand to her forehead. "And now," she said briskly, "we must return to the trail at hand. My mates are preparing food. We must eat well, with obvious pleasure, or they will be disappoined."

"Suddenly I'm starving."

"Sometimes you lie very badly."

Lhar smiled unconvincingly, then set to work rearranging himself around his inner numbness. When the meal was set before him he ate, and his smile seemed genuine. By the time they were ready to continue their journey he doubted that he could haul himself aboard his taman. His only consolation was that Syza had eaten with a good appetite—and Kaffi was as uncomfortably full as he was.

Lhar groaned softly as he settled into the riding harness. "Lightly," he said to his taman, "or there will be Lith's own mess to clean up." His taman snorted and danced when Kaffi came riding alongside.

"I suppose we have to gallop out of here," said Lhar hopelessly.

"Lith forbid such waste," muttered Kaffi. "We'll go sanely. A slow canter?"

"Very slow," agreed Lhar as he turned to make sure everyone was ready. "Isn't Birol coming?"

"Not unless you want Feyl, too."

Kaffi was saying she felt no need of her hunter's deadly skills; but if she wanted to act as though it were nothing, so would Lhar. "Tokor?"

"I live badly without Tokor," said Kaffi matter-of-factly. "He is the river in my desert."

"Not true," said Tokor as he brought his taman up behind them. "She is the river."

"Let's argue about it," said Kaffi, smiling. "To-night."

Their eyes met for a moment and Tokor was still smiling as he turned toward Lhar. "Your animals mixed well with ours. Birol's skill wasn't needed even once."

"With your skill, how could it be otherwise?" said Lhar.

As he watched Tokor ride to the end of the line, Lhar suddenly realized that Tokor's eyes were brown, as brown as Feyl's. Lhar searched his memory but could not remember another dark-eyed man in Kaffi's khaner.

"Does Tokor have any other children?"

"We'll know before Festival," answered Kaffi, and Lhar felt the fear that flickered in her mind.

The trail away from Kaffi's khaner led above the highest water mark of the shrinking lake. There was enough forage for their few animals, and they would pass well above any other khaner. There were eight more plateaus, eight more waterfalls, eight more shallow lakes and flood plains to be negotiated before they would come to Tal-Senet. Along the margins of the shrinking lakes they would see khaner animals feeding on the plants that flourished as the cold water retreated. Here the various khaners harvested fruits and reed hearts and the strange, twisted ssan stems.

The sky was cloudless and dry, burnished by a cold sun. The days were growing shorter, the shadows longer, the air colder. Soon the lakes would be memories, the river a diminishing silver promise. With the end of melting season would come ice and desicca-

tion and fear that the next melt would be late . . .
or never.

As Lhar rode he sensed impatience in the Tal-
Lithens; impatience and frustration at being locked
into cycles that brought nothing but declining hope.
And beneath the frustration, violence lurked and
waited to be released.

VI

LHAR SHIFTED HIS WEIGHT FORWARD TO HELP THE TA-
man's scrambling climb through the notch onto another plateau. The last twelve days were a blur of
cold meals hastily eaten and of stiff hides thrown over
rocky ground. They had changed mounts every day
to rest the taman, but there had been little rest for
the riders. As his taman clawed over the last loose
rocks, Lhar sighed and guided the animal off the trail
to wait for Nevin. Far below, the narrowed river
thundered and seethed cold mist.

T'Mero and Diri passed by, close together and
silent. Though Lhar could not discern any expression
through Diri's concealing veils, her posture was upright. Each night Syza had discreetly checked the
dancer's health; if Diri's strength were failing, he
would slow the pace no matter how Kaffi objected.

Syza looked stronger than he had ever seen her.
Kaffi gave her a small package of spices, then made
sure that Syza used them in her morning ssan. The
result was a doubling of Syza's appetite and strength.
In spite of the grinding ride she was no longer gaunt.
Whether the renewed strength was reflected in her
mind, he had no way of knowing; Syza kept her
shields locked even in sleep.

When Nevin's taman finally came through the
notch, Lhar moved back onto the trail.

"Notice anything in particular about the country?"
said Lhar.

"There's too much of it," Nevin said, trying to ease

his tired body into a more comfortable position. "And the higher we get, the colder it is."

Lhar laughed shortly. "No argument there. Anything else?"

Nevin was silent as he reviewed the long days on the trail; then he looked around to make sure that Kaffi and Tokor were out of hearing.

"I'm an anthropologist, not a planet man. But whatever collision of forces built—or rebuilt—the Ramparts, is still very active. I'd guess that the Ramparts used to be old, so old that they were eroded almost flat, just a ripple in a wide plain of their own debris. Then something snapped. As the second Ramparts rose they dragged up the plains until the plains faulted in great chunks, making these accursed steps."

"So far we agree. That all?"

Nevin glanced sideways. "You worried about something special?"

"At each notch we've crossed there were fresh rock-falls, bigger each time. At this last notch there was a strip of new cliff-face that was taller than a rearing taman."

"Fault line," said Nevin casually. "It stretched across the cliffs as far as I could see."

"Exactly. Now, what kind of earthquake could heave up a wall like that?"

Nevin emptied his lungs in a rush. "I see . . . and I should have seen sooner. I'm so used to earthquake signs that I don't even notice them. Remember that first quake we felt?"

Lhar grimaced; he was not likely to forget it.

"Along that faultline you noticed, at the bottom, a band of rock no wider than my palm. It was very fresh, completely unweathered. I'd guess it was the result of that quake.

"And the rest of the cliff?" demanded Lhar. "I didn't see any other stripes."

"The rest probably went up all at once."

"Sweet Lith!"

"Yea and believe," muttered Nevin. "Tal-Senet is

mainly built of stone. I'd hate to sleep under stones in faultline country."

"Tal-Lithens should know how to build against earthquakes."

"Anything else? Kaffi has been telling me about the local city life."

"Listen and learn, my friend," said Lhar, reining his mount away. "You'll find no better teacher."

"Lhar?" said Nevin, urging his taman closer.

"Yes?"

"How much does Kaffi know about us?"

"I'm not sure. She's psi. Untrained, of course, but still potent."

Nevin looked uneasy. "I—can we trust her?"

"Do you want to?"

"Yes."

"Your instincts are good. Don't let her psi scare you. She knows less than you do about the subject. But be careful all the same. And try not to fight your imprinting."

"You mean Kaffi and Tokor and . . ."

Lhar waved his hand casually. "You know better than I what part of your native culture conflicts with your Contact conditioning."

"Don't you have any conflicts?" said Nevin with a trace of bitterness. "No, you wouldn't."

"Don't count on it." Although he wanted very much to kick his taman into a run, Lhar held the pace at a walk. He was not sure enough of his own control where Syza was concerned. The impasse was too new. A single, simple irrational impulse might unravel everything.

"Sorry," said Nevin quietly.

"No need. Like the rest of us, you're doing the best you can with what you have. No one can ask more."

"But what I have isn't—"

"Don't belittle yourself." Then, more gently, "Are you edging up to a request for integration?"

"I don't know. Kaffi."

Lhar waited.

"The khaner. Tokor is her half-brother. One of the men we met is probably her father."

"Biological?"

"Chosen, and probably biological as well."

"And?" said Lhar.

"Isn't that enough?"

"On your planet, yes. On many of the other civilized planets it doesn't mean a kerden thing."

"So I learned."

"Was your first integration successful?"

"I'm here," Nevin said carefully.

Lhar said nothing.

Nevin mumbled, then said clearly, "Some days I'm not sure who I am. I've broken almost every one of my own cultural taboos but I don't feel like a monster. I could love Kaffi and Tokor in spite of myself. I wish . . . sometimes I wish life were as simple as it used to be," finished Nevin with a tired laugh.

"And the rest of the time?"

"I rather enjoy it."

"You don't need integration," said Lhar drily. "You need sleep. Tell them to skin other hides for a few nights. Kaffi will understand. And if you can't tell her, I will. When we get to Tal-Senet I don't want my miran stumbling around half asleep."

"When the khaners all return, anyone who is fully awake is suspect. The city is like a river in flood until after the Festival."

"The usual 3b orgy?"

"Ummmmm . . . yes and no. Yes in that sexual relations are obligatory. No in that beatings, murders, rapes and general mayhem are not condoned."

"Not enough population to spare?"

"Right."

"Are there laws to that effect?"

"More of an implicit cultural taboo. Oh, I'm sure some people lose control, but they're brought back to the herd very quickly. I suspect that yefa helps. When the last khaner arrives, yefa is taken in every conceivable manner—baths, rubs, three kinds of drink, chewed, burned, smoked, eaten, sniffed. I might have missed a few."

"Better yefa than—"

"Than what?"

Lhar looked around, but no one else was near.

"Better than jexn, the preferred drug on a 3b planet I once worked. Jexn does for people what too much salt does for a taman."

"Remind me to give that planet a pass."

"Exactly what I recommended. Thousand-year proscription. In that time the culture will either learn to handle jexn or die."

"Rather harsh."

"It's their population, their planet. If they want to destroy either or both, it's their problem."

"But I thought that Contact saved cultures for potential Concord membership."

"Contact intervenes in natural, not cultural, emergencies. If Tal-Lith's sun were stable we wouldn't be here. And if we succeed in transplanting this culture to Seytal-Lith, we will let the culture develop in its own way. No further interference."

"How much time do we have?" said Nevin quickly. "I have an uneasy feeling about the sun."

"Officially we have eight Tal-Lith cycles before burn-off is expected. Unofficially," Lhar's hand moved in a flowing Tal-Lithen gesture of ambivalence, "killing flares are very unpredictable. The sun could go today."

Nevin stared at Lhar in disbelief.

"But," continued Lhar, "I calculated that we have a ninety-four percent probability of making it through Festival. After that the probability drops off a cliff. About eleven percent each tenth-cycle. If Diri does her job, though, Festival is all we'll need."

"Festival," muttered Nevin. "By the Sacred River and Each One of Her Drops. Festival! The people will be too full of yefa to care."

"What better ending to the Festival than to wake up on a rich, new planet warmed by a stable sun?"

"It's not that simple."

"If it were," agreed Lhar, "we would just set up Accesses, fill the natives with ecstasan, and transport them to Seytal-Lith. We'll do that if we have to."

"Shock. You'd lose the culture, most of the people, and any hope of a representative gene pool."

Nevin was silent for a long moment, obviously troubled. "Does Diri know how absolutely vital she is?"

"I hope not," said Lhar grimly. "If she gets too arrogant I'll have to make Syza bring her back to reality again."

Distaste twisted Nevin's usually smooth face. He exhaled noisily. "It's a good thing Diri's brains are in her genitals."

Lhar laughed softly. "We counted on that."

They continued the ride in a silence broken only by occasional comments on recent rockfalls and apparent faultlines. As the sun arced across the sky toward evening, the land gradually changed. Wild plants were replaced by orderly orange rows of ssan shrubs, green pools of reeds, red fodder fields and long stretches of stubby lavender grain. These were khaner holdings, harvested by people made tiny by distance. Irrigation ditches turned silver, then bronze, then molten red-gold in the waning sun. The trail avoided the fields, threaded up rocky ridges, clawed through yet another narrow notch where the river thundered and breathed icy mist over tired riders.

When everyone had safely passed through the slippery pass, Lhar urged his taman close to Kaffi's.

"How much further to Tal-Senet?"

"Three days, if Jyll hasn't begun his harvest." At Lhar's quizzical look she added, "Jyll would be furious if we trampled through his ripe reedhearts. He tends those reeds like the children he's never had."

"Is he of your khaner?"

"No. Didn't you keep your fertile lands in common, all khaners working together?"

"We had no fertile lands."

"Forgive me. I should have guessed by the small number in your khaner."

"How many are in your khaner?"

"I'm not sure. People drift into different khaners, find other lovers. Probably one thousand."

Lhar remembered Feylin and wanted to ask if Feyl was the only child among one thousand adults. Even if only one quarter of the adults were women of child-bearing age, there must be more than just one child.

"That must seem like a lot of people to you," said Kaffi, mistaking the reason for his silence. "Only eighty-four of us follow the herds. The rest work the fields."

"May I ask questions about khaner relationships?"

"Nevin has asked so many questions I'm beyond offense," said Kaffi drily.

"Then perhaps I should ask him."

"His questions concerned city power structures and religion. Miran matters. You, naturally, would be more interested in khaners."

"Does your whole khaner live in the same compound? Are you equally familiar with each member?"

"That would be impossible. Of course we all act as if we love every khaner member equally. As for living together, only in the frozen season. The khaners, and the guilds as well, are almost separate cities. We care for our own and trade the surplus of our work to the merchant guild. The khaners feed the guilds, a fact that the guilds would like to ignore."

"It must be very difficult to live with one thousand people."

Kaffi laughed suddenly. "I wasn't clear, Lhar. Normally we live in small groups, i'khaners, within the khaner compound. A single khaner is like a ssan shrub; the i'khaners are stems and leaves and roots and buds. All different, but all part of the same whole. My i'khaner has eleven members in the melting season, twenty-three in the shrinking, and thirty-one in the frozen."

"Are khaners entered by birth or choice?"

"Khaner membership is usually determined by birth. I'khaners are chosen fathers, mothers, brothers, sisters and friends. But nothing is fixed. Khaner born or raised may prefer the guild life. The same for guild people. Nor are i'khaners carved out of rock. Anyone is free to join another i'khaner, a separate khaner, or any of the guild levels."

Lhar rode in silence, correlating the new information with the information he had been given by Contact. The concept of i'khaners had not been part of that information. The automatic monitors had seen the compounds, dissected the language, and concluded that khaners were endogamous clans. The living groups within the khaners were assumed to be based solely on genetic relationship. Perhaps it had been that way in the past, but customs had changed. Khaners were actually more a socially than a genetically determined structure. The i'khaner was the basic unit of living, and was determined by personal, mutual choice. His extrapolations about Tal-Lithen society must be changed on the basis of new information. He studied the ramifications from all angles, riding silent and relaxed while his mind performed intricate calculations. Finally he asked, "Are mirans separate from their khaners and guilds?"

"Only during the training period."

"How are mirans chosen?"

Then, fearing that he might have trespassed on a social taboo, he lightly touched Kaffi's mind. But all he sensed was her patient willingness to educate the remnants of a former culture into the complexities of a new one.

"Six cycles from the day of birth, all children are taken to the g'mirans. After three days the khaner or guild is told whether the child has the qualities necessary for miran training. And no, I don't know what the g'mirans look for."

Lhar silently wondered if psi was the essential

quality the g'mirans sought, but Kaffi's mind was as empty of knowledge on that point as his own.

"Do khaners and guilds ever war?"

"They used to. Then the g'mirans decreed that every fourth child born to either khaner or guild must be exchanged. When the child is twelve, the exchange is made."

The monitor had missed that, too; ritual hostages to peace. Lhar rode silently, making rapid correlations.

"Feyl is your i'khaner's only child?" he asked finally.

"He is my i'khaner's only child," said Kaffi in a thin voice, "and the only living child born to my khaner in three years."

Even as his hand covered hers in silent comfort, Lhar's mind was reeling at the ramifications of her statement. That was less, far less, than the monitor's extrapolated birth rate. Machines had watched and gathered information for six cycles, a highly risky process in Tal-Lith's clear skies. The last three cycles had been used for finding and preparing a planet for the exodus from Tal-Lith. Surveillance had been reduced to a single moon-based monitor capable only of detecting gross deviations from the norm as perceived in the last six cycles, changes such as wars or extreme famine or violent solar flares. Six cycles of machine-gathered information, with all its inherent lack of subtlety. Two cycles with virtually no information gathered. Eight cycles in all. Not enough. Not nearly enough. The Contact team knew Tal-Lith's language, had an outline of gross cultural and geographic realities, a thorough familiarity with taman and drifs, and little else. Eight cycles. Most planets were monitored by machines for at least one hundred cycles, and by living intelligence for fifty more, before Contact was attempted. If Contact was attempted at all.

Lhar fingered the concealed psitran and wondered if his Contact superior knew that Tal-Lith's sun had defied the odds in the last two cycles and taken a quantum leap in instability, shifting its radiation patterns so that the intricate dance of gestation and birth became aborted travesty.

One child in three years.

"When does the Festival begin?" he asked abruptly.

"When the last khaner returns."

"How long?" he demanded.

When he saw the sudden fright on Kaffi's face he eased his grip on her hand and softened his question with a smile.

"Seven weeks. But the river has been erratic. It may take longer."

Erratic river. A warming sun softening more of the massive icefields at both poles of Tal-Lith and

water

flowing, river growing, plants reaching, sun growing and flowing and reaching out

"Lhar, what's wrong? What's wrong!"

Abruptly Lhar remembered Kaffi's psi. Before he released her hand he shoved back his vision of flaring sun and substituted a kaleidoscope of plateaus and strange customs and fatigue. Though Kaffi received only hints of emotions, they were emotions she could understand. When he was certain that she was no longer frightened he pulled his hand away.

"Nothing's wrong," he said, letting tiredness roughen his voice. "My khaner has traveled far, we have further to go and we have to wait until after Festival to know whether your people will accept us."

"Is it only that?" said Kaffi.

"Isn't that enough?"

Kaffi did not answer. Lhar cursed his carelessness in touching her when his mind was undisciplined. His own control decreased every day. He knew that he needed time, silent time to integrate personal and professional imperatives. Two weeks, one week, even a few days. Yet time was the one thing he no longer had. He would have to go on waking up and working with his mind in the quiet hours before dawn, knowing as he worked that self-integration cannot be accomplished in scattered hours by a tired mind. But he had no other choice.

He wondered how Syza was sleeping, what her dreams were.

Jyll's reedhearts had not yet been harvested. The weary riders made a long circuit of the flooded area. The air felt unusually moist, almost humid, as the taman scrambled over the rough trail. When the taman walked instead of cantered, Lhar rode beside each member of his khaner, trading inuendos with Diri and measuring possible dangers with T'Mero. Nevin, refreshed by six hours of unbroken sleep, was questioning Kaffi about miran powers while Tokor listened with a bemused expression. Syza, as usual, rode alone. Lhar hesitated, then fell back to the end of the line where Syza and the drifsen oversaw the fractious taman.

"Sorry," said Lhar stiffly, "but it would look odd if I continued to avoid you."

Syza's face remained expressionless, her mind impenetrable. He felt unreasoning anger at her composure, then told himself he was a fool for expecting anything else. She, at least, was able to stand by her pragmatic appraisal of the impossibility of their relationship. If the impasse upset her she kept it well hidden. But then, hiding was her specialty. Nothing ventured, nothing lost. Maybe she was right; the less he saw her, the less he was close to her, the easier it would be to accept the necessity of being apart. If only he could excise the memories from his mind.

"Tokor told me the crops were maturing oddly," said Syza.

"Kaffi mentioned it too. That, plus the extremely low birth rate, means trouble. The sun is closer to burn-off than Contact thought."

Syza drew in an uneven breath. "How long?"

"We should make it through Festival. Seventy-nine percent chance. Are Diri's rhythms consistent?"

"For her age, yes. The ride has been hard on her. And T'Mero."

"T'Mero?" said Lhar, surprise making him look directly into her clear green eyes. For a moment his attention scattered, then with an effort he focused on her words.

"I've been checking Diri every night. Last night T'Mero woke when I touched her."

"You mean that he hasn't been waking up when you approached? He's our guardian!"

"He slept all but last night. When he woke up he grabbed me hard enough to leave bruises. I felt fear and anger from him before he recognized me. Everything faded but a deep tiredness, a sense of dissipating rhythms. He concentrated, evened out his rhythms and fell asleep again."

Lhar remembered the song that had triggered T'Mero's violent attachment to Diri, the incident with Nevin and the yefa leaves, the guardian's subtle disregard of his duties in favor of Diri's presence. And Diri herself, suddenly content to be exclusively with T'Mero. He wondered what they symbolized to each other, why their sudden and total intimacy had occurred. It could hardly be a mental bond, for neither one had the psi potential to realize, much less accomplish, a relationship of complements. Nor could it be purely physical; according to Syza, neither one had the stamina to sustain such a bonding.

"Why?" he mused aloud. "Why T'Mero, who hasn't had an exclusive bond with a woman since his first maturity? And Diri. Her promiscuity is legend."

"Does it matter?" said Syza, her voice tight. "They're not harming anyone."

"Unlike me?" shot back Lhar. "But maybe you're right. It doesn't matter why. Maybe I'm just jealous of two people who found a means of enriching duty with pleasure. Obviously I need integrating more than anyone else. Question:" he said coldly, "who will integrate the integrator?"

"Do you think I enjoy this?"

135

"You chose it over integration."

"As you chose Tal-Lith. Will cutting at each other make our choices easier to live with?"

"Syza," said Lhar hesitantly, "if I opened my mind to you, let you know the details of my life and essence, but did not touch your mind at all, would you trust me then? Would you let me integrate your past and present?"

"I trust you. I don't trust myself. I know now that if my integration fails, it can be no worse for me than it was. But for you, for Tal-Lith—too much to lose. That's half of my fear. The other half is my fear of knowing what I have been. And another half," she laughed raggedly, "—if there can be such a thing—is my fear that I will destroy you as I have every person whose mind I touched."

"The last two are almost the same fear, Syza," he said carefully, keeping the sudden hope out of his voice. She had begun to peel back the layers of amnesia, begun to remember what had happened on Bjmsk. Perhaps integration would be possible after all.

"Are they the same? Yes, I see that they could be. In my dreams I destroy faceless people. And laugh. My laughter is worse than Zomal's. I can't trust myself."

"You can't trust nightmares."

"They feel like truth."

"Half-truth."

"Maybe. Can we risk Tal-Lith to find out?"

Lhar remembered the wrenching joy of sharing just an instant of her mind. "Tal-Lith may already be lost to her sun."

"Then what we do or don't do no longer matters?"

"It matters more than ever," said Lhar tiredly. "We have to convince the natives to leave at the end of Festival."

Syza was silent for a long moment. Then, "Diri."

"Yes. A messenger is not good enough. We'll have to let her be Lith. A commanding god, in effect."

"She'll like that. She didn't come here for a few short hours of adoration. Don't trust her. Or T'Mero."

"T'Mero? He's spent six maturities as a Contact agent."

"Diri seems to be the beneficiary of his skills."

"That will change. If the Tal-Lithens turn against us," said Lhar, touching his rough belt, "T'Mero will be our best chance to make it to the emergency pickup point.

"I might," Lhar hesitated, "I might have to use you again. With Diri."

"I know."

"Why don't you trust T'Mero?"

"I don't know. Something about how he felt when he touched me."

"Have you been in his mind?"

"No!"

Lhar wished he could mesh with her, know directly the source of her vague unease over T'Mero. But that was impossible.

"If T'Mero shouldn't be trusted, I have to know why. I'd rather be controlled Diri than you. We don't have much time; all of Contact's calculations have to be changed. Help me."

"How?"

"Touch people. Become part of them. Let them react with you in ways they never would with me. Monitor Tal-Lithen minds. All our minds, for that matter. Make your own theories, measure them against mine. You have a unique mind. I respect it even if you don't. Use it.

"And then maybe, if we're lucky, we'll get off this zarfsucking planet before either one of us cracks."

"Not you," said Syza certainly. "You'll never crack."

Lhar laughed without humor. "Before Tal-Lith I might have agreed with you."

He urged his taman into a canter and rode up toward the head of the line of taman. Through the long cold hours of afternoon and wind the animals cantered and walked, walked and cantered past the irridescent rustling reeds. At sunset Kaffi kicked her taman into the lead, heading toward a distant jumble of rocks that was the only path up onto the highest plateau. Two of the three moons rose, yellow and silver pouring over the black land. And still the taman cantered.

In a hollow near the base of the pass, Kaffi signaled a halt. When Lhar caught up with her, Tokor's taman was already at the base of the ragged notch. Hooves rang against crystalline rocks, there was a tumble of pebbles, and then Tokor disappeared among the huge boulders.

"We'll rest here," said Kaffi. "When the third moon rises, the light will be too dangerous for climbing."

Lhar looked into the distance where Tokor had gone.

"Tokor knows Tal-Senet's Gate," said Kaffi. "He'll be as safe as anyone in sunlight."

"He's tired."

Kaffi spread her fingers in a gesture which indicated both agreement and disagreement. "Someone has to reach g'miran Firn. If I went it would be noticed. Tokor can be as inconspicuous as a drop in the river."

"Then what happens?"

"If word of you has already reached Tal-Senet, g'miran Firn will meet us at my compound. If you're still our secret, she'll ride out to meet us."

"If we aren't accepted what will happen to us?"

Kaffi paused halfway through unsaddling her taman. The belly strap flapped awkwardly in a newly born wind. She caught the strap and coiled it carefully before turning to face Lhar.

"I don't know. There are no rituals or rules for dealing with your khaner. The worst punishment we have is to be sent out to die in n'Lith, but you have already survived that. Who are we to punish or dispose?"

"And those who are our friends?"

"N'Lith."

"No one who helps us will die in n'Lith."

"Who would want to live there, or beyond?" asked Kaffi calmly.

"There are other choices."

"Tell me one." But when Lhar hesitated, Kaffi's hands opened in a gesture of resignation. "I know," she said wearily. "I must trust you fully though you trust me incompletely. An uneven bargain, but I'm too tired to protest it."

"Kaffi—"

"We'll talk when you have something new to tell me."

Lhar watched her as she went through the motions of caring for her taman. Once she stumbled and would have fallen if he had not steadied her. When his hand touched her he caught a confusion of emotion-images blurred by fatigue

Tokor gone, cold brittle suspicions, Tokor, tired and alone and a dry wind blowing.

"Like us, you're tired and cold and almost frightened. For once let us take care of you." He led her unresistingly toward a pile of bedding.

°T'Mero.°

°Receiving.°

°When you're finished with Diri, bring some food and hot ssan for Kaffi.°

°Diri's asleep. Small fire?°

°Very small. Kaffi wants us to remain a secret.°

A small flare of orange appeared at the base of a rock pile. Kaffi started to protest, but Lhar pushed her gently onto the warm hides.

"No one but us will see the fire."

The flare became a small glow overshadowed by the scent of ssan brewing. Soon everyone except Diri was sitting and sipping at scalding ssan. Kaffi ate lightly, then dragged her hides over to a place that was almost level and free of rocks. Lhar waited a few moments before he followed.

"Do you prefer sleeping alone?"

"I'm too tired to do more than sleep. But I would enjoy a warm body or two nearby. Nights at the Gate are always bitter."

Lhar returned to the already dead fire and began picking up bedding. Only Syza and Nevin remained; T'Mero and Diri were asleep together. Lhar quickly laced three hides together, beckoned to Syza and Nevin, and returned to Kaffi.

She shouldn't be alone tonight, thought Lhar to Syza. *She's cold, tired, lonely, and more than a bit afraid.*

He began arranging bedding on either side of Kaffi. When the biggest rocks were out of the way, he shook out the laced-together hides and crawled in next to Kaffi. He was debating whether or not to curl up with her when Syza's delicate thought brushed his mind.

She needs to hold and be held.

Behind Syza's calm thought was a restless universe of similar needs.

In the pale light of the moons Lhar lay next to Kaffi. Her body shifted, inviting him to move his arm so that his shoulder would become a pillow. With a murmured sigh of appreciation, she turned on her side and curled up against his warmth. When Nevin burrowed in beside her, she automatically drew his arm across her body. He obligingly turned on his side and snuggled against her back, giving and receiving warmth.

Lhar touched her mind lightly; loneliness and cold were receding.

There was a rustle of hides and Lhar felt the sweet pressure of Syza along his back and legs, her arm across his chest, her quick apology in his mind. He brushed his lips across her hand and willed himself asleep.

When he awoke it was with a sense of danger. Only the third moon remained, golden, balanced on the brooding rim of the plateau. His mind searched outward until he remembered Kaffi's latent psi, and

140

the search faded to a thread of awareness-seeking. He had an instant of surprise when Syza's mind joined his, then he accepted her piercing clarity, guided their joined minds with all the subtlety of his training.

They discovered three people silently walking, descending the lowest portion of the Gate. Syza whispered in his mind without disturbing the delicate search.

Tokor's in front, the rainbow with the core of gold. He tastes of reedhearts and dawn.

One of the others must be g'miran Firn.

Which one woke us?

Lhar probed with incredible delicacy, retreated in puzzlement. *Neither one feels dangerous to me. Their psi is greater than Kaffi's but still untrained.*

And then two of the minds blended with surging power. Immediately Lhar clamped a shield around Syza and himself. His warning trickled through her surprise.

They're complements. Untrained, unknowing. Complements. When they touch each other.

Like our minds when we called T'Mero?

Like ours when we're unaware and touch casually.

Can they see/sense us?

Only if I let them.

He held the shield and quickly sorted through possibilities, probabilities, hopes and difficulties. He reached out for T'Mero, found him deep in sleep. He smothered a flash of irritation that the guardian slept while three people walked closer to them each second. He woke T'Mero, told him the new problem, and turned his mind back to Syza.

Can you touch my mind so that no one would suspect?

Even you?

Lhar laughed silently. *That would be too much to hope.* But before he had finished the thought, his awareness of Syza vanished. With growing surprise he searched his mind for her presence. A long time

141

passed before he finally sensed a distant flash of emerald, crystalline yet warm, alive with potential.

Beautifully done, Syza. Now stay there.

How long?

Is it a strain for you? I'd go into your mind, but—

I know. I'm sorry. Better this way.

Stay there until you can't hold. Tell me when you leave so I'll know to go back to the old way of mind-touch. It's harder to shield that way, but it can be done if this is too uncomfortable for you.

A feeling distinctly like a drifsen's satisfied murmur spread through Lhar, emerald-tinged and alive. He laughed silently and told Syza to sleep. The arm that had unconsciously tightened across his chest relaxed and the breath warming his back slowed and deepened.

T'Mero?

Receiving.

Don't try mindspeech unless it's an emergency. I can shield my contacts with you, but I can't shield a contact I don't know is coming. I'll check with you when I believe it's safe.

Kaffi stirred. Lhar eased carefully onto his back, trying not to disturb either of the women. Both women shifted, unconsciously seeking their lost warmth. Nevin also moved. When everyone was quiet again, Kaffi's and Syza's hair tickled Lhar's neck, and Nevin's long arm stretched almost across all of them.

Lhar moved his legs cautiously, then gave up. He could avoid more rocks if he slept alone, but it was not nearly as pleasant. He gently worked his fingers into Syza's long hair and was rewarded by a subtle increase in the pressure of her body against his. He stifled a flash of desire by concentrating on Tokar's advance. Lhar opened his eyes but remained utterly still, hoping Tokor would not be fool enough to approach without the ritual greeting to the khaner's hunter.

"It's Tokor, hunter. May my two friends and I pass?"

Tokor's voice was barely a whisper.

"Your friends are ours," came T'Mero's soft answer.

Lhar felt the subtle tightening of Syza's body and knew she was awake again.

"Tokor," whispered Lhar, "you're as silent as a rockfall."

Tokor's quiet laugh came from no more than an arm's length away. His robes rustled as he sat near Lhar's head. In the waning light of the golden moon, he saw Tokor's eyes flash as he counted heads among the tangle of bodies and hides. A hand squeezed Lhar's shoulder.

"Good," murmured Tokor. "Kaffi told me she would not be alone."

"But still missing you."

Tokor chuckled. "That's good, too."

"Is g'miran Firn with you?"

"Yes. And g'miran Daal."

The satisfaction in Tokor's low voice was unmistakable. "Daal is a leader, too," said Tokor. "He is always finding ways of keeping Tal-Senet from fracturing into warring guilds."

"Does g'miran Firn trust him?"

"They are as close, closer, than Kaffi and I."

"Then I'd better get untangled and greet them properly."

Tokor's hand pressed lightly. "Wait. It would be good if they saw their daughter sleeping among friends."

Lhar wondered what Kaffi had told Tokor, then realized she had probably told him everything she knew or suspected or hoped. He listened to two people approaching very quietly.

"Lhar wanted to get up, but I told him that Kaffi's sleep was more important to you than ritual," explained Tokor softly.

"She's never learned her limits," said a woman's low voice, half laughing, half concerned, reserved.

"She's your daughter," answered a man's voice, wry and admiring, reserved.

Soft as the whispers were, Kaffi stirred. Her hand slipped beneath Lhar's skindrape. As though reassured by the smooth resilience of chest muscles, her fingers curled and relaxed, and she slipped more deeply into sleep.

"Forgive my informality," said Lhar very softly. "I intend no disrespect."

Robes rustled, brushing his cheek as g'miran Firn reached down to her sleeping daughter. He sensed a flare of psi as fingers touched Kaffi's forehead. After a moment the older woman's breath came out in a soft sigh.

"She is well and free, Daal."

"Would I leave her otherwise?" said Tokor sharply.

"Not if you had a choice," murmured Daal. "We just weren't sure you had that choice."

"If you can tell all that just by touching," said Lhar casually, "touch me."

G'miran Firn hesitated, reached for Daal's hand. Orange and silver burned in Lhar's senses. He braced himself for the inevitable roughness of untrained mindtouch. Through his shields he sent a mixture of anticipation and friendship. He barely sensed Syza's deft maneuvers, his shields opening further to reveal depths of silence and heights of immense power. Had there been time or opportunity, he would have argued with Syza. He was not that powerful, and even if he were, this might not be the time to announce it.

A long sigh and Firn's fingers lifted.

"Daal?" she said softly.

"Yes," he answered. "He could have crossed n'Lith."

"Yet he belongs to the Ramparts."

"Her Ramparts."

"The symbol of Her anger," countered Firn.

"And the source of Her water."

"You trust him, then?"

"He could have killed us if he had wanted to," said Daal.

Lhar waited, outwardly relaxed, while the g'mirans discussed him.

"Could you kill us?" said Firn, as casually as if they were discussing the weather.

"Why would I want your deaths?"

"But you do have the ability," said Daal.

"Yes," said Lhar, knowing that the time for evasion was over, had been over since Syza opened his shields.

"Could we kill you?" asked Firn.

"Yes."

Tokor muttered that he would hate to be the one to try. Daal laughed softly.

"Kaffi trusts you," Firn said musingly. "Why?"

"Ask her."

"Later. Why does she trust you?"

The truth, urged Syza deep in his mind.

Xantha! What is the truth? he shot back. Kaffi's body tensed, and he knew she had awakened.

G'mirans Firn and Daal waited.

"Kaffi . . . to Kaffi I symbolize change. She hopes the change will be good."

"And if it isn't?" said Daal.

"She said she would rather die in a rockfall than be smothered in dust."

"That's Kaffi," said Tokor with grim amusement.

"You trust Lhar?" Firn said, turning on Tokor and examining him with luminous amber eyes.

"I left Kaffi with him."

"Why do you trust him?"

Tokor mumbled random curses; being interrogated by a g'miran was unpleasant. Kaffi opened her eyes, abandoning all pretense of sleep.

"Tell her, Tokor," said Kaffi.

Tokor opened his hands, flexed his fingers. "So many things. Lhar—forgive me Kaffi—he's the best leader I've ever known, yet he treats all of us as honored equals. He and Syza both risked their lives to save me from a salt-crazy taman."

"As you risked yours for Syza," said Lhar.

"I am First Herder."

Tokor's tone left no doubt that it was his unquestioned duty to protect khaner members from vicious animals.

"You killed the taman, Tokor?" said Daal. "Where were your hunters?"

"Too far away," snapped Tokor. "Lhar killed the taman. He broke its neck with his hands."

There was a very long silence.

"And when the taman was dead," continued Tokor, "Syza and Lhar healed a crushed drifsen. With their hands."

"You're a healer?" demanded Firn.

"Syza heals," Lhar said, trying to keep the irritation out of his tone. Firn was needlessly unpleasant. "I help when I can. The gift is erratic."

"Feylin," whispered Kaffi.

"Ahhh," said Firn. "Of course. If we accept this meager khaner, Feylin will be healed."

Lhar felt anger uncoiling in his mind despite Syza's efforts to soothe him. As he spoke he saw himself through Syza's eyes, and it warned him: his face looked dark and harsh, his gray eyes were hard with anger, and power surged around him like dark lightning.

"Believe whatever comforts your fright," said Lhar coldly. "I won't lick your salt and call it sweet."

Kaffi reached toward him with an inarticulate sound. He looked at her face, pale and tight, and he took her hand, saying only for her ears, "We'll do what we can for Feylin, unless g'miran Firn forbids it."

Kaffi regained her tongue; she turned on her mother with tumbling words of anger and insult.

"No," said Lhar, muffling Kaffi's tirade against his chest. "Don't. G'miran Firn has made her peace with the future. You can't force your hopes on her. You can only hurt yourself."

Kaffi's arms closed around him convulsively. He held her in return, not knowing whether the frustration and despair he felt was hers or his or Syza's. G'miran Firn hostile, g'miran Daal neutral at best. So tired, so much to do, so little time.

146

He felt sudden pain as Daal/Firn touched him. In the instant before his shields closed, agony exploded in his mind and his face ran with sweat. Immediately Syza was there, damping the pain. Even as he drew a long breath, her hands ripped the g'mirans' fingers off his forehead. He sensed the lethal flash of her fury and gathered his mind to stop her, but there was no need.

"They didn't want your death," she said coldly. "They're merely clumsy."

Lhar felt Tokor's bewilderment and Kaffi's sudden horror.

"You forced g'malk on him!"

"We had to know." Firn's voice trembled. "He's miran, g'miran, more. Our apology, Lhar. We have never caused such pain, never known such pain."

Firn and Daal sat down suddenly on the cold earth.

"You need training more than I need apologies," Lhar said.

"The green-eyed one," said Daal hoarsely. "She wanted to kill us."

Firn's lips shaped a half-smile. "Not unreasonable. I'd want to kill anyone who hurt you that much."

Firn breathed deeply until the trembling in her body was gone and her mind no longer echoed Lhar's agony. When Daal glanced at her she gestured agreement. Daal spoke slowly, carefully.

"When Tokor came to us, we sensed so much potential. We wanted to believe that change, good change, was possible. We wanted it so much that we were frightened. We couldn't trust ourselves. So we goaded and insulted and used g'malk. You were angry and in violent pain and yet you didn't destroy. We know you could, know you can. Perhaps you will. But . . . may we begin again?"

"It couldn't be worse than the first time. You have met me and Syza and T'Mero. Diri is still asleep; there's little point in waking her. The fourth body under the hides is Nevin. He's an unusual miran; he knows how to be quiet as well as how to argue."

Nevin sat up and made formal greetings to the g'mirans. They returned with equally formal speech, then Firn asked yet another question. This time her tone was without malice.

"Your khaner has no g'miran?"

"There was only one g'miran left among our people," said Nevin. "He did not believe your people existed. He believed only that life ended in the salt desert."

"Yet you came," Firn said wonderingly.

Nevin glanced quickly at Lhar. Though he was not sure what point Nevin wanted to make, Lhar gestured for Nevin to continue.

"Kylith could be no worse than our lives there," said Nevin.

Then Lhar realized what Nevin was doing; kylith to the natives was the rest of the universe. Nevin had begun his work of undermining the natives' pathological fear of space.

"Tal-Lith is heaven, fulfillment," said Daal firmly.

"You can afford to believe that," Nevin answered, his voice an odd mixture of anger and compassion. "Your people are many and they still bear children. Sometimes. Our portion of Tal-Lith was an ugly death with no chance of rebirth."

Firn's hand lightly touched Daal's wrist. Whatever Daal was going to say died on his lips.

"Your words are heresy." Firn's voice was cool, controlled.

"And the punishment for heresy is never to be reborn," said Nevin wearily. "How many true and faithful believers cry their betrayal from the Ramparts?"

"That's a jagged truth," said Lhar to Nevin. "We've had cycles to explore its cutting edges. Don't expect—"

"Don't expect the g'mirans here to be any wiser than the ones we left gasping for Lith?" said Nevin bitterly. "When my mother was a child there was water and food and a city. When I was a man there was no water and no food and no city. And not one child."

Silence stretched into darkness and waiting and a cold wind scratching on the rocks.

"Like Lhar," said Daal finally, "we can't lick your salt and call it sweet. Without our illusions we would die."

Nevin looked at Firn curiously. "You will die because of your illusions."

"What can you give us to replace them?"

Lhar gestured Nevin into silence. "What we give will seem like heresy to you. You would reject it without thought. Wait, know us, let us live among you until Festival is over. Then we will talk again about choices and children."

"And if we don't like your choices?"

Daal's voice was almost lazy, but Lhar sensed the menace implicit in it.

"We'll leave," said Lhar, "more quickly than you would believe possible."

VII

AFTER A LONG RIDE THROUGH DARKNESS AND CRUMBLING rocks, Lhar sensed again the presence of the river. He stood high in the stirrups, looking left. The first moon rose, spilling thin gold light over the land. Yellow light lay sullenly on the distant, heaving water. Though the river was narrower here, narrower with each successive plateau, the water was still an immense expanse of turgid power. He looked away, relieved that no khaner would have to face the crossing on an unstable collection of inflated skins and slender reeds; ritual suicide had no appeal for him.

The stone smell faded as though overpowered by the second rising moon. In the unstable shadows he thought he saw vague patterns, suggestions of roads and streets and compounds; but the shadows slid and regrouped like black flames, defying knowledge. He closed his eyes and turned inward, balancing flawed certainties with perfect unknowns. Nothing disturbed him until the third moon rose, bright and slow, deep gold.

"The river is behind us," said Nevin's voice, soft and dry and perhaps frightened. "I can't see the city ahead."

"We're cantering over the bones of a city right now."

Nevin's teeth shone in a vague blur of white, then vanished. "No bones, just rocks in empty dyn fields."

"More than fodder grew here once," said Lhar indifferently, still half-withdrawn into himself.

Nevin stared intently but the triple shadows defeated him. "Our eyes see differently. Is it my imagination or are those black humps the outline of granaries?"

"Granaries. And this is as close as we'll come to them on this trail. It seems we're to be the g'mirans' secret for a bit longer."

Neither Lhar nor Nevin said anything more. The first moon, its brief hours of glory past, sank into blackness, taking a pale gold veil of light with it. Lamayryll, the natives called it, the one that runs; it would rise again before dawn, sending vague light over the forgotten ruins of a city.

The ruins weighed oppressively on Lhar's mind. Not their age, not the inexorable pressure of time, but the opposite. Tal-Senet was not ancient; nor were these crumbled, unremembered ruins. The city was young, no more than a few thousand cycles, but it was fading nearly as fast as Lamayryll's thin light.

Syza . . .

He felt her sudden presence, but had nothing to exchange with her, nothing but the sight of rocks and dust and the dreams of men long dead. When he realized that what he felt was like a distant tremor of her own nightmare, he started to close the link between them. But the link remained open, blossomed into humming strength. He drank thirstily, letting her pour into his emptiness an emerald rain so perfect that he forgot the dry land, the sullen river, the dead ruins and the dying city. And when he could drink no more, the song remained. His thanks were soundless, as her song had been.

Small return for all the nightmares you eased.

Syza's thought was warm with pleasure at having helped him. He felt vaguely ashamed of his undisciplined shadow fears.

Not all yours, corrected Syza. *Daal's. Your minds were ill-matched. He cut himself and bled his fears into you. I didn't realize it until you called me. I'm sorry. I should have known immediately.*

I'm the one who is supposed to be trained in the mental arts.

A breath of Syza's laughter curled in his mind.

It happened to me, too many times, before Zomal taught me to heal without joining minds.

In that, at least, Zomal was worthy of your love.

Syza was silent and Lhar cursed himself. As long as Syza believed in her dead lover Lhar would only drive her further away by pointing out the truth.

I'm human, Syza. Jealous.

It was a half truth, but she accepted it.

He's dead.

He lives in your mind.

Is that wrong?

Your mind, your choice.

Because the words felt cold in his mind, he warmed them as best he could. It was a poor effort. He found himself alone again. The two slow moons crawled across the night, chill and remote. Dawn brought a cold meal, a dirty wind, and restless sleep. At sunset they rose and resumed their distant circling of the unseen city. When the pace finally slowed to a walk, Lhar brought his taman up next to Kaffi's.

"The g'mirans must have ridden on the wind to reach us in one night. But then, the city was not closed to them."

"They rode fast and straight," agreed Kaffi. "The city sprawls like a man with too much yefa in his blood. But we'll sleep tomorrow in my compound."

"And then?"

"Firn hasn't told me."

Lhar pulled his taman back, held it firmly until the last rider passed by him. As he followed he tried to reconstruct Tal-Senet in his mind. Since they had passed the Gate they had walked on ruins, young ruins for all their battered invisibility. Crops grew on the forgotten memory of the city, and taman grazed. Nevin had told him it was a no-man's land pre-empted by the residue of formerly large khaners, by people unaffiliated with guilds, and by the random poor.

They all lived in crude, temporary shelters during the shrinking season, worked the hostile land, then returned to the city for the long, frozen season. It was an uneasy compromise of a life; if the melt delayed, starvation did not. The further the land was from the river, the closer the people lived to hunger.

Tal-Senet itself was little better off. In the frozen season, water was scarce. The river, silent beneath a treacherous lid of ice, was a two- or three-day ride from the edge of the city. The water guilds labored to keep the high flumes ice free, the aqueducts repaired, the ancient underground cisterns full and unfrozen. Ice haulers and water carriers hawked their cargos in the streets and the wind became a blessing for it removed air fouled by thousands of dung fires. Khaners sold crops and frozen meat to hungry guilds; mirans gave food to those who were too old or ill to work. And when the brief sunlit hours drained into Long Night, people abandoned the dark streets and huddled around little fires fueled by braided straw or reeds or dung.

Lhar shivered and drew his worn robes closer, wishing that he were as well prepared for the high plateau as his taman. He thought longingly of other desert planets he had known, hot deserts under molten skies, a lavender oasis where water neither froze nor failed, rare rivers that were sweet and bright and small enough to be understood.

With an inner sigh he pulled his mind back to Tal-Lith. This planet, too, had known beauty. Before a neighboring star had gone nova, the land had been warm, fertile, and blessed with rain. But the star had exploded, disrupting Tal-Lith's atmosphere. Cosmic storms and savage winds had come, with Tal-Lith's oceans evaporating and descending as polar ice, ice which reflected back the heat of the sun to an atmosphere too thinned out to retain it. Caught between drought and ice, the surviving natives lived on a narrow strip of land at the base of the Ramparts. Below the city, on Namaylith's vast, salt-crusted plains, the river disappeared. Above the city, on the shoulders of the Ramparts, ice sublimated into an atmosphere barely more dense than space itself. Drought and ice owned the planet now, but not for long. A few major sun flares, a vast surge of stripped atoms blowing off, and Tal-Lith would become a sterile rock wobbling around a slightly diminished sun.

Half sleeping, filled with uneasy dreams, Lhar swayed on the taman's narrow back. When he awoke enough to notice his surroundings, the sky was empty of all but the piercing eyes of scattered stars. It was the time that Tal-Lithens feared most, when their guardian moons slept and kylith crept closer.

The taman snorted and stopped. When Lhar urged it forward, the taman refused. Before he could urge it further he sensed the ground trembling. The taman's ears fanned, flattened; the beast rippled with nervousness. He heard the hoarse sound of distant rockfalls before the taman snorted again and moved forward slowly. He let it choose its own pace. Another taman condensed out of the darkness, black on black. Nevin's voice came to Lhar, too soft to be overheard by the riders ahead.

"I'm glad we weren't in the Gate."

Lhar grunted agreement. "How did the others react?"

"Kaffi called it sela, a baby. She said it was the season for them."

"Temblors don't have seasons."

"Tal-Lithens believe they do. A reminder of Lith's displeasure. Helps everyone to approach the Festival of Union with proper humiliation."

Lhar suddenly thought of the river, the immense silver weight of meltwater sliding down the Ramparts, sinking deep into a crust riddled by faults, a crust still adjusting to the sudden redistribution of the weight of oceans. Perhaps quakes were more common after water lubricated the faults. Perhaps not. He said as much to Nevin.

154

"Then maybe we won't get any more big ones for a while," said Nevin.

"Comforting. But I wouldn't depend on it."

"I won't."

The sound of taman hooves changed from the muted clicks of rocky land to the dry crackle of dead vegetation. Lhar bent low over his taman's neck and grabbed blindly in the darkness. His fingers curled around fragments of dyn straw. A pale scent of stored sunlight and dust tickled his nose. He suddenly wished for light to see the land and the hidden city that grew somewhere in the darkness. But there was no light. He heard Nevin's taman trotting ahead, and his own taman responded. He adjusted to the uncomfortable gait, trusting to the taman's superior night senses.

Just when Lhar had decided that he could endure the trotting no longer, his taman slowed to a walk, stumbled, steadied itself and walked briskly. He guessed they had just reached the first of many dry irrigation ditches. Hooves striking stone beneath a thin layer of dirt confirmed his guess. Kaffi's voice drifted out of the darkness ahead. He returned her call and urged his taman to a faster pace. Soon Kaffi's mount joined his.

"We're in Tal-Senet's high fields. There will be many ditches and a few canals, so ride alert."

"I'm glad the first one was dry. I nearly fell into it."

"All the high fields are dry. The river has shrunk below the water guilds' highest irrigation trough."

Lhar made a puzzled sound.

"Didn't you water your crops?" she asked.

"Irrigation lives only in our legends. Tell me about it."

"After break-up, when the river is free of its ice top, there is a great flood. In the foothills high above the city there are troughs hammered out of solid rock. As the river rises, the troughs fill. All the troughs run down to canals which empty into ditches that water the fields. All but the highest troughs and canals and

155

ditches and fields are buried beneath the great flood. As the high crops grow, the river shrinks. The first trough dries up, but by then the high crops are ripe and the lower fields are ready to plant."

"But what do you do for water when the river freezes and all troughs are dry?"

"Only the top of the river freezes," said Kaffi absently. "The drinking troughs, four of them, are at a place where the river moves so fast that the top can't freeze. This place is very high; getting there requires many days of riding and scrambling. I've only seen it once. The troughs stand on stone legs and wind down canyons to the city. Most of the time water remains water. When it freezes the guild begins to earn its very high fees." She laughed shortly. "No khaner pays for ice."

"The water guilds must be powerful."

"They are. They used to be separate and quarrelsome but Daal united them, even down to the stone masons who repair the troughs."

"What do you think of Daal?" said Lhar casually.

"As my mother's lover, I think he is a good man; they water each other's deserts and fine crops grow. As a khaner leader I fear Daal's power. I would rather ration water because of quarreling guilds than see the guilds become united and powerful. But as a miran I understand the necessity of power. Twelve shrinking seasons past, there was a great quake. I was a child, but I remember sucking ice and shivering while the water guilds argued over who would be paid what fee for repairing which trough. Daal ended the arguments, rebuilt the damaged troughs, wept prayers for the dead—and brought water to Tal-Senet. Firn helped him in ways I don't understand."

Lhar remembered the sudden power which had wrenched his unprepared mind, but said nothing. He doubted that Firn or Daal understood either.

"Will Firn and Daal be neutral toward my khaner?"

"I hope for more than that," said Kaffi tightly.

"And you fear less."

Kaffi was silent.

"How much do they love power?" asked Lhar.

"Well enough. It's the only way to get results."

"Are they narrowly devout?"

"Are you planning further heresies?"

Lhar waited. Kaffi swore.

"I've met more garrulous rocks," she said acidly. "Firn and Daal are g'mirans. They are required to be devout."

"If the requirements of survival changed?"

"How?"

Lhar did not answer.

"Lith's silver ass," hissed Kaffi. "You cover my eyes and demand that I see!"

"Kaffi," said Lhar softly touching her arm. "Do Firn and Daal have the courage to cross n'Lith, and beyond? Would they dare even kylith so that their people would have children, a future?"

"Kylith has no future," said Kaffi, her tone every bit as inflexible as Firn's.

Lhar removed his hand and fought a rising tide of irrational fury. "I see," he said, his voice cold. "You'll make a fine g'miran some day—ignorant, devout and doomed."

Silence seethed between them. At last Kaffi spoke, her voice thick with the effort to restrain her emotions. "What you are saying is that I cover my ears and demand that you make me hear."

"You're not the only person who would rather not hear unpleasant truths. It is easier to writhe in fear of kylith than to realize that kylith exists only in your mind."

The bitterness in Lhar's voice made Kaffi wince.

"My apologies, Kaffi. When I can't make my own khaner feel secure I shouldn't ask for your trust."

He pulled his taman away from hers, back into the night.

"Give us time, Lhar."

"I wish I could."

Lhar held his taman until he could no longer hear

157

hoofbeats. Then he loosened the reins and let fatigue settle over him like a heavy robe. His body demanded sleep but the taman stumbled often, forcing him to concentrate on making out obstacles before his weary taman blundered into them.

Gradually the dyn fields gave way to lower fields of ssan bushes. Their scent was like a knife in his nostrils. The bushes bent beneath his stirrups, releasing sharpness into the night. The leaves and stems had either been harvested or shed as the plants prepared for cold and drought. Only the leathery main branches remained, shrunken yet resilient, impervious, waiting for water and a new cycle. He felt an irrational pity for the patient plants; there would be no more cycles for Tal-Lith's life.

Night hung interminably around him, punctuated by the slithering of ssan branches and an occasional hoof scraping over dry stone ditches. The wind coiled, colder than before. Scents rode dry eddies, smells of burning dung and dyn straw, dust and old hides, smoke thinned by distance, a faint promise of warmth. Then the wind shifted and only the penetrating odor of ssan branches remained.

Lhar stared into the darkness where the wind had been, but Tal-Senet was still invisible. Ssan bushes gave way to clumps of loh, waist-high limber wands whipping in the wind, black by night and scarlet by day. From loh fibers cloth was woven; oil was pressed from its seeds, and a protein-rich flour, ground from its tubers. As valuable as the quantities of water it drank, as tenacious as the wind, loh was the staple of Tal-Senet.

Lhar's taman fanned its ears suddenly. Expecting another quake, Lhar settled more firmly into the stirrups. The taman whuffed several times, but then the wind shifted yet again. The vagrant scent the taman had picked up now faded, and the animal subsided into indifference. Lhar wondered if the taman had smelled others of its own kind, or drifs, or drifsen

—any of the multitude of animals which ranged the outskirts of Tal-Senet.

He strained into the darkness, trying to spot animals moving. He saw nothing but night. He inhaled deeply, smelled nothing but the vague spice of loh.

After a long time of half sleeping, Lhar was brought fully alert by his senses. Though his eyes saw nothing, he knew that the city must be near. Barely sensed shapes slipped by, low walls and outbuildings, granaries and loh presses; the piercing scent of crushed ssan was everywhere. Dyn straw rustled in the gentle breeze; somewhere close by, a mound of straw waited to be twisted into mats and used as fuel for winter fires.

He heard faint sounds of confusion ahead: taman milling, drifsen coughing, Syza's low whistled commands. He urged his taman forward. Its heavy trot shook Lhar's cold body. Tokor's voice momentarily rose above the whistles, then all was still except for the snorts of uneasy taman. Kaffi appeared suddenly beside him.

"We'll leave everything here."

"Where are we?"

"A field near my compound. It has food and water. The drifsen will guard the taman."

Lhar dismounted stiffly, shivering as the bitter cold of night swept through legs accustomed to the relative warmth of saddle and taman. He tied a walking hobble with numb fingers, stripped everything off the taman, and turned the animal over to the drifsen. Though the saddle was little more than an ellipse of tanned hide and various flapping straps, it felt as heavy as stone. He staggered slightly until feeling returned to his feet.

T'Mero's broad-shouldered form loomed suddenly ahead. Lhar saw that he was carrying two saddles. He paused, surprised that he could see at all, then realized that Lamayryll must be rising again.

"Is Diri all right?" asked Lhar softly.

"Too tired. We should have waited for light."

"Tal-Lith doesn't wait for Diri's convenience."

"Not yet," muttered T'Mero.

In the faint light of the unseen moon Lhar quickly counted the group. Two missing. He walked back toward the taman.

"Syza? Tokor?"

His whisper carried across the sound of milling animals. A figure walked toward him, loaded down with saddles. He picked off the top two.

"Lith be loved," said Kaffi breathlessly. "I sent Tokor and the g'mirans ahead."

"Where's Syza?"

"She'll come when the taman settle down. Tokor will—"

"What about me?" said Tokor's voice.

"You're supposed to be getting the talmare rooms ready."

"They were ready yesterday."

"Good," said Kaffi, dumping saddles into Tokor's arms. "I'll get Syza. Those taman are too tired to fight. And the moon will be up soon."

Lhar turned and followed Tokor out of the field.

"Watch the ropes," said Tokor.

Lhar looked down and barely made out the shapes of ropes folded on either side of the gap in the chest-high stone fence. It had been too dark to see the fence on the way in, much less the woven rope mesh which served as gate. He shifted the saddles and walked carefully. Tokor turned into a low stone shed.

"Hand the saddles in to me."

Gratefully Lhar passed the saddles into the black opening. When Tokor emerged, Lhar fell into step behind him. He followed Tokor over ditches and past more small stone buildings, through small fields and around stone fences. He tried to memorize landmarks in the vague light. After a time everything looked alike—angular or curved shapes that were buildings, low fences of piled stone, darkness. Ahead, the night was a cold impenetrable black that defied knowledge;

then Lhar realized that it was high walls rather than night that he was trying to see through.

A faint creak, a wash of air redolent of smoke and people, and Lhar was inside the compound. As he passed through the gate he ran his fingertips lightly over it. With a muffled exclamation he stopped and touched the gate more slowly while Tokor disappeared into the darkness. The gate was made of wood, dense and nearly as heavy as stone. His fingers traced whorls and bumps, fine-grained irregularities that spoke of slow growth and difficult life. Suddenly he hungered to see trees again, strong and thick, lifting to the sky with wind singing through their crowns, huge forests heavy with time, alive. He pressed his palms and forehead against the wood as though he could feed his hunger with mere touch. In his mind grew the towering forests of his childhood, awesome and serene and perfect above the dark head of a small laughing boy.

A hand lightly touched his cheek. There was a hiss of indrawn breath and he felt his memories shared in the second before his defenses closed.

"Where?" said Firn's voice wonderingly.

Lamayryll rose as Lhar pulled his hands away from the ancient wood, saying nothing. Firn stepped backwards when she saw his face.

"We—it was an accident," said Daal. "We thought you were ill. We meant no wrong."

Lhar hesitated, struggling with a baffling rage. Not at Daal or Firn or even himself; just a shattering blind anger that Tal-Lith's forests were dead, never to be reborn, never to hear laughter and the running feet of young children. Never.

"We're sorry," said Daal.

"I know," said Lhar thickly. "My error."

"Those trees," breathed Firn. "Where are they?"

"Nowhere. A dream."

"Not a dream . . . they're alive," said Daal, his voice a blend of apology and anger and yearning.

"I know that you can't share their place; they are mur-Lith. But don't lie to us. Those trees are alive!"

"They must grow beyond n'Lith," said Firn slowly. "Why did you leave them?"

"Why does anyone cross n'Lith?" said Daal with sudden coldness. "What hideous act did your khaner commit?"

Lhar looked up and saw Daal's expression change from contempt to something close to fear. Lhar sensed what he must look like, gray eyes glittering obscurely in the flat light of the racing moon. He laughed; the sound made them flinch.

"The truth will be unpleasant," said Lhar softly. "Do you really want to know where those trees grow?"

"Any truth is worth those trees," said Firn quickly.

"Kylith."

"What?"

The negation and contempt in the g'mirans made Lhar's anger writhe. He took their clasped hands between his own with painful force.

"The trees grow in kylith."

"No!"

Lhar held their struggling hands and his voice was as inexorable as night.

"Does your training fail you, g'mirans? Can you no longer find truth with touch? The trees grow in kylith."

"You have eaten too much salt," said Daal.

The conviction in his voice brought forth Lhar's terrible soft laughter again.

"Of course," said Lhar, releasing their hands abruptly. "Of course. The trees were a dream of madness."

"No," snapped Firn. "Memories."

"Then," said Lhar, leaning against the ancient wood gate, "you have a problem worthy of a g'miran's mettle: can madmen have sane memories?"

Silence spread and stretched like light from the racing moon. He straightened and moved away from

162

the gate. "I'm sure you're as tired as I am," he said quietly. "Where is my khaner's sleeping place?"

Wordlessly Firn and Daal gestured toward a large stone building.

He entered the building and followed the muted flickering of candles until he came to a large room. The loh fiber wicks in the candles burned a fine bright gold. Fresh mats of dyn straw filled the room with a smell reminiscent of sunshine. Piles of supple hides and loh blankets were piled along one curving wall.

With a deep breath he walked slowly toward the hides, measuring his tiredness in his heavy movements. He sorted through the hides. Neither T'Mero nor Diri moved as he shook hides over rustling mats. Nevin woke, mumbled something unintelligible, and slept again. Lhar went back to the bedding pile and dragged out more hides. By the time he had finished making a second warm nest he heard Syza's footsteps in the hallway. He fell asleep before Syza entered the room and found her bed waiting.

Lhar awoke to a subdued play of rainbows across his face. On the wall to his left a small prismatic window divided light into a clear fall of colors. He stood, ignoring the chilly air penetrating his skindrape, and tapped the window lightly. A faint crystalline sound shimmered in the room.

Nevin stirred, awoke with a harsh rustle of reeds. When he saw Lhar at the window he whispered softly.

"Careful. Some of that silica stuff is brittle."

"Not this," said Lhar quietly. "Crystal. Thick enough for a—" He stopped abruptly. The carved crystal pane was indeed thick enough for the viewport of a primitive spaceship, but it was hardly the type of comparison he should think about, much less say.

Nevin smiled knowingly as he pulled on his heavy robes. "It is, isn't it?" he said, yanking the robes into place.

Lhar hurriedly put on his robes. "My tongue wakes up sooner than my mind."

"Does it, now?" said Kaffi's voice from the hallway. "Remind me to wake you up some day. I may learn interesting things about trees and kylith."

At Nevin's startled look, Lhar signaled him to follow. The tapestry dividing the room from the hallway rustled as he pushed it aside. Nevin looked from Lhar to Kaffi, a questioning look on his face. Wordlessly Kaffi led them to a small room where another crystal window shattered light into colors.

"Well, miran," said Kaffi. "Do trees grow in kylith?"

Nevin's face became carefully expressionless. He drew a slow breath and his eyes glowed like brown amber in the shifting colors.

"Is your tongue asleep, miran?"

Kaffi's taunting voice echoed in the stone room.

"Many trees grow in kylith," Nevin said. "More trees in more colors than you can imagine."

Lhar felt tight muscles relax; though young, Nevin was as professionally quick as anyone he had ever worked with.

"You are as mad as your leader."

"Perhaps," said Nevin, spreading his hands in a graceful, neutral gesture. "In that case, only the insane survived. The rest died gasping dogmas through withered lips."

"If you aren't mad, you're demons. Either way we would be fools to listen to you."

"Is that you talking, or Firn?" said Lhar.

"Me."

"Then you are a fool." Lhar ignored Nevin's dismayed expression. "Tell me how many children your people have. Tell me about your sweet future. Tell me about death."

Kaffi aged as he watched; her yellow eyes became dull, her skin dry and lifeless as stone.

"No . . ."

"Yes."

Silence and rainbows filled the room. Kaffi's eyes closed, then opened slowly, clear again.

"What do you want of me?" she whispered.

"Nothing. Everything. Your trust."

"But you don't trust me."

"Trees in kylith. Such a small heresy," Lhar said, his voice soft and inflexible.

"I . . . see. Then there is worse to come?"

"What could be worse than your future?"

"Yours. While you slept, the g'mirans met."

"And when do we meet with them?"

"You don't."

"Oh? No questions that need answers?"

"I told them where I met your khaner. It's obvious you aren't from Tal-Senet. You aren't Wanderers; we haven't had any of them for over two hundred cycles. Where else could you be from except the Forgotten Lands?"

Lhar ignored Kaffi's probing eyes and said blandly, "Where else indeed?"

Kaffi's mouth twisted. "So the g'mirans will whisper and weigh whatever Firn and Daal tell them. I'd bet my khaner's water that it won't be trees and kylith. That would shame me, ruin Firn. So the g'mirans will mumble heavy words and trade stupidities and decide how to use you for their greater power. I wish them luck; I'd sooner try to ride a salt-crazy taman. Until they have divided your prestige—or shame—among themselves, you will be our honored guests."

"And what are your rules for such guests?"

"You will not leave the compound unless I or a g'miran allow it. Your hunter will not leave this building. Your miran will be available to discuss . . . heresy. Syza is free to tend your animals. Diri," Kaffi made a dismissing motion with her hand, "will stay with T'Mero."

"Can we join in the Festival?"

"You will be required to participate. Pray to Lith that you do well. You will be judged after Festival, when all khaner, guild or miran disputes are resolved."

165

"Diri will need room to practice her dance."

"This building is the First Khaner's talmare. There is a room set aside for large khaner meetings; it should be big enough for your purposes."

"And does this magnificent gathering place have a cooking room and a latrine?" said Lhar. At Kaffi's sudden change of expression, he laughed. "What? Aren't demons supposed to need such things?"

"I'll have to consult the Enigmatic Scrolls," said Kaffi drily. "I'm sure that some g'miran has solved the difficulty. Until then, I'll show you through the talmare."

Kaffi led Lhar through fourteen rooms lit by restive candle flames and crystal windows. The rooms were all curves and domed ceilings built of rocks so carefully shaped that no mortar was required to hold them together. On the walls hung tapestries which outshone the colors spilling through the windows. The floors were resilient with fresh reed mats and lush rugs woven of soft hairs from a drif's middle coat.

"Beautiful," breathed Lhar.

"Useful, too. Our place of honor. Living here will raise your prestige. Or lower ours."

"I'm surprised Daal and Firn allowed it."

"This is my khaner; I am miran and leader."

Lhar glanced at her out of the corner of his eyes.

"Surprised?" said Kaffi. "Whatever my own doubts might be, I'll keep them private."

"Except when Firn touches you."

Kaffi stopped, turned to face him. "I am what I am. What seemed possible in Namaylith seems incredible now."

"Namaylith is the truth."

"Your truth."

"Why are you fighting us, Kaffi?"

Kaffi said nothing.

"Is heresy worse than unborn children?"

"Liar," said Kaffi, her voice shockingly soft.

"What is it?" said Lhar, sensing the agonized feeling of betrayal that radiated from Kaffi's untrained mind. His hand reached for her taut face, hesitated, dropped back to his side.

"Kaffi, what is wrong?" he asked gently.

"Trees in kylith! Firn touched you, knew you thought it truth, said you were mad. I know you are not mad. You are a clever liar."

Lhar sighed wearily. "Or else I'm stupid but truthful."

"Stupid?" Kaffi's derisive laughter raked over him. "Don't play your games with me. You are the Ramparts to our dust. I know that, know it as surely as I know that water freezes in the Long Night. Why do you play with us? Does it amuse you to see our pitiful hopes? To laugh at our ragged illusions? And when we are stripped of our beliefs will you smile as we freeze and die?—No! Don't touch me! Don't force your mind on mine and give truth to lying dreams!"

"I've never forced my mind on yours."

"Then why do I believe what can't be true?" said Kaffi fiercely.

"Because you want to."

"Or you've made me want to."

"If I did that, why would I leave doubts?"

Lhar waited while Kaffi fought against herself with an intensity that was painful. The sound of Tokor calling her seemed loud in the silence.

"Feylin . . ." Kaffi's whisper was prayer and fear and a silent mental scream.

Lhar noticed for the first time the fatigue that thickened Kaffi's movements and thoughts.

Tokor's voice, urgent, came again. "Hurry, Kaffi."

Kaffi's robes flared as she turned and fled. Lhar followed, summoning Syza as he ran out of the talmare. The sun was a hard white light. He stumbled, yanked up the trailing edges of his robes and ran after Kaffi. Behind him he heard Syza's light running footsteps.

They followed Kaffi's flying robes past low stone markers and down narrow paths that twisted among crowded i'khaner homes. A stone arch, a stone-paved courtyard, sudden darkness. Lhar slowed to match

Kaffi's walk. Though she had not acknowledged his presence by so much as a glance, Kaffi began speaking in the colorless tones of exhaustion.

"She was very weak when Firn left. When we arrived last night I went to her. She did not know me. She called my name again and again. I could not make her see me. I could not reach her. I lay down next to her and held her and listened to her call my name. I watched the window, watched every color call my name in her voice. When I thought I could take no more, she slept. I left her to go to you." She laughed hollowly. "That's when Firn told me, and I knew."

"What did you know?"

"It doesn't matter. Feylin is dying."

Lhar heard Syza's hissing breath, but said nothing. He could not force her to heal. He followed Kaffi through a hallway hung with ancient tapestries. At the end of the hall was a small curved room filled with rainbows. Feylin lay on a pallet piled high with soft rugs and softer blankets. The glowing colors in the room emphasized her shrunken flesh. She had been beautiful once. He vaguely heard angry words, Firn and Daal demanding, Kaffi repeating that it did not matter; Feylin was dying.

And Syza was paralyzed by fear.

"I'm not asking you to heal her. Just touch her, try to find what's wrong. If nothing else, ease her death. Can you do that?"

Syza walked slowly toward the bed, knelt, and touched Feylin's wasted hand. Lhar saw Syza's hand shake, then it steadied as she drew a scarlet blanket aside. Her fingers moved slowly down Feylin's body; Lhar sensed distant pain and negation, heard Syza's clear surprise.

"She's starving. She needs food."

"She can't eat," said Kaffi, tonelessly. "It was the same with the other pregnancies. No, not the same. Each time was worse."

Lhar felt Syza's puzzlement. "But there's nothing wrong, no physical reason. Except for lack of food, she is whole."

"And the child?" said Lhar.

"She is also whole. Starved, but better off than Feylin."

"She?" demanded Daal. "How do you know?"

Syza's hand dropped. "I know."

Kaffi's unasked question burned between them.

Lhar. Fear cold and naked. *I can't.*

Won't.

Feylin wants death. Her choice. I have no right, even if I could!

You're sure?

In an instant he felt Feylin as Syza had, a deep river of negation draining life.

Can you give her strength?

I'm no longer a healer!

Syza's denial exploded in his mind, echoed with a dead man's laughter. He knelt by her, controlling her fear and his own. When she no longer fought against her nightmare he murmured wordless apologies into her hair and felt her relief that he did not despise her for her weakness. Fingers laced through his hair like fire, then she stood and faced Kaffi.

"Feylin has chosen death."

Kaffi offered no denial to Syza's words; she seemed to shrink into her robes, barely noticing Tokor's supporting arm. Lhar saw Firn and Daal touch, sensed their joined minds comforting each other.

"You don't question this?" said Lhar, then knew as he spoke that they had sensed Feylin's choice long ago.

"Why? Why!"

"We don't know."

"You've used g'malk."

"Too late. She was beyond even our . . . us."

Lhar turned and looked at Feylin, motionless, gaunt, ugly, the random casualty of a restless star.

Rage welled up in him. He worked with the irrational surge until it became a profound source of power controlled by a calm mind.

"See that no one touches me, Syza. Not even you. I'll try to integrate her."

He sensed Syza's lurch of fear at the mention of integration, dismissed it as irrelevant. Gently he took between his fingers the emaciated claw that had once been Feylin's graceful hand. As his fingers lightly stroked her lifeless palm, his mind delicately sought to know hers. Patiently, skilfully, he probed beyond the superficial levels of her mind. It was like walking through empty rooms. She had withdrawn, was absorbed inward, hoarding herself so that her will to die would outlast her body's will to live.

He paused to flex himself gently against the abandoned structures of her senses. He had never integrated any but a trained, willing mind. If she were grossly incompatible as well as unwilling, he might easily kill her.

Pain coursed through him. He withdrew quickly, hearing himself moan as though at a great distance. He breathed slowly, deeply, until the pain faded. In control once more, he filtered back into the silent spaces of her mind. Pain returned, thrust, was deflected by his will. He held pain at bay and studied her with infinite patience, time suspended, turning. Gradually he inferred the strengths and dangers, impossibilities and invitations of her mind. With a caution exceeded only by gentleness he sifted more deeply into her. Pain again, but different. Hers. Starvation's howl reduced to a feeble whimper, ignored as the erratic beating heart, the thin shallow breaths were ignored; indifference waiting for death.

He called to her.

A flicker, no more. He called again, sweet and compelling. He sensed her confusion and soothed it tenderly.

Only a dream, Feylin. A dream ... dream.

She did not resist him He spoke soft words into

her mind, familiar words, water and dust and sun. She accepted each one indifferently, dreamed small dreams of river and windsong and dawn. He took the dreams and gave her warmth, spoke a single word. *Child.*

He rode the storm of negation easily; he had expected it. When she was quiet again he murmured into her exhausted silence. Slowly her dream coalesced, Tal-Senet and a silver river shrinking, gone, people crumbling into dust blown by dry winds over stone plateaus, a child's despairing cry, Feyl lonely and lost and innocent as the stars reached down to consume him, the last life on Tal-Lith.

Feylin's scream tore through his mind. He shook as her conflicting desires fought for supremacy; awful guilt that she should allow a child to be born, determination that she would bear no more, cold emptiness that she should aid in her people's extinction, aching desire to hold another child in her arms.

He took her nightmare and gave her warmth. And a dream. Water and wind and rock, Feyl's despairing cry transmuted to delight as stars reached down singing of a universe of life. The child blinked and found a new planet beneath his feet, water flowing through fields heavy with harvest, a sweet clean wind lifting through his hair, the sound of his mother as she crooned to the baby smiling in her arms.

The dream repeated itself, waves upon the shore of an ocean she had never seen, each wave a separate thing of beauty flowing from an immense sea of assurance. Waves became the steady beating of her heart, strengthening and demanding life. Her mind stirred, unfolded, expanded to reclaim what had been abandoned. He melted away before her advance.

Feylin's eyes opened, pale lavender glowing with dreams. With utmost care he dissolved the link. No sooner was he free than an irresistible darkness claimed him. He was unconscious before his body sank into the soft rugs.

* * *

". . . still sleeping."

Syza's low whisper became part of Lhar's dream, candles flickering, voices fading.

". . . five days!"

Nevin's voice, harsh with concern; a dream?

". . . reasonable." Syza's voice. "First n'Lith . . . nearly died . . . salt-crazy . . . riding riding riding . . . and me."

Lhar gathered his concentration, managed to keep Syza's voice from fading.

"He has limits like anyone else. He reached them. I'm doing all I can. He's exhausted; salith just makes him sleep and eat; his mind has shut down."

Points of bright gold burned in the darkness. Candles. Night.

"Then get out. Let me stay with him. Kaffi says you're on the edge yourself."

"No."

Lhar tried to reach her with mindtouch, but found himself slipping into darkness. The pattern—or was it a dream—repeated itself each time with people drifting through, concerned voices fading, Syza's voice harsh with tiredness and worry.

"I've half a mind to call T'Mero . . . carry you out." Nevin angry.

". . . half a mind . . . let T'Mero touch me!"

The menace in Syza's low voice frightened Lhar. He forced his eyes to open and saw rainbow light. He tried to speak but could not. Soft and limitless, sleep invited him. He fought and felt pain like white light lancing through his mind. He fought and finally managed to form her name in his mind. As he fell into darkness he felt his name called softly against his hair and cheek and lips; another dream?

Candles golden and warm, ssan and salith, sleep. Colors falling across his eyes, the warmth of another body next to his.

Syza . . . ?

Lhar? Lhar, is it you? I lost you . . . couldn't find you. Empty. So empty.

Her thought was chaotic with remembered horror. Sliding deeper and deeper into Feylin's mind, Syza's subtle link with him stretching, thinning, snapping soundlessly. And he was so still but for

his fingers stroking Feylin's palm, his eyes like silver pools focused on infinity, candles glittering into day and rainbows into night and day, and still he and Feylin writhed and laughed and sighed and screamed and she could not reach him, could not.

I didn't know. Pain surged in his mind, then subsided, tolerable now. *You kept our link?*

You said I was to stay in your mind until I had to leave. But I didn't leave. You did.

Lhar felt the salt-sweet warmth of tears. *I'm sorry; didn't know. Should have . . . you're so skillful that I forget . . . no training.* His mind cleared a little, making communication possible though still difficult. *I had to be her, not myself. We fit badly, steel and dough. I had to dissolve . . . .*

A tidal wave of darkness claimed him, tumbled him, cast him up on a shore of candlelight, small flames, eyes watching him.

"Praise to Lith," breathed Kaffi.

Lhar attempted a smile, then decided speech would be easier.

"Feylin?" The word came out more croak than name.

"Recovering rapidly," said Syza. "She's still very weak, but both she and Seytal will live."

"Seytal?" Better, but still more dry cough than speech.

"Drink this," Syza said, handing him a bowl.

Lhar sipped cautiously while he listened.

"Seytal is Feylin's unborn child," said Syza. "When I told her the baby would be—was—a girl, she named it Seytal."

"Seytal, Where the Sun Rises After Long Night," murmured Kaffi. "What did you do, Lhar? What did you tell her?"

173

"Not now," Syza said. "He needs more rest."

Lhar set the bowl aside, having taken only enough to wet his throat. "I'd like to be awake for awhile," he said, answering Syza's questioning eyes.

"It's not a soporific, unless you need sleep," said Syza.

"I've had enough sleep for three men."

"Then salith will keep you awake," said Kaffi. "You've certainly eaten enough for three men."

Lhar tried to remember eating, but could not. He had very few memories of the time since Feylin. Syza put her hand on the curve of his neck. He vaguely sensed her awareness searching through his body.

"Finish the salith," she said, removing her hand. "You're too exhausted for true sleep; your mind won't permit it."

"Later. As for your question, Kaffi, I can no more tell you what I did than Syza could explain how she healed the drifsen."

"I expected as much," said Kaffi without rancor. "Firn may not be so easily satisfied."

"About what?" said Firn's voice.

Kaffi turned quickly, making candle flames bend. "You're very quiet tonight, Firn."

"Why don't you just say that I'm sneaking about like a hungry drifsen?" Firn laughed lightly. "No matter, daughter. I'll not touch Lhar unless he requests it. Ever." She turned to Lhar, smiling at his puzzlement. "When you were . . . with . . . Feylin, she moaned and screamed. But your pain was worse. Your face was terrible to see. We thought that Feylin was beyond help, that there could be no purpose to your suffering. But when we would have stopped you, Syza—" Firn's hands moved in an abrupt gesture of total negation. "We could not move. Not one step. All we could do was watch your agony and listen to your screams. If I had known what it would cost you I would never have permitted you to touch Feylin, even to save her life. Are you truly well? Could any mind survive such g'malk and still be sane?"

Lhar's eyes sought and held Syza's. "Thank you. If even you had touched me at the wrong moment . . ."

"I wanted to," she whispered. "I could bear the agony because I shared it. But when you no longer screamed, you were so still, so empty."

Firn waited, then eased a diffident question into the silence.

"Do you know why my daughter desired death?"

Lhar hesitated, tongue working in a dry mouth. Syza handed him the bowl of ssan and salith. He sipped, though he wanted to gulp; when he handed the bowl back to her it was less than half full.

"Feylin was fighting against herself. We all do sometimes." He glanced quickly at Kaffi. "But Feylin's fight was at the deepest level of her being. Her mind had no hope for the future; she saw that Feyl could be the last of your people, alone and crying on a barren world, and it would be her fault for allowing him to be born. Yet she wanted children; she hungered for them as you hunger for sun after the Long Night."

The memory of Feylin's impasse condensed in his mind like a moving shadow of agony.

"As long as she wasn't pregnant she could endure hopelessness; there was enough good in her life that she lived willingly. But when she became pregnant she couldn't tolerate the guilt of bringing another child into life, knowing that the child would die alone, the last of its race."

Absently Lhar rubbed his cheek and beard against Syza's hand, accepting the comfort that flowed from her.

"You're tired," said Firn. "You don't have to remember your pain for an old woman's curiosity."

Lhar smiled, small and weary. "It's important. Feylin isn't the only woman suffering and refusing to bear futile children. Ask Kaffi. But Feylin's will

175

alone couldn't prevent conception. During each pregnancy, the battle with herself became worse. Her mind won all battles but one, Feyl. This was to be the last. Without consciously knowing it, Feylin decided that the only way to end the battle was to die. But because her mind and body were divided, she couldn't die quickly. Starvation was slow; so slow, so painful, yet she endured it. All I did was show her . . . ."

Syza handed him the bowl again. He drank.

". . . gave her a dream . . . truth," he said, letting himself drift. "She . . . chose."

His last thought was surprise that he had not tasted the drug that was sending him so irresistibly into sleep.

VIII

LHAR SAT BENEATH THE WAVERING GOLD LIGHT OF A stone lamp set high in a wall niche. A bowl of ssan laced with salith smoked between his hands. "What did the g'mirans say then?" he asked, his breath a long cloud of silver in the cold room.

Nevin warmed his numbed fingers over the ssan brazier before he answered.

"They didn't like it. But they haven't liked much that I've said in the last tenth-cycle."

Lhar grunted. "Did they believe you?"

"They didn't want to. Who could blame them? My words were their death carved in stone."

"G'miran Urari?"

Nevin flexed his stiff fingers. "About what you'd guess. He loathes all talk of decline. If he were powerful enough he would have killed rather than listen to our story. When I talk about no children he yells and curses . . . but he listens. He isn't stupid. He has to act as though I'm lying, but he can count children as well as I."

"Is he trying to bring his cult around to reality?"

Nevin laughed soundlessly and his face looked old. "That would be a miracle. And G'miran Rik's people still roam the city destroying unused buildings, hiding the dead, and saying Lith has answered their prayers." Nevin swore tonelessly. "Some cultists even tried to get into the Ninth Khaner's compound. They were turned back at the inner gate, but it was an ugly brawl. They got what they came for in the end."

"Which was?"

"A corpse. But they had to wait the full term."

Lhar grimaced. "Death-guild rights?"

"No corpse can be buried or burned or otherwise disposed of within a day's ride of the city, and all corpses must—"

"—be given to the guild within two days. I know. A sensible system until Rik made it a cult of hysteria and stupidity. Go on, what did Rik do to you?"

"Nothing new. He's still trying to have us exiled, of course. G'miran Urari won't hear of it since I pointed out that our story fits very neatly with his cult of sin and punishment and penance. And while Urari's followers are the unaffiliated poor of Tal-Senet, he rules them with a stone fist. Not that he likes us, either. He just dislikes Rik more."

"The other g'mirans?"

"Like the river—first expanding, then shrinking, then frozen. If it were just a matter of accepting or rejecting us it would have been resolved after a few meetings. But until each g'miran decides what will be gained or lost or unchanged by our arrival, there will be no resolution."

"Festival."

"Yes."

Lhar swore. "Kaffi was right. But I'd hoped to at least get the local equivalent of a vote of confidence before then."

"I could try to force a decision."

"No. I trust your instincts. We'll try something else. Have you talked with Syza about this?"

Nevin's face assumed a look of distaste. "I haven't spent much time here since Feylin . . . you weren't well and there was a lot to do."

"And," added Lhar, "you might have met Syza if you came here."

Nevin was silent.

"Diri and T'Mero?" asked Lhar.

"They're too busy for politics. When he isn't guarding the practice room for her, she's setting up targets

178

for him. I doubt that they would be much help anyway. Their understanding of politics is zero."

"Syza's isn't."

"Oh? Then if compassion failed her," said Nevin bitterly, "why didn't her political acuity demand Feylin's healing?"

Lhar waited and felt the chill in his mind congeal into ice.

"The talmare is too large," Lhar said slowly. "In a tent or around a fire we were forced to live with each other. But now . . . T'Mero and Diri ignore everyone else. They have skills they must perfect for the Festival; in any case, they prefer to be alone. Syza sleeps in a room, alone. Her choice. You sleep with Kaffi's i'khaner. Your choice, and perhaps politically motivated."

Lhar stopped and watched Nevin, obviously expecting some comment. There was none.

"I could," continued Lhar, "require us to sleep in a single room. Diri wouldn't notice; she's too tired to worry about such details. T'Mero prefers to keep Diri alone with him. I see little to gain by objecting; his job is to ensure that no native sees her skin before Festival. Syza might object, but not forcefully."

"Why should she? No one would disturb her sleep. Not after Feylin."

"Do you love as easily as you hate?"

"Does it matter?" said Nevin stiffly.

"Yes. Unless we forget our preferences and begin to work together, Tal-Lith is lost."

"But Diri and T'Mero are doing what they prefer."

"And what they prefer also helps Tal-Lith."

"I'm doing all I can."

"No."

"Just how would my coping with Syza help Tal-Lith?"

"Did I suggest that?"

"No. All right. But the thought of touching Syza is impossible. I'd sooner cope with a river in full flood."

179

Lhar hoped that the emotions twisting through him did not reach his face. "Have you considered something like simple ability to exchange information with her?"

"Just sit down and chat with a force of nature?" Nevin was half laughing, half incredulous. "Sweet Lith! Syza can control me as easily as wind controls dust. What under seventy-six suns could I talk about!"

"You talk to me easily enough," said Lhar drily.

"But you can't control me," said Nevin. Then, weakly, "You wouldn't?"

Lhar finished the last of his ssan and carefully set the bowl aside. "And if I would?"

"I wouldn't like it."

"Naturally. That's why I've done nothing about your fear of Syza. I could have. I will if I must. I'd rather give you information and let you make your own decisions." Lhar absently ran his finger around the rim of the ssan bowl. "Within the parameters of your own culture, you've had a frictionless life. Agreed?"

"What does that . . . yes, I suppose so."

"Have you ever been absolutely without simple touch, simple laughter, a mutual bond of affection and respect with other intelligent life?"

"No."

"Were you ever told, repeatedly and smugly, that you were hopelessly evil? Unfit to live?"

"No."

"Then it's no surprise that you don't understand Syza. She was told all that, and worse, yet she refused either to wholly believe or wholly become what everyone told her she was. Nor did she destroy them, which she could have done easily. She even tried to love them, and not to hate herself."

Lhar felt his eyes narrowing as he looked at Nevin. Lhar raised his eyes and murmured meaningless words in his own mind; his control was very ragged since Feylin. When his heart once again beat slowly he opened his eyes. Nevin was watching him with an uneasy mixture of compassion and fear. Lhar took Nevin's hand between his own.

"Sorry, my friend. Syza means more to . . . . But that's no reason to frighten you. Or to force you to be kind to her. I had hoped, though, that if you understood what Syza's life has been you might find it more difficult to hate her."

"I don't think I hate her," said Nevin slowly. "Not really. I am afraid of her. And she condemned Feylin so coldly. If it weren't for you Feylin would be dead. And you almost killed yourself saving her. Syza did nothing for either of you. That's hard to forgive."

"Does Kaffi feel as you do?"

"Kaffi is too kind."

Lhar laughed shortly. "Kaffi can be as mean as a taman. But that's irrelevant. Would you force life on someone who wanted death?"

"Anyone who wants death is not competent to have an opinion."

"You condemn Syza or me for interfering with other minds, but proclaim that some minds need to be controlled. Now I suppose you'll plead morals to explain your difficulty."

Nevin studied his hands. "You don't believe in morals?"

"Whose: yours? Mine? We could sit and argue morals until the last star in the universe froze without settling anything. You work for Contact. If the time comes when you feel that Contact does more wrong than it does right, then you leave and find work or a culture you're comfortable with. You'll discover there are few cultures that demand life at any cost."

"Are you saying that you forced Feylin to live because it would help us with Tal-Lith?"

"I forced nothing. I simply told her that there was a future worth having children for. She decided to live. Her choice, not mine."

"If she hadn't chosen your way?"

181

"She would have died. Desire for life is the one aspect of mind that cannot be indirectly controlled. I can kill, but I cannot create. I'm not a polished glass god."

"Could Syza?"

"Syza could have kept Feylin's body alive for a time; the body wanted life. I could have kept her body alive for a time by destroying her mind. Satisfied?"

Nevin shuddered. "Why are you doing this? Why does it matter that I like Syza?"

"Because a broken team is dangerous. I expected to have problems holding us together. This has been a snarl from the beginning. Diri isn't even Contact trained; her services were bought. T'Mero is in his sixth maturity, experienced, yet his actions do not fit the profile I was given of him. For now that doesn't matter; it could be crucial under certain circumstances. Syza is Contact trained, but remembers little of the experience. This is your first assignment. Incredible. If there hadn't been such a long-nailed rush to make up a team, you would have been sent to a nice placid planet not dissimilar from your own.

"But we're here. Our chances would be much better if we were a team rather than—if, if, if! We should be living together, discussing possibilities, offering ideas, resolving difficulties. Instead, I have to summon you for a conversation because you have been avoiding me out of fear you might meet Syza in the hall. That will end. Today. Now!"

Lhar examined Nevin in silence, wondering whether he had penetrated Nevin's innocence. It was important to shake him up without making him lose all confidence in himself.

"I didn't know I was so obvious," said Nevin finally.

"You weren't, until Feylin. And it's not just Syza. Part of it is inexperience. The deeper you get into a native culture the less real any other life seems. It becomes easier to drift away than to maintain the connection between off-world and native thinking.

There are times when you hardly believe a Concord of planets exists out there."

Nevin's expression told Lhar he was right.

"It's a common problem of first assignments," Lhar said calmly. "Usually there is only one inexperienced team member. Usually the team understands and helps a person learning to live a double life. But we haven't got a team. All we've got is a collection of skills held together by habit. And our habit isn't very strong, is it?"

Nevin sat motionlessly, his face bathed in the white-gold glow of burning oil. "No, it isn't. And I haven't helped much."

"Don't take all the blame yourself," said Lhar wearily. "Since Feylin, I haven't been much help either." Lhar's lips twisted over the sour understatement. He had not been worth a zarf's dirty ear. Only in the last eight days had he been able to walk across the compound without getting dizzy. And while he was recovering, the team was quietly disintegrating. "It does no good wailing over yesterday's water," said Lhar softly. "I'm reasonably whole again. And I'm tired of being caged. With Kaffi's gracious permission, you and Syza and I are going to ride up to Miran Ridge. By the time we get back I'll know whether to call in the ecstasan experts."

"But why? The g'mirans have accepted us no matter how they argue. Feylin's recovery is not lost on them. It will—"

"It was a mistake! A calculated action that came out on the short end of the probabilities. It cost what little the team had."

Nevin said nothing, but his expression said he refused to accept Lhar's words. Reflexively Lhar checked again that no natives had entered the talmare. The constant checks were habit now, and required as little attention as breathing.

"Nevin," he said patiently. "When I accepted this assignment, Contact's calculations—and mine—for the probability of success were mainly based on three things. Time. Culture. Team. Not Diri alone, or Syza, or you. Team. We are much more than our total of individual skills, just as the Access is more than the sum of its machinery."

"I just can't believe that we've failed," said Nevin.

"We haven't, quite. But we're close. If I hadn't been asleep for the last tenth-cycle, if we had functioned as a team, we'd be walking Tal-Senet with the g'mirans' blessings. Minstrels would be singing of our heroic conquest of n'Lith, nurturing the idea that if you dare, all things are possible—even trees in kylith. People would trample each other to touch the ground where we walked. We would be living symbols of hope. Your heresies would be eagerly accepted by a population whose women are barren because fertility is a tragedy.

"But there are no new songs, are there? We're treated with suspicion when we aren't ignored. Instead of new heresies, new songs of hope, you're compelled to argue the pitiful notes of a stillborn melody."

"Diri will convince them."

"By the Nameless Gods!" exploded Lhar. "You can't just drop Diri on them without preparation. The people have to suspect that salvation is possible or there will be utter chaos."

Nevin's fingers laced together, then separated into fists.

"Then Tal-Lith is doomed," whispered Nevin. "The g'mirans will never release us or our story in time."

"It's hard to control a song," said Lhar flatly. "Syza says that rumor of us has seeped through the city. With her feel for music, your knowledge of key religious phrases, and my estimate of what the people must know, we might manage to plow up fertile ground."

"Greater than the parts."

"Exactly. Ready for that ride?"

Without answering, Nevin rose and followed Lhar out of the compound to where Syza waited with the taman. The drifsen silently led the taman along the trail Syza had chosen. Wordlessly, singly, the riders pushed into the formless night. When half the trail had gone by, Syza ventured a question into Lhar's brooding mental silence.

Why Miran Ridge? Now, in darkness?

Nevin needs distance from the city before he can think. Maybe sunrise over a dying Tal-Senet will galvanize him. And we need privacy to make the song.

Are you going to trip the signal?

Lhar touched his belt, felt the reassuring strength of concealed wires. *You guessed?*

It wasn't hard. Ten days to Festival and we've made no progress. And while you slept the river rose.

I know. The water callers were puzzling and chanting.

The lower fields are under water again. As far as I've been able to find out, this has never happened before. I'd use it if I knew how, but I don't.

Does Nevin know?

I don't see how he could avoid it. It's the talk of the marketplace. But then, he's been mainly with the g'mirans. They tell him only what they want him to hear.

And you?

Since Feylin, he has spoken to me less than before.

Syza's thought was totally disinterested; he could sense none of her emotions. The contact was as clear and colorless as an information cube. He probed lightly, discovered a vague whisper of tension humming and tightening, contact thinning. He stopped. Contact renewed. He accepted her boundaries sadly. When he was sick, there had been neither fear nor boundaries. For an instant he longed to be weak again.

Cold penetrated his robes, but the wind was no more than a sigh. The Long Night was breathing over

185

the land; two tenth-cycles of nothing more than pale moons and candles to hold against the stars. And when the treacherous sun slid behind the Ramparts for the last time, the Festival would begin—frightened voices singing in the icy twilight, reassuring each other of Lith's abiding love.

When the taman could scramble no further, Lhar dismounted and went on foot across the last obstacle, a steep talus slope. As he climbed, the black night faded into slate, then light gray, then vague translucence. At the top of Miran Ridge he eased himself onto a rock cushioned by a closely knit, hairlike growth. He waited for Nevin and Syza to complete the climb, waited and watched Tal-Senet emerge into the truncated day. Shapes slowly condensed out of the silver light. The First Khaner's compound became a large, irregular lump of buildings surrounded by a twisting rock wall. Height and distance made the huge compound trivial, no larger than his fist.

Other lumps emerged, guild compounds where potters and tanners and weavers and masons and water masters lived. The edges of the compounds sprouted straggling growths of thatched and hide huts laced together by footpaths; the huts of the unaffiliated city dwellers. Many of the huts were empty, their inhabitants hired to help the khaners harvest and store crops. And when the harvest ended, the people would go back to their huts, back to overflow guild jobs, struggling gardens and miran doles.

Lhar drew his robes closer as the chill wind moaned into life. The river leaped out of the darkened land, burning silver in the rising sun. Lhar blinked, then peered past his breath condensing in the dry dawn. On the far side of the river a shadow city rose, sinuous lines surrounding shapeless lumps, vague roads and blurs that could once have been river gardens.

"Eerie, isn't it?" said Lhar as Nevin sat nearby. "Even though I knew Tal-Senet must have been on both sides of the river once, it's like meeting a dream. How long do you suppose it's been abandoned?"

"I don't know," said Nevin, pulling up his feet to let Syza pass. "Three, maybe five hundred cycles. Maybe much less. Earthquakes and winds don't leave monuments."

"There was a bridge once," said Syza softly.

"Where?" said Lhar.

"When?" said Nevin.

Syza tucked the hem of her robe away from the reaching wind. "I don't know how long ago. But just above the Gate, where the river drops into a deep, narrow gorge, I thought I saw crumbled piers. I pointed them out to Tokor, and he said there were legends of men crossing the gorge as easily as the wind. At one time each notch was fortified against invasion. But that was long before the bridge was built."

"They don't have enough people for war now," Nevin mused. "No 'other' to fight against."

"Tal-Lith is all the enemy they need."

A cold exhalation of wind slid down the talus slope. They studied the ruins until the climbing sun flattened shadows.

"What about the Wanderers scattered over what's left of Tal-Lith?" said Syza into the silence.

"Contact's doing what it can," Lhar said. "As tribes or clans or families are found they're given a knock-out dose of ecstasan, lifted to the second moon and loaded into the Access. They wake up on Seytal-Lith. Crude, but we don't have a lot of time."

Syza's expression was rueful. "I wonder how many have died, will die."

"With subsistence groups like the Wanderers, the usual death rate is less than two percent," Lhar said tonelessly. "Another three percent never fully recover from ecstasan. The rest are helped by special teams in native disguise. There will be a rash of new religions for the first thirty or forty cycles, but by the time the Wanderers discover the new city, Seytal-Lith's major culture should be stable enough to absorb them."

Lhar glanced at Nevin, subtly urging him to participate. But the urging was not necessary; the vague ruins had made Nevin forget Syza's presence.

"What are their chances?" said Nevin, studying the city far below.

"The same as ours," Lhar said. "Poor to fair. The khaner leaders are neutral; they don't have time for their own problems now, much less ours. The g'mirans are uneasy about us in spite of Firn's and Daal's efforts. The rest of the people who know about us are more interested in Festival preparations than in strangers."

"What's your mimax for getting this culture off Tal-Lith?" said Syza quietly.

Lhar controlled his impulse to stare at her. Mimax was a rather unusual term used mainly by synthesists —the minimum and maximum probability, within given parameters, of achieving a goal. The only synthesist Syza had ever met before him was on Bjmsk. He wondered what other scraps of memory were surfacing, and what effect they would have on her and him and Tal-Lith.

"Parameters?" he said casually.

"Only the obvious ones; g'mirans, Diri, Festival, time."

"Can I include you?"

"As I am, not as healer. I couldn't even heal . . . you."

Lhar sensed the effort it cost her to speak neutrally. With a similar effort he matched her tone. "Between thirteen and thirty-one percent."

"So little! Why?"

"Diri."

It was only half the truth; he wondered if Syza knew it.

"She's well enough to dance. I've checked her every night."

"But ill-trained for anything else. If she could just dance, announce us as messengers and vanish as we had planned, the mimax would be thirty-six and seventy. But the population isn't prepared for that. Unfortunately, the sun won't wait for us; we don't have nineteen or twelve or even two cycles. Diri will have to stay and do a bit of godlike persuasion. She has neither the training nor the personality for it."

"Then let's go back to dance and vanish," said Syza.

"Five and twelve."

"Why?"

Lhar waited for Nevin to answer her question.

Nevin shifted his position on the cold rocks and sighed. "Same reason—no preparation. If Diri disappeared and we told them that they had to live in kylith because their planet will be destroyed, we'd survive just as long as it took the mob to catch us. Like a lot of religions, Tal-Lith's is rooted in fear and guilt. When Lith appeared for the first time, she was taken away to kylith because her followers hadn't the power or courage to rescue her. Tal-Lithens would see us as god stealers."

"And if I could heal?" said Syza tightly. "If I could be a walking miracle for all to wonder at?"

"You can't," said Lhar in a tone that left no surface for questions.

"If I could heal," repeated Syza.

"No."

Syza's hood fell back, and her bronze hair fanned out in the wind as she swung around to face him.

"Tell me."

"Why? What good could it do? You're too pressured as it is."

"Then healing could be crucial," said Syza dully.

"You're no longer a healer."

"But she healed the drifsen," Nevin said. "And your face."

"In both cases it cost her too much."

"Too much? Too much!" Nevin swore. "Just how much is Tal-Lith worth to you?"

Syza pulled her hood into place and huddled against the merciless wind. She looked at Lhar; her green eyes shone in the shadow of the dark hood.

"Tell him the truth," she said. "After what I did to him with my song, I owe him at least that much."

Lhar hesitated, then opened his hands, fingers wide. "Ever heard of aversion training?"

"It's the basis for most cultural conditioning," said Nevin impatiently.

"Of course. I'm not thinking." Lhar struggled with the emotions twisting in his mind—Syza's, Nevin's, his own rage at Syza's pain. When he heard his own voice it was too cold, too angry. "Healing is a gift, a prize in the genetic sweepstakes. It's involuntary, like breathing, yet it can be trained to an art, the highest art known to us. And the people who raised Syza did their best to destroy her. They used her gift, then abused her for having it."

Lhar stopped, fighting the sweeping anger that threatened his control. Then he dismissed Nevin's growing fear and as he spoke, his rage unfolded, uncontrolled.

"Then Syza met Zomal. They entered into an exclusive lifetime marriage. Zomal was a Contact agent; he should have known how to help her. But Zomal was entering Decline. He cared for his health more than he cared for a friend, a lover, a brilliant mind, more than all that was Syza. But as cold as Zomal was, he was better than anything she had known before. She loved him. She healed him until she was beyond exhaustion.

"She reversed Decline."

Lhar turned toward Nevin for the first time and his rage leaped with frightening force.

"You can't possibly understand what that means. No one, ever, has reversed Decline. Ever! If Syza brought down the Ramparts with a whispered word it could be no more astonishing."

Lhar noticed his own clenched hands, hard and heavy and powerful. He breathed deeply and put his hands inside his sleeves.

"I would have enjoyed killing him. I don't know

190

what he did to Syza. I can guess, though. I hope the zarfsucker died as horribly as he made her live."

"Don't," whispered Syza.

Lhar ignored her. "Whatever happened was so destructive to Syza that she will not, cannot, remember it. It had something to do with healing, for with amnesia came a loss of her gift. Her amnesia is a survival reflex; the only time she can drive herself to heal is during or just after the moment she believes her life is threatened, when her mind is fully awake and willing to do what it must to survive."

Lhar's burning gray eyes focused on Nevin; the younger man's face was drawn, and he did not notice the icy wind combing through his dark hair.

"Questions?" said Lhar, using what remained of his control to make his voice pleasant.

"Why can't she sing to the natives? Force them like she forced Diri and T'Mero. And me."

"She doesn't fit their god myths. What would happen if we forced a conflicting religion on their culture?"

"Shock."

"A delicate word used to describe cultural murder. I'll call for ecstasan drugs before I'll ask Syza to sing."

"But—"

"Stop it." Syza turned slowly toward Nevin. "I forced no one. All my song did was distill what already existed in Diri and T'Mero and you." She looked away, out over the darkened city. "Both you and Lhar are assuming that if I sang and offered Tal-Lith Feylin's choice, they all would choose as she did. Life. They would not. Many of them would rather die than change."

"If you believe that," began Nevin coldly.

"I know it."

"Then why did you come here—to watch them die?"

"I was given a choice: Tal-Lith or forced integration. Death."

Nevin let out his breath explosively. "So you get revenge by refusing to heal."

"You weren't listening," said Lhar coldly.

Nevin scooped up a rock and threw it toward the city with force enough to split a skull. "You said it yourself. She can heal when she really wants to."

Could you fight what she fights and win even once?

As Nevin reeled with the power of Lhar's question, Lhar forced a direct link between Syza and Nevin, and her fear went through his mind like an explosion of

blackness and desiccating laughter, crumbling, supports dissolving, feet sliding, hands clawing, spinning, falling in laughter more terrible than unwanted death
    NO

Lhar held their minds together with a ruthlessness he did not know he possessed, held them until Nevin screamed, the deathcry of a mind breaking. Lhar released Syza abruptly, held Nevin's body, which was drawn up in fetal travesty. Syza's fury raked Lhar.

You almost killed him! He can't survive my past!

Then he can stop judging you.

Lhar worked with Nevin's mind, coaxing, draining away terror until Nevin's body relaxed, trusting. When Lhar was finished, Nevin felt nothing worse than a vague slinking memory—and a shame which he fought to keep intact.

"That's mine," Nevin gasped. "I earned it. Syza . . ."

Even as Nevin tried to apologize, Syza was speaking over his words, her voice tight and strained. "And I earned what you thought of me. You are right. I could heal if—"

"And taman could fly if they had wings," Lhar said harshly. "Stop punishing yourself. Or do you enjoy it?"

"No more!" said Nevin. He drew a deep shuddering breath. "There's been enough cruelty." He leaned over to Syza, pulled her hands out of her sleeves. "I'm sorry, Syza. Such a futile word. But I mean it. Touch —touch my mind."

Lhar's senses leaped; he knew how deeply Nevin feared mindtouch.

"Please."

Lhar sensed a faint breath of contact sliding deeper. He waited and hoped and waited while shadows shortened and wind moaned. Slowly Nevin's body relaxed; shame receded into wonder. When Syza withdrew as lightly as a breath, Lhar felt a relief so great that it was painful.

"Kaffi understands too," said Nevin. "Somehow she knew."

Syza's arms went around Nevin, holding him as he held her. Nevin's untrained mind radiated sensations —surprise that he had never noticed her beauty, pleasure in the breath against his neck and the suggestion of strength and heat and softness beneath the muffling robes.

Lhar shut Nevin's sensations out, but it was too late. Desperately he closed his mind so that Syza would not know what it cost him to be always close to her, always far away. He fed his mind numbers and estimates for success and failure, trying to bury needs and pain beneath numbers. After a frighteningly long time, the numbers won. When he became aware of Syza again, she was watching him and he felt himself sliding into her eyes, sensed depths of hunger as great as his own. Syza moaned softly and hid her eyes behind her hands.

Nevin looked from one to the other, afraid without realizing it. "It's too soon after Feylin," he said urgently. "You're not well enough to be up here."

Lhar closed his eyes. "I'm fine. A little tired, but it was worth it. The new mimax for Tal-Lith is twenty-four and forty."

Syza lifted her head suddenly. "Is that why you forced a mesh?"

"I wasn't thinking about Tal-Lith when I forced the mesh. I shouldn't have done it. The odds weren't encouraging." Lhar laughed shortly. "If Contact knew, I'd be shoved through the nearest Access. And they'd be right. My decisions should be pragmatic, not personal."

"But you're an integrator. Can't you help Syza? Or would it be like Feylin all over again?"

"Worse. I'd be dealing with a will to live. Syza forgot in order to survive. She'll fight integration with the same ferocity you'd use to save your life. Her mind is too powerful for me to force integration. One or both of us would break."

Nevin looked unhappily at Syza. "Isn't there anything?"

"Nothing," she said, her voice thin and brittle. "I've got to want integration. I don't. I can live with my fear, but I don't know whether I could live with what I've forgotten."

Nevin groped for sharp pebbles and threw them down the slope. His arm whipped forward and the pebbles flew. When the last pebble at his feet was gathered, launched, gone, he rubbed his cold hands together.

"Let's make a song," said Nevin grimly.

Syza leaped upon the new subject with an eagerness born of relief.

"Tokor is vague about the details of Lith's arrival, life, and leaving. What have you learned from the g'mirans?"

Nevin answered mechanically, then became involved as he spoke. "Stripped of religious rhetoric, the story is rather short. Just before, during, or after some natural cataclysm—probably just before—Lith arrived on the planet riding either 'a piece of the sun' or 'a falling star.' The first records call it a star; the later ones call it the sun."

"Meaning that after the stars came to symbolize kylith, g'mirans thought the sun would be a more suitable vehicle?"

"Exactly." Nevin looked at Syza approvingly. "Took me a bit of time to figure that one out."

"I'm not buried in rhetoric."

Nevin smiled fleetingly. "When She came to Tal-Lith—then called just Tal, or Place—this was a rather ordinary planet, about center on the Concord scale of habitable worlds. Lith traveled from city to city inspiring the people with Her beauty and Her dance. In turn, they gave Her the treasures of their world."

"Was dance a form of worship before Lith?" asked Lhar.

"The g'mirans say yes; the Scrolls and Stones don't mention it either way. They do mention Lith's difficulty. Apparently she was having a problem with Her entourage. The Scrolls say first that She was accompanied by strange people creating beautiful sounds. Then She traveled alone, danced with only native singers for music. Then Her people reappeared, but they are described as monsters this time. Demons. They overpowered Her native protectors and carried Her off to a high valley. A star reached down, took Lith and the demons, and withdrew. A short time later Tal was racked by a cataclysm that resulted in dried up oceans, devastating crustal adjustments and huge ice fields growing out of the poles. All caused, say the Stones, by a star that grew until it 'ate the falling day,' whatever that means. After that the story is mainly composed of chanted dirges and prayers and penances and death."

"How much of Lith's visit do you think is true?" asked Syza.

Nevin's hands moved uncertainly. "There have been lightships for eleven thousand Centrex years. It's possible that one orbited, sent down a landing party, looked around, and left. Put that event next to a natural cataclysm and at least one new religion is inevitable—especially when the natives don't have even intrasystem flight. I'm no synthesist, but I don't think the coincidence of contact and cataclysm is impossible."

Syza and Nevin looked at Lhar.

"Nothing's impossible," said Lhar, "but some things are more probable than others. That's one thing Contact was really interested in; they hinted that they would be very grateful if we could explain the circumstances of Lith's visit." Lhar sat quietly for a long moment. "Do the Scrolls describe more than one Lith?" he said finally.

"Yes . . ."

"But?"

"Two problems: name and description. I can think of at least three other planets that have the word 'Lith' in their native vocabulary." He looked at Lhar.

"Eighty-one planets," said Lhar. "I punched it up before we left. Also, Diri's home world is spelled six different ways, depending on the source you happen to use. Lythe and Lith are the two favorites."

"So the similarity of name is just a coincidence?" said Syza.

Lhar spread his fingers. "Could be. How do they describe Her?"

"That's the other problem," said Nevin. "She's described as wearing silver clothing. Only the Third Enigma hints that perhaps the clothes might have been something other than fabric. But even that isn't definitive. How many races have skin that could be described as silver?"

"Between eighteen and twenty-six, depending on the eyes of the seer," said Lhar. "And six other races commonly wear tight silver clothing."

"How many of them dance? How many of them had lightships thousands of cycles ago?"

Lhar smiled at Syza. "Exactly what Contact asked."

"And?"

"Three. Of them, the Lythens are the best dancers. That's why we persuaded Diri to come with us. But whatever happened was a long time ago. The monitoring machines saw the Festival, the ceremonial silver clothing, the dancers, and decided that a Lythen would be the best galactic analog to Lith. More effective than, say, a Semerel contortionist."

"Do the Scrolls describe more than one Lith?" asked Syza.

Nevin looked confused.

"More than one silver skin or cloth or whatever," explained Lhar.

"Yes. That's the Ninth Enigma. A bare hint," said Nevin drily, "but all that's needed for sixteen religions. It's only mentioned once, vaguely. The Scrolls only describe one Lith."

"How is She described?" asked Lhar.

"'Cloth of silver alive with Her flowing grace, and shining.'"

"Eyes? Hair? Ears? Number of digits?"

"Four digits on each hand. That's why the most devout dancers cut off their smaller fingers. Eyes as blue as ice caves. No discernible hair or ears."

"Diri," whispered Syza.

"Or a Semerel, or Nvstm, or a few others I could name," said Lhar. "But Contact chose well. They could have given us a green-eyed, blue-skinned Lythen. At any rate, Lythe was among the first planets to have lightships."

"Then you think the legend actually tells of a First Contact?" said Nevin.

"That's what Contact wants to know."

"Almost all cultures see their gods in their own image, or in fantastic images of the mind," said Nevin slowly. "Originally, Lith fit neither category. But the g'mirans have been working on it."

"Silver cloth for skin?" said Lhar.

"Yes. And a tight hood to explain lack of hair, ears, et cetera."

"Do the Scrolls describe Her dancing?" said Lhar.

"Yes, in great detail. The movements would be difficult or impossible for a race with Tal-Lith's skeletal structure."

Lhar sat motionlessly while the wind hummed down from the Ramparts, icy and powerful. "Do the Stones say why She came here?"

"She came to dance for a doomed planet," said Nevin.

"You're sure?" demanded Lhar.

"The symbol for impending death is unique; there's no possibility of error. But I can't accept that as literal truth," said Nevin. "It could easily be a religious flourish; Tal-Lith didn't have the scientific understanding to know that a nearby nova could doom their planet. In retrospect, added to Lith's disappearance, it would be an inevitable association to make. The Stones mention that Lith's coming was preceded by a huge star that 'ate the sky.'"

"How much of this does Diri know?"

"None."

"Good. We have enough problems with her arrogance."

Nevin looked startled, then said, "I see. If she started to believe that a Lythen really came here once . . . . But that's insane. Why would a Lythen come here, especially with a nova nearby?" He waved his hand abruptly, cutting off Lhar before he could speak. "All right, assume that they saw the nova and came for a look. That still means nothing. No one would stay around for a few cycles and take a chance on being caught in the backlash."

"A Lythen would," said Lhar. "Their arrogance is the despair of the Concord. A Lythen does what he or she kerden well wants to." He turned to Syza. "Have you talked with Diri?"

"A few times. I check her every day. Once when I was watching her practice I told her how very beautifully she danced. We talked together while T'Mero used the throwing stones. She told me her culture is ancient, uninterrupted by wars for thousands and thousands of cycles."

"How do they control their arrogance?" asked Nevin.

"Lightships and colonization," said Lhar briefly. "Go on, Syza."

"Lythens worship the body; dance is considered the highest Lythen art. Diri told me that even before the Concord, Lythen dancers traveled to all the civilized planets to perform, and their greatest dancers . . . ."

"Yes?" said Lhar, his voice sharp with interest.

"That's all. T'Mero told her to be quiet so he could concentrate."

"Sucking zarfs," muttered Lhar. "Well, Contact will be glad to know that much."

"Why?" said Nevin.

"Lythe was very reluctant to join the Concord. They have told us almost nothing about the years before Concord. We know they were great explorers and suspect that they have colony worlds they haven't mentioned and we haven't found. Did you ask more about the early dancers?"

"She seemed indifferent. She talked only about her own life, the days when she was Lythe's greatest dancer."

"She was the greatest dancer in the known galaxy," said Lhar flatly. "She was younger then, more resilient."

Syza's fingers moved in a graceful gesture of disbelief. "I've watched Diri. She's as supple as water. She makes me feel like a twelve-toed zarf. Have you seen her dance?"

"I recruited her off a backside planet," said Lhar. "She was dancing on a coarse stage as part of a traveling circus. The planet was wealthy; she had many debts. Contact is paying them now."

"From worship to that," said Nevin softly. "Sad, and somehow unfair."

"Nothing's fair," said Lhar. "Not one zarfsucking thing. Look down there and tell me how they earned extinction."

Nevin looked gloomily at Tal-Senet, so small beneath the slanting sun.

"Would it help us," said Syza, "if we could prove to them that a Lythen or some other race had come here and danced and ended up a god? If they could see their history as something other than well-earned destruction?"

"But if we could convince them of that," said Nevin, "we could make them believe anything, including the fact that there's another planet waiting for them under a different sun."

"I agree," Lhar said. "Unraveling the various truths out of Tal-Lith's legends is useful only up to a point. We know enough symbols to begin the song: gentle world, catastrophe, ravaged world, long struggle against death, victory possible for those who dare to grasp it."

"When Lith returns the ice will melt, the seas will fill, water and warmth will fall from the sky," said Nevin. "Let's just call it a new world. Vague enough not to panic the g'mirans, solid enough for our purposes."

"Seytal-Lith?" said Syza.

"Why not? We have to introduce it sooner or later."

"At the end of the song, then," said Lhar. "Syza—a melody for our lovely half truths. Simple but resonant. How much time do you need?"

"None. The planet and legend cry out for a song; I've thought about it often since we landed."

Syza's lips parted slightly and a clear note filled the air. The note rose slowly, golden as a stable sun, became a fall of light and warmth over fertile land. Rills of water danced, spinning, children laughing

congealing into wind moaning icy notes over crumbling walls; huddled people croaking prayers for water. Laughter mocked them, horrible laughter rasping dried flesh from wind-blown bones. People dying childless, alone,

cold laughter rose, stirring dust, spreading despair's contagion while people prayed and died.

The melody shifted subtly, became the rhythm of a taman running, running, low and urgent, dry laughter howling behind, wind scouring stone troughs, purple Talkyer. Demon laughter like a storm gathering behind fleeing riders, dark and climbing, devouring light

grit rasped living flesh, drying flesh, dying flesh.

Rhythm faltered, slowed, stopped. A single consuming note of human defiance rose above the storm, divided storm into silence and jeweled stars reaching down

singing with the distant liquid notes of an alien river. Taman walking, rhythm blending with the silver water. A joyous flight of notes, hope and children's laughter beneath a gentle veil of alien sunlight.

Lhar and Nevin opened their eyes, surprised to find the world unchanged.

"That . . ." Nevin gestured helplessly. "It doesn't need words."

"Not when Syza sings it," said Lhar softly. "Thank you, Chanteuse. If we do a tenth as well with words, I'll be satisfied. Can you simplify the melody so that it's within reach of a normal voice? I can't sing a duet, much less a chorus, with just my natural equipment."

Syza hummed quietly in a voice that was haunted by subdued echoes. The melody was pellucid, the rhythm irresistible; Nevin and Lhar found themselves humming.

"The refrain was so subtle when you sang it by yourself," said Nevin. "I didn't notice the repetition until the second time around. But it's perfect. Simple and addictive."

"A distillation of experience," said Lhar reflectively, his mind analyzing the resonances of the notes. "Like atoms, capable of infinite variation with only subtle shifts of energy-emphasis. Brilliant." He looked wryly at Nevin. "Our turn, miran. I want whoever hears this song to think of the five who refused to die, who crossed n'Lith to find water, and who would cross kylith rather than give up. By the time the song ends, I want kylith to be challenge rather than horror."

Nevin sat quietly, clicking more pebbles between his fingers. A sudden excitement came over him.

"Yes—yes! With a song it will work!"

"What will?" asked Lhar.

"Have you noticed how jumbled their language is? Oh, it's smoothed out in common speech, but the

Stones and Scrolls contain what could be a mix of several languages. Obviously the languages merged as the survivors trickled into the only habitable areas left on the planet."

Lhar suppressed his impatience and made encouraging noises.

"Take n'Lith and kylith," said Nevin. "They originally meant the same thing in different languages. The 'nuh' and 'kyl' sound carry the meaning of without or absent or negation. On my native world we would call n'Lith or kylith 'pimt.'"

"Pimt?"

"A very unpleasant place," explained Nevin, "where very unpleasant people—usually dead ones—are punished for very unpleasant acts."

"Sihólitel," murmured Lhar in his native tongue.

"Hell," said Syza in hers.

Nevin laughed shortly. "The concepts of sin and punishment are almost universal. The cultural variations are immense, of course, but the themes remain basically intact."

"How does that help us here?" said Syza.

"N'Lith is semantically equal to kylith. In common usage, they're interchangeable. Only g'mirans and some mirans make a distinction between the two. As far as most people are concerned, the land we crossed to get here is kylith. In the song's refrain we should use both words, often, and blur whatever distinctions remain."

"Or start out saying n'Lith, then mix the two, then use only kylith," said Syza thoughtfully.

Lhar listened while Nevin and Syza exchanged ideas, words, bits of melody. Satisfied, he let them work with no more than an occasional nudge when they strayed too far from the basic theme he had outlined. By the time the sun neared the end of its shortened arc, the refrain and six verses of the song were complete. Syza's full, haunting voice began the song. He listened and watched shadows rise on the far side of the river, calling up the ruins of dust and neglect. The lament for the Forgotten Lands keened through him, telling of thirst and unanswered prayers and despair. The refrain was a bare whisper of daring hope, desperate will, a fragile embryo of victory that would grow with each repetition until the refrain was born into potency and a universe of hope.

The last vivid notes shivered through him, and he prayed that their promise was as true as the lament which still keened in his mind.

IX

"YOU'RE FREE," SAID KAFFI SIMPLY.

Lhar put aside the harness and oil and wiped his hands carefully.

"Heresies and all?" he said, without looking up.

"No dogma can stand against that song. Every khaner singer sings it in every part of the marketplace." She waited, but Lhar said nothing. "The g'mirans are searching for the source of the song. It's very elusive. Singers just spread their hands and say they heard the song in the market or outside a khaner wall or in the fields."

Lhar finished wiping his hands in silence.

"You do know which song I mean," said Kaffi, her voice sharp with exasperation.

"I've heard it."

"And?"

"It's contagious," he agreed.

"Where did you hear it?"

Lhar spread his hands and smiled. Kaffi hissed her frustration.

"You created that song," she said flatly.

"I lived it."

"G'miran Urari is furious. He has turned against you for your heresies. His people meet and whisper of pain and penance and death."

"Tell me something new. Tell me why you're angry."

"Confused. And, yes, angry. That song is like the wind, shifting the land here and there, building new hills and scouring away old ones, changing and confusing what used to be a clear trail."

"The old trail clearly led to death."

Kaffi's yellow eyes flashed and narrowed, then her face relaxed in soft laughter.

"I knew it was your song. I see you riding through it, a man like the Ramparts with eyes of ice. You have a frightening strength around you. Lith help anyone who tries to change your trail."

"You didn't fear me when we met."

"I didn't know you then. I hadn't heard your song."

"It's not my song. The song I heard held no fear, only hope."

"Hope can be terrifying."

"Why would singers love a song of fear?"

"They hear only the hope."

Lhar stood and held Kaffi's face between his hands. "Then listen to them, Kaffi. If you listen, the song won't betray your hope."

"And you, Lhar. Will you betray me?" At Lhar's surprised look she said, "You are planning something . . . final. I sensed it when I first touched you. I sense it now. Your khaner is not like others I have known. Diri and T'Mero wear secrets like dark robes. Nevin twists our dogmas as easily as I twist straw. Syza . . . she lives with an unspeakable private horror. Yet the song promises a reborn world of light and warmth and children's laughter."

Lhar touched Kaffi's mind lightly, found explicit the fear and mistrust and confusion implicit in her words.

"I can't promise you a world without pain . . . or change without loss. Tal-Lith is like the river in winter, trapped beneath a thick lid of death. The break-up is wrenching, yet without it, life would be impossible."

He felt Kaffi tremble beneath his hands, her mind responding to his grief as he tasted again the death of Tal-Lith.

"But I can promise you a new world," he said softly. "A world of beginnings."

"New . . . not reborn?" she whispered.

Kaffi's eyes searched Lhar's for a denial. She found none; only compassion was there. He felt her mind recoil from his certainty. He held her while his mind helped hers to accept an unknown truth. At last she took a slow breath and looked up at him with surprising calm.

"You're not from the Forgotten Lands."

"There are many Forgotten Lands."

She hesitated, wrestling with conflicting needs.

"Lhar, has Nevin been told of the Vile Stone?"

Her words tumbled out from some inner urgency he could not fathom.

"No. Is it important?"

"It's the g'mirans' greatest secret, and shame. The Vile Stone talks of many lands, worlds like ours among the staring white eyes of kylith. That surprises you— but the stone is old, very old. It is said that the Stone talks with Lith's voice. I will show Nevin that Stone, though the cost may be exile. It is the Stone of dissension and heresy and curses."

"Don't risk it," said Lhar, excitement rising in him. "Just tell me what this Stone says."

"It's not really a stone, at least not like the others. If you touch it in the Long Night it burns the skin off your fingers. Only in sunlight and warmth is it safe. It's bright and silver, not heavy like stone. It was a gift from Lith. But some ancient g'mirans were offended by its words. They dared not destroy Lith's gift, so they ignored and later reviled it as containing demon lies. The Stone's words are like what I sometimes feel when you touch me. Other worlds, other people, kylith seething with life and suns. But if that were true, Tal-Lith must be kylith, and the stars must be miur-Lith, and Tal-Lith will die as the Stone said it would."

There was a long silence.

"I'm not surprised the g'mirans rejected that Stone," said Lhar slowly. "Its truths are without comfort."

"They reject the Stone and they will reject what

you say. They will call you demon. Even I didn't want to believe you, and I saw your agony with Feylin. Must you tell the g'mirans?"

"What about Firn and Daal?"

"They'll trust as I do. But the others—no. Isn't there a way to tell without telling, to hint without—the song!"

Lhar smiled. "Yes, the song. You're very quick." He looked at her searchingly. "You're also very calm, Kaffi. Too calm. Do you really understand what we have talked about?"

"Understand?" She put her hands lightly over his. "No, I don't understand. I accept. I started accepting the first time I touched you and sensed strangeness and distance and change, always change. I'm a coward, Lhar; I fought change even while I worked to help you. And then I fought myself. I thought I believed after Feylin, but it was too good. Too perfect. Everything I had ever longed for given to me. Like bread with no crust. A trick."

"Then why do you accept now?"

"You told me there was no change without loss. You grieved for . . . what? No, don't tell me the price we'll pay for our future. Not yet. I want to be able to walk the market streets and laugh like the others. I want to eat sweet loh and drink ssan laced with yefa. I want to stop and listen to the old songs and sing with my people. I want to find Tokor and feel his fine strength. I want to forget."

"Yes," he said gently. "That would be good."

"Then eat this."

Surprised, Lhar looked at Kaffi, then at the moist crumbling cake she had pulled out of a pocket in her robe.

"Yefa," she said. "I can't forget or enjoy if you're sitting longfaced in a cold stone room. Syza said it wouldn't hurt you."

"Has she eaten any?" he said curiously.

"Of course. She's waiting for you. She wants to see the market streets."

207

"Done," said Lhar suddenly, scooping the cake from her hand.

The cake was a flavorful mixture of fine loh flour, sweetberries, and just enough fat to make the mixture hold together. He thought he tasted the spicy, almost astringent flavor of yefa oil, but he could not be sure.

By the time he found Syza, he was sure. Yefa was spreading through him like echoes through a canyon. Pleasure and relaxation loosened him. When he saw Syza, he smiled widely.

"Yefa may be mild," he said, "but it's fast and thorough."

"Isn't it, though?" she said, taking his hand.

"What does it do to reflexes?" he said, savoring the feeling of her palm against his.

"Nothing permanent. Just don't go climbing rock-falls. You may feel like you can fly, but the landing would be sudden."

"And the mind?"

"Try to think an unhappy thought."

Lhar tried. The thought slipped away. He stopped walking and concentrated. By summoning all his will he could hold the thought of Tal-Lith's destruction.

"How long does it last?" he said wonderingly. He would have been worried, but the drug made it almost impossible.

"An hour, maybe more. It breaks down very quickly."

"An hour," murmured Lhar. "So little, and so much."

Syza looked at him; her eyes flashed green in the late morning dawn. "We're like rope-dancers balanced over a void," she said softly. "Don't question the illusion of safety."

Lhar moved his fingertips slowly over her forehead and cheeks, traced the smooth curve of her lips.

"No questions," he agreed, abandoning the last of his controls against the yefa.

They walked slowly to the market area, letting the scents of hot bread and ssan and sweetberries wash over them. Permeating the food smells, a subtle hint of spicy yefa rode on the light breeze. Lhar stretched and thanked his private gods for the freedom the g'mirans had given them. It was good to walk streets, which were seething with laughter and excitement. It was good to feel the deep current of pleasure that surged through the crowds. Even the rising river and the coming night could not destroy the Festival spirit.

Khaner and guild singers, singly and in groups, wandered slowly about. Their melodies wove together strands of the crowd as people stopped to share a favorite song. Some singers were accompanied by musicians, but most sang unaided, confident that the purity of their voices needed no embellishment. The songs were mostly secular, telling of sand and windstorm and water, brave riders and salt-crazy taman, laughter and the pleasures of love.

Lhar and Syza stopped to listen to a song called "The Great Thaw." The song compared an indifferent lover to the river in the Long Night. Stanza after stanza detailed the khaner's intricate and ingenious efforts to effect a thaw. When the orgiastic break-up finally came, Lhar whooped his approval as loudly as any Tal-Lithen.

"That's the first time I've heard you really laugh since you helped Feylin," said Syza.

"Only a stone could resist that song. I'll have to try that eighth stanza sometime—when I find a taman good-natured enough to carry three riders."

Lhar's hands and body moved suggestively, evoking a ride that left Syza helpless with laughter.

"Stop," she gasped. "I can't even walk."

Lhar smiled down at her and realized that he felt very good, like a man seeing light after blindness.

"A bargain," he said, lifting her off her feet. "You laugh for me and I'll walk for you."

He ignored her sudden silence as he shifted her weight in his arms and set off through the crowded streets singing snatches of "The Great Thaw." When a passing man offered new verses, Lhar stopped to debate biological improbabilities with him. As the suggestions became more and more outrageous, Lhar felt laughter ripple through Syza's body.

"That's impossible," she sputtered finally.

"Don't bet on it."

The stranger laughed and melted away as Lhar's mouth closed over Syza's. He expected her to resist, but her lips opened with a hunger that matched his. They held each other as though flesh could dissolve barriers of mind and circumstance. Slowly he put her down, released her, and let her stand close to him. He felt an angry hunger searching through him, then anger was overwhelmed by yefa. He still wanted Syza, wanted her as he had never wanted any other woman, but there was no room for bitterness or pain. All he felt was the memory of her lips, the moving warmth of her tongue. How could he be angry at that?

"I'd still like to find that taman," he said, "but there's no hurry."

They walked close together, weaving through the crowds of people. Everywhere they looked they saw stalls filled with the products of careful labor. Cloth dyed with all the colors the eye could hold, leather tanned to incredible softness, stone carvings of uncanny simplicity.

"Wait," said Lhar suddenly.

He watched the stone carver work, turning a dark gray oval of rock in his hands, shaping lines in the soft stone. The man worked quickly, expertly. A ghostly face appeared.

"Water rock," said the man as he examined his work carefully. "It's rare. Not many people can work with it. It keeps its color when it dries, but it dries very fast. Take this piece, for instance. The surface is already dry. If I had one more line to make, I couldn't do it."

"Can't you just get it wet again?" asked Lhar.

The man laughed shortly. "I could, but I'd leave

white marks. Ruin it." He looked at Lhar, sensing real interest. "Like it?"

"Yes."

"I've done better."

He picked up some stones no bigger than his palm. As the stones moved, lines like running taman turned and twisted in the thin light. He set the stones down.

"I just finished a head. Best I've ever done."

The carver turned abruptly and went to a shelf at the back of the stall. Lhar glanced at Syza but her hood was up and her face hidden as she admired the taman stones. A soft thump brought his attention back to the carver. With a flourish the man removed a leather covering, revealing a small carved head. A woman's head, proud and strong and beautiful, with hair piled up above high, slanting cheekbones, a face drawn with suffering. In the place of eyes were two tilted ovals of deep-green crystal.

"Syza . . ." Lhar's word was barely a whisper.

The stone carver grunted his satisfaction. "That's what he called her. The woman in the song."

"He?" said Syza softly, not looking up.

"G'miran Daal," said the carver with barely concealed pride. "We're chosen brothers. He told me about her. He's a bit afraid of her," he added to himself, but Lhar heard.

"Will you sell that statue?" said Lhar.

"It's for Daal."

"No," said Daal's voice behind Lhar, "it's my apology to Lhar. And my thanks for Feylin."

Lhar turned quickly but before he could speak, Daal bowed to him. When Lhar would have returned the bow, Daal restrained him.

"Leten," he said to the carver, "I came as soon as I heard you were finished. Apparently Lhar and Syza also heard, somehow."

"An accident," said Lhar. "We were just walking."

Leten looked quickly at Syza's bowed head. When she looked up and met his eyes they heard his sharp indrawn breath. Then Leten slid the hoof off of Syza's

211

head and studied her carefully, turning her face slowly with a callused hand beneath her chin. At last he sighed.

"Better than I'll ever do. Daal, you might have told me about her smile."

Syza laughed, a sudden warmth that softened the planes of her face. "He's had little cause to see me smile."

"My loss," said Daal.

Syza turned and looked at the g'miran gravely. Daal returned her glance without uneasiness.

"Our loss," said Syza, smiling suddenly.

Leten covered the head and reluctantly handed it to Lhar. Though the carving did not smile, it was a masterwork of subtle power. Lhar hesitated before returning the head to Leten.

"Keep it for me until after Festival," said Lhar slowly. "Keep it here, uncovered. Let anyone with eyes admire your artistry. Let this carving tell them that only a fool follows a smiling face through ky-lith."

Leten locked his hands together in the sign signifying a fair bargain made and kept, and bowed to Lhar. When Leten looked up again, his pale blue eyes were alive with shrewd humor and his voice carried no further than the three people standing close.

"I've heard the song," Leten said carefully to Daal. "Remember that a drifsen without fangs is useless for herding."

"A thirsty drif doesn't need to be driven to water," countered Daal.

Leten laughed softly and whispered, "No? You never were a herder, were you. Look to your fangs, Daal. You'll need them clean and sharp and quick."

Irritation crossed Daal's face, followed by sudden thoughtfulness.

"Urari?" said Daal very softly.

Leten snapped his fingers in agreement.

"Thank you, brother. Anything else?"

Leten's fingers snapped again.

Daal's fingers responded with a swift sign Lhar had never seen. Again fingers snapped.

"The carving," said Daal in a normal conversational tone, "is excellent. I would like a gift for Firn, also. The drifsen you mentioned would be very nice."

"I haven't found the right stone."

"Find it. The carving should be a Festival gift."

"I'll do what I can."

Lhar knew that more than a carving had been discussed. He considered lifting the details from their minds, but decided it would do little good; Daal was in a better position to understand city intrigues than Lhar was. He walked with the g'miran into the crowd.

We're being followed.

Syza's thought condensed in his mind with amazing subtlety. She had renewed the silent link that had broken with Feylin.

Hostile, curious, excited?

All. The two men behind, one on each side, are afraid, hostile. A third man, ahead of us now, is excited; he overheard our names. He's telling those singers about us. And . . .

Yes?

Daal knows someone, expects something, but not . . . just . . . yet. I can't make out the details unless I use real mindtouch.

Don't. He might sense it. But monitor the hostile ones.

Lhar and Syza walked slowly through the crowd, following Daal's lead. The g'miran moved with the ease of a powerful man among affectionate subjects. But for all his confidence, Daal's eyes moved ceaselessly and his mind was fully alert; he, too, sensed the change rippling through the crowd, the silence followed by murmurs which grew louder with every step. Above the sound of the crowd rose the opening notes of "The Forgotten Lands."

"Stand beside me, as equals," said Daal. "Let them see you as they hear your song."

213

Lhar and Syza stepped forward. The crowd withdrew slightly, expanded, and waited expectantly. The clear keening notes of song fell across sudden silence. When the chorus came it was a mere whisper, a subdued breath telling of many broken hopes. Several voices in the crowd echoed each line of the chorus softly, and the effect was a catechism of desolation.

Lhar listened closely, hearing new words and nuances, sensing currents flowing unknown among minds. As the song progressed, the people around him echoed each line of the chorus, more hopefully with each repetition. The singers felt the current building, skillfully dammed a phrase here, opened a new verse there, allowed the crowd to become the leader of a catechism of growing hope.

The weight of massed emotions pressed against Lhar and Syza. The feeling was at first uncomfortable; then it became a force not weighing, but lifting. They were the center of song and hope and sudden, fierce love. The crowd's strength became theirs, a thousand hearts pumped their blood, a thousand minds focused on them like a great lens.

The final chorus was a roar of acclamation.

Before the last notes of the chorus had died, Daal pulled Lhar and Syza through a nearby door leading into a large stone building.

"It's Lith's own blessing we were on the edge of the crowd," said Daal when they were safely inside. "I didn't expect that many people. And there was something else, like faint g'malk. Frightening, yet . . . I paid twenty people to seed a crowd for you. Only one was out there. They weren't expecting the three of us until tomorrow. When Jile overheard your names he went ahead anyway. The crowd loved it but there's such a thing as too much love. That song is like the moment that the river sheds its lid of ice—necessary, unpredictable, and dangerous. We'll have to plan your appearances very carefully from now on. We could easily have been trampled into the streets."

"I hope that doesn't mean back to the talmare for

us," said Syza. "Crystal windows are beautiful, but I'd rather watch the Games."

Daal started to speak, then hesitated. Lhar exchanged glances with him.

"I know, I know," sighed Syza. "Back to crystal windows. What about T'Mero? Is he safe at the Games?"

"The song barely mentions him," said Daal.

"But—" began Syza, then stopped.

Daal laughed softly. "The song has changed since you first, ah, listened to it. Am I correct?"

"Yes."

"Such things happen," said Daal smoothly. "Singers like to leave their mark on a song. And Firn disliked having Diri and T'Mero presented as your equals."

Lhar's dismay did not show in his face. He thought rapidly, assessing how a changed song would affect their plans. He sighed.

"Did she say why?" asked Lhar.

"She distrusts them."

Lhar did not press Daal to be more precise; in a few days Firn's distrust would no longer matter.

Daal gestured reassuringly. "Don't worry, my friend. Kaffi will not exclude Diri and T'Mero from the First Khaner in spite of Firn's distrust. The First Khaner gained much prestige when you became their i'khaner. Kaffi is a leader; she knows that you two are necessary if the First Khaner does not want to become Second—or dead."

"I don't understand," said Syza.

"No? Of course . . . how different your lives must have been in the Forgotten Lands. It's very simple, Syza. Lhar will inevitably be named First Leader, just as you will inevitably be named First Herder."

"Inevitably?" asked Lhar drily.

Daal looked at him. "Yes. And not because of khaner or city politics. Politics may decide who is named the best tanner or weaver or singer or dancer; the titles of First Leader and First Herder are matters of survival. You brought your khaner through

215

n'Lith alive. Syza brought your animals through alive. If a time comes when the First Khaner must cross the river, you will be our best hope of bringing the First Khaner through alive."

There was a long silence.

"We understand," said Syza finally. "We are honored."

"Tell me that when river ice numbs your body."

Daal's voice had overtones of immediate concern, as though he anticipated a river crossing soon.

"The river worries you," said Lhar.

Daal was silent for a moment. The noise of the crowd faded as he led them toward a room filled with the sharp smell of curing hides.

"Yes, the river worries me. It has been as unpredictable as a salt-crazy animal. The melting season was more than a tenth-cycle early. The flood was the greatest in memory. Then the river waned—far too early. For seven days it dropped. Then there was a roar and a second flood. Then waning and rising, waning and rising. And not just small changes. The khaner farmers have lately become very devout," added Daal with a short laugh.

"But we heard that the crops were good," said Lhar.

"We were careful to give that impression. The crops are barely adequate. What we gained in high crops we lost in the lowlands. Worse, the lowland harvest has been delayed by the river. Late-maturing crops, rising river, falling light. They are harvesting by torchlight now. Not that it will do much for us; the last flood washed out even the deep winter roots of the loh.

"If the river is like this next cycle, the First Khaner will have to cross. If we have another flood in this cycle, the First Khaner must attempt a crossing in darkness. That has never been done. But there should be enough wild harvest on the other side to keep the First Khaner alive through the Long Night. And the Second. Perhaps even the Third."

Lhar and Syza looked at each other, memories of the sullen river heavy between them.

"Obligation, not honor," said Lhar finally.

"I'm afraid so. You came to us in uncertain seasons. But perhaps the river has purged itself and the next cycles will be regular."

"No," said Lhar. "The river will never again run smoothly."

"You're very certain."

"Yes."

"I wish I could dispute you, First Leader," said Daal heavily. "But I cannot. Firn and I will cross with you."

"But the city—without you," said Syza.

"The city is dying of fear. The next cycle or the one after, the city will turn on itself like a salt-crazy beast and tear out its own guts. Urari is almost beyond my control. With each fluctuation of the river he grows more potent. If I can take some guild people and several khaners across the river, we might have a chance to survive." Daal paused. "I've told no one but Firn of my fears."

"Don't worry," said Lhar with a faint twisting smile. "Syza and I know how to keep secrets."

"Do you also know how to share them?"

"More important, we know when."

"Don't wait too long, First Leader. Urari hates your song. He is trying to destroy you. If I knew what you planned, I could help."

"If I knew what I planned," Lhar said grimly, "I could help, too."

Daal spread his hands, palms out. "I'll take you to the talmare."

They followed Daal through storerooms filled with cured hides and rustling reed mats, fabrics worked with religious symbols and pallets of drying sweet-berries. Between the storerooms ran twisting alleys filled with silence and darkness. The short day was over; kylith had claimed the sky.

"Wait here."

Lhar and Syza stood quietly while Daal checked the open space they must cross. Lhar flexed his aching hands automatically, working the tension out of them, and thought wistfully of the long-dissipated yefa.

"Come."

They were halfway across the clearing when the earthquake came. They threw themselves down while the ground quivered, swayed, then settled, only to surge again. Daal lay nearby, praying quietly. They heard a burst of excited voices, then silence again; only very large quakes were worthy of much comment. Daal rose to his feet, shaking dust and straw from his robes.

"It's safe to stand now. That one was barely kanehi-mahn. At most a cliff-builder. Certainly not kanehi-n'gat, a cliff-destroyer. The aftershocks will be negligible."

Lhar stood quickly. Syza was much slower, too slow; the silent link between them was full of unease.

What is it?

Her cold fingers wrapped around his wrists and a single urgent thought came from her.

Listen!

He held his breath and listened as much with his mind as his body. And he heard it, a vague—

"What's wrong?"

Syza's hand silenced Daal. Lhar strained into the darkness toward the Ramparts. Yes, there it was again, pressure waves more felt than heard: a vague, melancholy rumble like thunder faint with great distance. He had felt something like that only once before, halfway across the galaxy when a far mountainside had sloughed off its burden of soaked earth and vegetation. This was similar, yet not quite the same. This sound had more sharp edges.

The noise faded and died.

"Is that sound common?" asked Lhar.

"I heard nothing," said Daal.

Lhar described the sound.

"I've never heard it," said Daal, his voice trembling

218

slightly. "But there is a name for what you described. Ssarrm, the Mourner. The—it is a portent of devastation. Come quickly. If Urari heard it, the streets won't be safe."

"No one in the city could have heard it," said Syza as she followed Daal. "A khaner herdsman might have, if he were alone and listening for it, but I doubt it."

"I hope you're right," said Daal softly. "But how did you hear if it was so very faint?"

"I didn't quite hear it. I felt it the same way I feel the wind building high on the Ramparts."

"And you, Lhar? Did you hear it easily?"

"Only after Syza alerted me. And," he added, "not easily at all. Mostly with my mind."

Daal stopped and seemed on the point of questioning them further but apparently decided that it was more important to get them to the safety of the talmare.

"We'll talk about this later."

In silence they followed him through narrow alleyways. They entered the First Khaner's compound through a hidden stone door. Once inside, Lhar oriented himself.

"Can you find the talmare?" asked Daal in a whisper.

"Yes."

"Good. I'd rather not be seen just now. Go quickly and tell no one about the—it. I'm going back to the city. Someone else might have noticed it. I must know."

Daal disappeared through the wall; the only noise was a very slight scrape as the heavy block of stone turned on its pivot. Even under the clear light of the racing moon the wall looked solid.

"Remember that door," he murmured. "We may need it."

They hurried noiselessly to the talmare. Diri and T'Mero were not there, but Nevin was.

"Sweet Lith!" Nevin said, grabbing both of them.

"I thought the crowd had gotten you. Kaffi and Firn are beating the alleys looking for you."

"Daal got us safely back," said Syza, smiling slightly, "in spite of crowds and earthquakes."

"Just a medium shaker," said Nevin offhandedly. "I'd better find Kaffi and tell her you're safe."

"You'd better stay here. An order, not a request," said Lhar. "Daal will tell her we're safe."

"But—"

"You're in the song, miran. And you're also the only man I can safely question about earthquakes and Ssarrm."

Nevin took a deep breath, but curiosity won over arguments.

"Ssarrm?"

"The Mourner."

"The—Lith's blue eyes! Did someone hear it?"

Syza shivered in the chill room and looked longingly at the dark brazier.

"Ssan first," said Lhar, deftly filling the brazier with straw braids.

When each had a bowl of ssan steaming between their cold hands, Syza quickly told what had happened.

"Pray to Lith no one else sensed it," said Nevin grimly. "That's all Urari would need."

"What kind of devastation do the legends tell of?" said Lhar. "Stripped of religious flourishes."

"Ummmm. Without rhetoric, it condenses to a fluctuation in the river's volume."

"But there have been several changes this cycle, and no one has mentioned Ssarrm."

"A disastrous fluctuation," amended Nevin.

"How much truth to the legends?" asked Lhar.

"How long is the wind?" countered Nevin. "Oh I know, I know; you want a trained guess." He frowned in the wavering gold light, looking suddenly older. "I can only reason by analogy. Is it safe to talk?"

"Yes."

"On my home world we have a lot of earthquakes,

mountains, plus a few glaciers and icefields. Sometimes a quake shakes loose mountain ice and rocks, which choke a riverbed and make a natural dam. A few of these lakes last for a long time. But most of the debris either melts away or is swept away when the weight of the water gets too great. The result," he added unnecessarily, "is a rather total devastation on the downhill side."

"Syza?" said Lhar.

"What I sensed," she began, then stopped. "Movement and violence and grinding, a . . . a vast breaking away. Terrible, yet somehow beautiful because when silence finally comes, the world is balanced again."

"Yes," whispered Nevin, his eyes unseeing as he remembered something from his past.

"Then you believe there was a landslide or an ice fall or both," said Lhar. "I agree. The edges of the icefields and glaciers must be riddled with weaknesses after the long season of warmth. The question is— how much damage can we expect?"

"The river will tell us," said Nevin. "If there's a severe drop, then we'll know that some major valley was thoroughly plugged."

"When will it break loose?"

"Not even a guess, Lhar," said Nevin slowly. "Even if I saw the dam I couldn't guess. Too many variables."

"At worst?" pressed Lhar.

Nevin moved restlessly. "I just don't know. The city is above even the highest spring floods. If it were light I would ride the hills and look for ancient flood marks. But it would probably be futile. The wind scours away everything."

"Is the city safe?"

"I don't know!" snapped Nevin. Then, more calmly, "You're asking me to give a life-deciding answer on almost no information."

"Welcome to the real world," said Lhar with a tired smile. "Syza?"

221

"The city has lasted this long. That's not an answer, just a feeling. I'll risk it. If we left the city the people would have no chance at all."

"Would you sense a flood coming?" asked Nevin.

"I don't think so. If we were otherwise safe I might sense a large flood coming, but our life here is shot through with so many personal hazards that my survival sense is sending out danger signals all the time."

"Shot through—how many dangers do you sense?" said Nevin curiously.

Syza looked at him for a long moment, her face drawn and her eyes flickering green in the shifting light.

"You don't want to know," she said finally. "If it would do any good I would tell you. It won't."

"The burn-off?" whispered Nevin hoarsely.

Syza looked puzzled, smiled slightly. "Not the sun. The people are the worst. They are unraveling, becoming animals. They have heaving currents of hate and violence in them that make the river look tiny.

"They are becoming extinct. They know it. They hear it in every silence. And they have nothing to blame, nothing to lash out at and destroy. They are a cataclysm waiting for the moment of nihilism." Syza shuddered uncontrollably. "I have felt them before, on Bjmsk. Who will be their destroyer this time, their Zomal?"

When Nevin would have spoken Lhar cut him off with a sharp gesture. He touched her mind carefully, sought the gathering threads of nightmare which were binding her. Yet he waited, needing to know if she could help herself—and wanting very much to find out what she had remembered of Bjmsk.

"It's all right," sighed Syza at last. "This time it's all right."

"I'm sorry," said Nevin, taking her hands. "I didn't mean to bring back your past."

"Not your fault," said Syza. "Tal-Lith reminds me more of Bjmsk every day."

"You saved Bjmsk," said Lhar evenly.

"So you tell me . . ."

"You don't believe it?"

"I wish I could."

"Then remember, and believe."

Her body stiffened.

She withdrew from both of them and warmed her hands over the brazier's dying fire. Nevin started toward her but stopped at a movement of Lhar's hand.

"Tell me more about Ssarrm legends, miran," said Lhar in a normal voice. "There might be something we can use, or keep from being used against us."

Nevin did not take his eyes off Syza, her hands opened over fading warmth.

"Do you like this kerden planet?" snapped Lhar.

"I—no."

"Then talk to me, miran. Give me ideas. Only six days until Lith's Dance. The more we know, the better chance we have. All of us."

With an effort Nevin organized his thoughts and began lecturing on the subject of Ssarrm.

TORCHES DANCED IN THE MID-MORNING DARKNESS, OUT-lining streets and compounds in blurred ribbons of gold. Eddies of expectation swirled through the marketplace and excited. Voices pressed back the darkness. With a last look at the light-shot darkness, Lhar slipped into the compound through the hidden stone door. Nevin waited nearby, seething with palpable tension.

"Well?" asked Nevin impatiently.

"Still dropping. The natives don't seem disturbed, though. The water callers accept it as normal for the season."

"It could be," said Nevin slowly. "The melting season officially ended a tenth-cycle past."

"Tell that to the sun. I don't like it. Too warm. Even isolated pools haven't formed ice yet."

"But higher up where it's colder?"

"Possibly there is ice."

Nevin sighed. "Not probably?"

"No."

"At least Urari's group isn't as active now that the river appears normal."

Lhar grunted noncommittally.

"Only three murders yesterday," added Nevin.

Lhar swore in a hard, low voice.

"That's three more than occurred in the last three Festivals combined! Worse, these were ritual murders, committed by religious fanatics, witnessed by slavering—" Lhar broke off in disgust. "When death is taken as proof of religious guilt, the trial is ugly."

Nevin said nothing; unlike Lhar, he had not witnessed any of Urari's impromptu street trials.

"Is there any danger to the dancers?" asked Nevin after a long silence.

"No. Even Urari is not that stupid. Officially he disclaims violence, of course. Unofficially he incites it. We'd better pray that he has as much control over his followers as he thinks he does; otherwise . . ."

"Bloody mess," finished Nevin. "Do you know who the killers are?"

"Everyone," said Lhar bluntly. "Some come to it eagerly, others very reluctantly, but everyone has the same need for a scapegoat, for revenging tomorrow's extinction."

"Hope Diri can handle them," muttered Nevin.

"She will. They're ready for her. God is just another word for scapegoat."

Nevin winced. "One Urari is enough."

"Despair is the other face of hope. Most of the people would hope, given a choice. Diri will give them that choice."

Nevin and Lhar walked silently into the talmare. When they were inside, Nevin looked quickly around. No one was near.

"When are you going to tell Kaffi?" whispered Nevin urgently.

Lhar was silent.

"You've got to tell her!"

A slight change in Lhar's expression told Nevin that someone had just entered the room.

"G'miran Firn," said Lhar into the silence. "We are honored."

"More than you know," said Firn. "Your dancer has been assigned the sunrise time."

"Doubly honored," said Lhar, bowing.

"See that she uses it to our advantage."

"She is the finest dancer Tal-Lith has ever known," Lhar assured her.

"Blasphemy," said Firn, but there was no censure

in her voice. She moved around the room quickly, restlessly. "Is her costume satisfactory?"

"Very. We're grateful for your gift; the art of weaving silvercloth was lost to our people long ago."

"She refused the eye jewels," said Firn suddenly.

"Graciously, I hope. If not, my apologies; her mind is fixed on the dance."

"As it should be." Firn hesitated, then continued. "I mean no insult. I know that a dancer's costume is unique, an object of near-reverence to its wearer, but are you sure that her eye jewels are suitable? The g'mirans are quite human; costume flaws might dim the brilliance of her dance for them."

Lhar took Firn's restless hands between his.

"We know how much of your prestige dances with Diri today. We will not shame you. The eyes Diri will use have been passed down to her from a long line of dancers. They are deep and round and flawless, utterly blue, and they do not baffle sight as your eyes do."

"I'd feel better if she had shown them to me."

"As you said, a dancer's costume is very personal. Diri's eyes can only be revealed on occasions of utmost religious importance."

"Yes, yes," Firn said impatiently, "but—oh, I'll be glad when this day is over!"

"We'll all be glad," said Nevin fervently.

Lhar smiled at Nevin and released Firn's hands. "Do you have any special instructions for me?" he said, still smiling. "I've never attended a Feast of Firsts, much less as a First."

"Eat well and ignore the fawning idiots," said Firn. "And wear your best robes."

"I am."

"Not quite," said Firn, waving Nevin out of the room. "Kaffi said you had no suitable robes for the Feast. She wanted to surprise you, but I wanted to be sure of the fit. Your costume is as important as Diri's. A shabby First Leader would be an insult."

"Ready?" said Nevin, returning with Kaffi. "The rest

of us have already gone through this. Now Lhar can join us."

With a flourish Kaffi shook out a bundle of clothing. Light ran like liquid over a long fur cape, and struck red sparks from jeweled fastenings. Lhar stroked the dark cape wonderingly; he had never seen a finer, more lustrous fur. It flowed like black water between his hands.

Kaffi smiled. "That's just the beginning. Take off those worn-out robes."

Obediently Lhar untied his belt and stripped to his skindrape, then looked questioningly at Kaffi.

"All of it. Weren't your winter clothes cut to fit around legs?"

"In the Forgotten Lands," said Lhar, pulling off his skindrape, "we were pleased to have any clothes at all."

Unhurriedly he put on a finely woven undershirt and pants. The material was very soft and slightly elastic, altogether more comfortable than he had expected. He pretended to fumble with the laces, not wanting to reveal his familiarity with pants. With an impatient gesture Firn brushed his hands aside and laced up the pants for him. When she was finished, she looked critically at the result.

"Say it, daughter. You were right."

Kaffi smiled. "The tailor will be pleased."

"They're almost too tight," Firn said admiringly. "I wouldn't have believed it."

Lhar waited, outwardly patient and inwardly laughing. Nevin, he noticed, had disappeared.

"Perhaps," said Kaffi, "he would make the greatest impression if we left off the outer clothes."

"Why don't you rebuild the fire while you decide?" said Lhar.

Kaffi relented and handed Lhar the rest of his clothes. The fabric of both the pants and the shirt was like a rainbow tapestry. It was heavy, yet supple enough to fit tightly. Best of all, it was warm. Fur socks, long gloves and mid-thigh soft-soled boots completed his finery. Jewels winked as he walked around the room.

"A fine First Leader," said Firn. "The women will weep. Urari will eat drifcakes tonight. Excellent. You'll be invited onto his hides before the Feast begins."

"Urari will have to wait," said Kaffi with a sideways glance at Lhar.

"The Feast would be long over before I got unlaced," said Lhar reassuringly.

"Oh, but the laces are very easy," laughed Kaffi. "Let me show—"

"Kaffi," said the g'miran firmly, "wait until after the Feast."

Kaffi bowed to her mother while a smile twitched over the g'miran's lips. Kaffi bent more deeply; her humble gesture was spoiled by barely stifled laughter. But when she straightened, she was no longer smiling.

"Is it time to share secrets, Lhar?"

"Thank you for the Festival gift," said Lhar gently. "I've never worn such beauty."

Kaffi's yellow eyes held his for a long moment before she bowed briefly.

"As you wish, First Leader."

Lhar watched them leave, then wearily unfastened his new gloves and cape. There was little time left before the dance, and much to do, beginning with Diri. He had seen too little of her for too long a time. Their few conversations had been crowded into even fewer minutes. Today he must talk with her, rehearse again the ways she would respond to the various possibilities that the day could bring.

Diri was in the largest room of the talmare. As always, T'Mero stood near the doorway, ready to prevent any native from entering.

"Congratulations, First Hunter," said Lhar. "To best a native at his lifetime skill is more than I had hoped for."

T'Mero moved restively; his vivid orange eyes reflected the wavering candlelight. "Birol is a better hunter," he said flatly. "The contest was a gift."

"Did Birol tell you that?"

"No."

"Kaffi?"

"No one. It's just something I know. Birol is trained to have a light touch as well as a killing blow. I'm trained only to kill."

Lhar felt uneasiness stir deep within himself. He sent out a very faint thread of mindtouch but discovered nothing more than impatience in the hunter's surface thoughts. Lhar stepped up the power of the touch. Just beneath the impatience, dark energy seethed. Something had shaken T'Mero's certainties; he was in need of integration.

Lhar withdrew and found T'Mero waiting, his face expressionless.

"Find anything?" said T'Mero, his voice neutral.

"Nothing you don't already know. You need integration."

T'Mero seemed on the point of disagreement, then he made a dismissive gesture. "We'll only have a few more days here. Or don't you think it can wait for a better time and place for integration?"

Lhar thought of the talk he needed to have with Diri about the coming dance and feast and the explanations that must precede exodus. He had neither the time nor the energy to spend on integration. He stifled his unease; T'Mero had many maturities of training behind him. More important, T'Mero's job was no longer crucial. It was Diri, Lhar should be concerned with now.

"We'll wait, T'Mero. But be careful. You know you can't trust your emotions now."

"If you want to see Diri you'd better go in. She'll begin her mental exercises soon, and shouldn't be disturbed."

Lhar pushed aside the heavy tapestry and went into the stone room. Diri sat wrapped in a fur robe. The room was chilly in spite of several braziers that were scattered about. As usual, Diri radiated an unfocused defiance.

"Syza tells me your health is excellent," said Lhar. Not exactly the truth, but there was no point in antagonizing Diri by emphasizing the years that had leached flexibility and vigor from her silver body. "And your eyes, as always, are more beautiful than lifsan jewels."

Her aura of defiance faded into a husky murmur of pleasure, and she invited him to share her fur robe. Lhar sat close, so close that her faint musk odor was warm in his nostrils. After the Lythen custom he leaned even nearer, bathing her face in his own breath, signaling a conversation between intimates. Diri returned the compliment; all residue of defiance vanished before Lhar's knowledge of Lythen etiquette.

"I've spent too little time with you," said Lhar softly. "You are kind to share your breath with such a wretched friend."

"I would be angry, but your breath is too sweet." The ritual satisfied, Diri smiled, a mischievious curve of the lips that could have been considered cruel. "You're smart to flatter the hidden God of Tal-Lith. Tomorrow I wouldn't have heard your voice among My million worshipers."

Lhar listened closely but heard neither humor nor irony in her voice. He touched her mind carefully; she was quite serious. He muffled a sigh and began to delicately approach the subject of her pending divinity. He did not want to shake her confidence, but neither did he want her to be inflexible.

"People are unpredictable, Diri. They might not name you God."

Diri leaned back sharply, and her voice became harsh with anger.

"You are the one who doesn't recognize Me. You and Kaffi and that dried-up Syza. But you will learn. All of you. You will know Lith!"

Lhar's probe was swift and conclusive. What he found was Diri's mind focused on a single goal: to dance and be proclaimed God. No matter how deeply he probed, the focus did not waver. He abandoned

230

any thought of discussing alternatives with her. She was wound tight with anticipation, completely obsessed with her role. He could break her but he could not change her. And if he broke her, who would dance?

"You are the greatest dancer in the galaxy," he said, coaxing her closer to him, whispering the words against her lips. "Taste the truth."

Diri held herself aloof for a few moments, then relented. "I taste the truth."

"You will dance with all the beauty of your body. And when they worship you, you will reward them with a new world, a world as sweet as your own breath."

"I will be their God . . ." agreed Diri slowly.

"What will you say to them?"

Diri sat silently. Her large eyes were unfocused, fixed on an event that had not yet occurred.

" 'Long ago you loved Me,' " prompted Lhar softly, giving her the first phrase of the speech she had memorized.

". . . you loved Me," said Diri, her voice husky in the twilight room, "but not well enough. You worshiped me, but not well enough. You measured your failure in barren women, barren land. You measured your failure in the unborn dead.

"I have come to you in your need. Because you loved me. I have come to you with . . . love . . . and a new . . ."

Lhar waited motionlessly in spite of his impatience; surely she could not have forgotten the speech he had made for her?

" '. . . a new world,' " coaxed Lhar, " 'a world as fertile as your love for Me.' "

Diri's eyes focused for an instant, then became vague again.

"Leave me," she said absently. "I must prepare myself."

Though the words were a dismissal, her tone was not hostile.

"How will you tell them of their second world?" said Lhar softly.

Diri did not answer; she had gone inside herself. When he used mindtouch all he found was a Lythen chant spreading through her mind. All Lythens were trained in the focusing ritual; the greatest artists mastered it.

With a sigh he did not bother to muffle, Lhar slid out of Diri's robe, wrapped it securely about the dancer and moved away. She did not notice his actions then, nor did she notice the sudden flares of light as Lhar filled the braziers. He watched her for a long time, uneasy about her inflexibility, wishing that arrogance and greatness were not so inextricably mixed in the Lythen race. With a last glance at her lambent blue eyes, Lhar left the room.

"She's deep in her ritual," he said to T'Mero.

T'Mero grunted. "Syza was here. She's waiting in the sleeping room."

Lhar walked quickly through the stone hallways, pulled the tapestry aside, and nearly knocked Syza off her feet.

"Sorry," he said, steadying her. "I was thinking about Diri."

"So was I. How did she treat you?" At Lhar's puzzled expression, Syza explained. "She was rather vicious to me when I touched her. Among other things, she told me that her health was no longer my business."

"She's just worried about the dance."

"If you say so . . ."

"What's wrong?"

"I'm afraid Diri is insane," said Syza bluntly. "She believes she is Lith. She barely restrained herself when I wasn't suitably abject."

"She is a Lythen who was worshiped and then humiliated. She sees her chance to be vindicated. Lythen pride and arrogance are legend; it's no surprise that her nerves are tightly drawn."

"Did you touch her mind?"

"Yes."

"And?"

"There was nothing in her mind but dancing and being God."

"No shrieking triumph?"

Lhar laughed. "Of course there was. A foretaste of victory after long humiliation."

"Our victory—or hers?"

"They are the same."

"Are they? What if Diri likes being God so much she doesn't want to give it up?"

"That was the first problem Contact considered," said Lhar reassuringly. "Of course Diri won't want to give up being Lith. She just won't have any choice. When she leads her worshipers through the Access, she'll be picked off and sent to Centrex."

"What if she refuses to lead them off Tal-Lith?"

Lhar touched Syza's mind lightly, and felt real fear.

"Has she entered Decline?" said Lhar quickly.

"No . . ."

"You're certain?"

"Her body rhythms are strong and harmonized. I don't know how much longer they'll stay that way, though."

"Does Diri believe she has entered Decline?"

"No." Syza's voice was positive. "She can feel her own strength."

"Then there is almost no chance that she will choose Tal-Lith and suicide over leading the faithful off this deathtrap they call home."

"You mean she won't be another Zomal, wanting a whole planet to die with him?"

"There's no reason for her to be a Zomal. She doesn't anticipate death. She knows she'll outlive this planet—if she gets off it in time."

Syza frowned and absently brushed a shining ribbon of hair away from her face.

"Is something else worrying you?" said Lhar gently, taking her hand. "Your dreams? Memories?"

233

"I hope you're right about Diri," she said uncertainly.

"Do you know something you haven't told me?"

"I . . . no. My dreams. Diri is mixed up with Zomal in them. I can't say whether my distrust of her is justified, or merely a residue from the past. I don't trust her, Lhar. I'm afraid of her, afraid of what she could do." Syza hesitated, sighed. "But that doesn't count for much, does it? I'm afraid of too many things. Including myself."

"Syza," said Lhar with quiet urgency, "if you have reason to believe that Diri will betray Tal-Lith, tell me. Now. I can stop her."

"You can control her mind without ruining her dance?" said Syza, relief making her eyes shine like clear green pools.

"I can break her. And I will if there's reason to."

Syza's eyes clouded and her hands painfully gripped his.

"You know everything that I know about her, about Zomal, about me. I don't know if Diri will betray us. I only know she can."

"Yes, she could," agreed Lhar. "But she has more to gain with us than against us. The probability is very much in our favor."

"Yes . . . numbers. Rational. Sorry, Lhar. I guess I'm more nervous than anyone."

"It's natural," said Lhar, holding her against him. "The closer you come to your goal, the more you fear something will go wrong. I'm the same way. I know it and allow for it. You'll be all right, Syza. You are stronger than you believe."

"I'll be glad when it's over," she said fiercely against his chest, "when everything is either right or wrong. Settled."

"So will I, Syza. So will I."

The doorway tapestry billowed suddenly and Nevin rushed into the room.

"Firn wants to see us as soon as we're dressed. Apparently there's a certain etiquette involved in the beginning of the Feast of Firsts. She wants to rehearse us."

Syza frowned. "What about T'Mero and Diri?"

"I'll cue T'Mero with mindtouch," Lhar said. "As for Diri, after she dances I doubt that anyone will care which knife she eats with. Or about us, for that matter. I doubt that the Feast will be as they expected. But we must act as though it will."

"I hope the feast goes as scheduled," said Syza with feeling. "I'm hungry."

"You'll get hungrier," predicted Lhar with a smile. "And so will I."

Shifting his position unobtrusively, Lhar tried to find a way to match his anatomy to the unforgiving block of stone which served as a seat. It was useless. He envied the many thousands of natives whose status was insufficient to allow them a seat in the natural amphitheater; he was certain that the surrounding rocky hills were more comfortable. The seven best khaner dancers performed in the amphitheater. And Diri, of course. That made eight. Six had already danced, some adequately, some well, and one with unusual grace. None of the dancers were as good as even an untrained Lythen; all were imitating moves that were possible only for the naturally flexible Lythen body.

What a sad waste. Syza's thought was in poignant parallel to his own musings. *All their pain and effort, all their creativity poured into copying the moves of what is probably a long-dead Lythen dance. It makes me ache to watch their helpless futility repeated and repeated and repeated . . . *

Only one more, Syza.

He turned and saw her tears golden in the blaze of the torches that ringed the nearby stage. Her sadness was a sigh in his mind, an echo of his own melancholy sense of Tal-Lith's history.

The seventh dancer, Bherme of the First Khaner,

appeared during the pause for a ritual prayer asking Lith's guidance in the coming dance. The privileged two thousand within the amphitheater and the countless others gathered on the hillsides silently repeated the prayer. Lhar tried to watch the dance as though he had never seen a Lythen perform.

Bherme was tall, thin, more fluid in her movements than anyone could reasonably expect. Her spins and leaps bespoke endless hours of effort as she told Lith's story through dance. As the story progressed the moves became increasingly complex, and alien; the effort of striving after what her genes denied her showed in Bherme's face. Her breathing quickened, deepened, could be heard above the singers' chants.

Yet there was an undeniable wholeness to her dance. She was so accustomed to the multifaceted world seen through her blue crystal eyeplates that she neither faltered nor appeared disoriented. Her leaps were smooth and her body, disciplined; only someone who had seen a Lythen dance would have known Bherme's performance for the inevitably flawed imitation that it was.

As the last chants of the singers died, hillside spectators took up the cry of "Lith! Lith!" Bherme was their First Dancer, their living incarnation of Lith. When Bherme did not respond, the cries gradually faded. In a moment the prayer would be repeated. In a moment Diri would dance.

Ready, Syza?

Yes.

Their minds flowed together. Kaffi was the first one they sought. While Syza prevented Kaffi's body from making any move that might betray her feelings, Lhar spoke quietly into the Tal-Lithen's mind.

The time has come for sharing, Kaffi. Diri's dance is the first step. As you have trusted us, I trust you to keep silence. Diri is not what she will appear to be. She is no more than a symbol, a message of hope from the place you mistakenly call kylith.

236

Lhar sensed Kaffi's initial fear. When she realized who had spoken so clearly into her mind, her fear dissolved into wonder and curiosity and excitement.

When Syza and I leave your mind, make no move. You must appear normal. Syza will give you control of your body . . . now.

Other than feeling an involuntary tremor, Kaffi handled the unprecedented transition well. Lhar praised her before moving on to Firn and Daal. Both g'mirans responded as well as Kaffi had, though Firn's incoherent questions were almost painful in their intensity.

As Diri dances you will know more, Lhar assured her. *But remember: Diri is symbol only.*

With his warning echoing in their minds the g'mirans signaled an end to prayer. Diri, completely covered by a long, hooded cape of silver-blue fur, glided slowly to the center of the stone floor of the amphitheater. Torches hissed in the spreading silence. With an experienced performer's sense of timing, Diri gathered attention to herself while torchlight ran like honey over her cape. In the instant before silence would become an intolerable burden on the audience, Diri faced the singers. Ten voices rose in intricate chanted harmony.

Diri's cape shimmered with light as she spun slowly, increasing her speed by increments until the eye perceived only a spinning mass of light; sweet voices chanted the story of Lith's arrival on a piece of the sun, in a spiral of sound that descended until voices and dancer hummed and Diri melted within the cape to a boneless heap which smoldered with barely perceptible movements. The audience sighed involuntarily in the silence between chants . . . and the watching native dancers knew they were seeing greatness, knew it from the first moment of Diri's impossibly fluid spin.

The singers' chant was like a heart, beating, and Diri's cape flared into a silver-blue cone concealing her as she rose from the ground. A supple twist, a blur of light as Diri threw the cape offstage, and she stood revealed as the Dancing God.

She's not wearing her costume!

Even as Syza's thought began, Lhar had realized Diri's nakedness. He quickly touched minds at random in the crowd, but sensed only pleasure and concentration upon a truly great dancer.

It's all right, returned Lhar with relief. *They see only what they expected to see; a dancer in silvercloth.*

Damn her arrogance! She could have ruined everything.

Lythens are also actors, commented Lhar calmly. *You must admit it was a riveting gesture.*

Syza grumbled wordlessly in his mind. Both returned their full attention to the stage.

Diri danced lightly, soundlessly, her movements essentially native rather than Lythen as the singers chanted about the first days of Lith. It was a simple exposition in dance and song, yet the consummate ease with which Diri moved made the old story fresh and vivid. As in a dream the audience saw Lith move from city to city of a vanished world, saw accolades for Lith become adulation and finally become worship.

Diri seemed to grow in height and grace as the dance gradually became more Lythen than native. Even the strident sweep of arms, the tumbling rushing moves as she fought the demons, were all incredibly controlled.

The wailing arrhythmic dissonance of the singers became a rhythmic triumph as Lith appeared to exorcise the demons who would remove her from her worshipers. Diri burned with sensual heat as she rippled and strutted, celebrating victory. Every step, every breath, the least curve of her fourth finger told of erotic delight. Life had vanquished evil; and life for the Lythens was celebrated in only one way.

Syza's wordless amazement at the spectacle was in counterpoint with the crowd's deep response. When

Lhar commented to her through mindtouch, Syza did not answer. He realized then that she was totally focused on the performance. He smiled to himself, and left her alone. A dancer such as Diri was born once in a millenium.

A low moan, mingling ectasy and sadness, swept over the crowd as Diri quivered in the aftermath of consummation. A wordless song was born in Lhar's mind, memories of the textures and liquid riches and ecstasy of love. But she did not know she was singing to him. She did not even know that she sang.

The singers' chant became a ragged sigh echoed by the audience. Before the singers could draw another breath, Diri changed her dance. Victory had been illusory; the demons had returned. No longer a burning silver passion, Diri was now surrounded by prophesies of despair.

The final passage of Lith's Dance began just as the first vague promise of dawn faded the stars.

Diri folded in on herself as though exhausted by her battle. Her collapse was slow, intricate, with the breath of life sighing out into darkness, leaving only an impossible boneless lump of silver flesh. The audience groaned and the singers faltered, fumbled over the ritual chant of love and encouragement to their stricken God. Diri's fingers opened into a fan above her hidden head, a single listening ear. The chant steadied, found its rhythm. A silver leg eased out and each toe straightened individually to form a second fan. The leg was at an angle impossible for a native; the resulting posture should have been grotesque. Instead, it was a moving representation of agony listening to hope.

Lhar's mind reached out and flicked invisibly through the entranced audience, sampling emotions. Astonishment, disbelief, vague fear . . . and a wave of awe. The people had seen their God unfolding. The singers' chant became ragged indrawn breaths, and silence.

The color of the sky thinned out to a translucent rose. Torches guttered and died in the unnatural silence, silence that coiled tightly around each mind, tighter and tighter until only a violent emotional explosion could release the consuming tension. Lhar felt insanity flex and strengthen, sensed person after person surrender his mind to group madness and the humming silence. He knew that the singers must chant; the dance must continue; some reassurance must be given, or the metamorphosis from crowd to raving Unity would be complete and Tal-Lith would be lost.

A single flawless note dispersed the gathering panic. The note twinned, became a sliding harmony of love and hope. There were no words, nor was there need of them; the voice was the essence of Tal-Lith's dreams, its own soul singing. The crowd's long sigh was an inarticulate cry of relief as Unity faltered and dissolved. Syza stood slowly and her arms reached out toward the huddled silver figure on the stage. Her matchless voice coaxed Lith to abandon despair.

Overhead, in haunting counterpoint, the sun overwhelmed the night.

Lith's limbs trembled at the sweetness of Syza's plea. With painful deliberation, an arm rose and swayed like river grass in a slow current. A cascade of melodic praise washed Her silver skin, yet still She hid Her eyes. Song pulsed visibly in Her body, strengthening Her. A rhythmic melody of hope tugged at Her, persuading Her of Tal-Lith's urgent need.

With a melting silver movement Lith rose to a crouch in center stage, all the improbable curves of Her body balanced on a single toe. Her round eyes burned like blue coals in the first light of dawn.

A low, involuntary cry was wrung from the audience.

As though released from great tension, Lith leaped to meet the rising sun. Syza's song followed Her sinuous flight, a rainbow of sound supporting Her silver leaps. Melody soared, lifting Lith to breathless heights until no one could say whether dance or song had originated the flashing silver arcs that consumed the stage. Music and dance rose in pealing grace, hung poised in the center of triumph with a beauty that made the watchers weep. Gradually, imperceptibly, irridescent movement condensed into the motionless grace of the Dancing God.

For the first time Syza's song had words, ancient words transformed by new hope:

> My River was as long as your memories
> As sweet as your worship
> As deep as your love.
> You drank of Me
> And you lived
> You danced with Me
> And you rejoiced
> You loved Me
> AND I WAS REBORN.

With a low tidal murmur, Tal-Lith prostrated itself before the living God. Syza sank slowly into her stone seat, exhausted by the effort of controlling a massed emotional response that came as close as Lhar had ever known to the awesome power of Unity. He stood and looked directly into Diri's blazing eyes: her husky voice rang in the silence.

"You have loved Me, but not well enough. You have worshiped Me, but not well enough."

Lhar moved uneasily; the speech was subtly changed. Diri's tone was wrong, more forbidding than forgiving.

"You measure your failure in barren women, barren land. You measure your failure in the unborn dead. I have come to you in your need."

The crowd moaned softly, hope and agony and guilt. Lhar fought the tension clawing at his mind. Though changed, the speech could be saved. He tried to speak gently, very gently, in Diri's mind, but she was impervious to his delicate prompting. As he watched, her silver lips curved in a cruel, triumphant smile.

"I have come to you in anger."

Diri's laughter rasped across the stretching silence.

Stop her!

It's too late. I can only break her. And if I did . . . . His grim vision of chaos and slaughter made Syza reel.

I'll sing.

No! One wrong response and Tal-Lith dies; you're too tired to control them. Wait.

But she's insane.

Yes.

Diri's husky voice continued relentlessly. "I know what you think, what you feel, what you dream. You do not dream of Me."

A long "no" flowed down from the hills, more in anguish than dissent.

"You have earned My anger. You can earn My love. Worship Me. Dream only of your living God. Love nothing better than you love Me. When each one of you lives only for Me, then will I give you fertile fields and fertile women. Then will I give you children. Then will you be reborn.

"Do not think you can deceive Lith with false worship. Your crippled souls scream your every sin. I know you. I will always know you. Love nothing better than Me.

"Or die."

Diri measured the wretched silence and found it good. At last she addressed their terrible fear.

"There will be no Feast of Firsts," she said scornfully. "There is only one First. Lith! Now crawl to your homes and count your sins and pray. Talk to no one! Each spoken word is a sin against your living God. A sin! Anyone who speaks threatens all your hopes, your very souls.

"Lith has spoken. Obey."

Slowly, very slowly, the people of Tal-Lith crawled

242

out of sight, the words of their vengeful God echoing in the silence.

Lhar waited until the last subdued native had slunk over the rocky hills. As he and Syza walked onto the stone stage, T'Mero appeared and stood next to Diri.

"So, guardian," said Lhar softly, "this is how you repay our trust."

"No," said T'Mero, pulling his crystal knife, "This is how I repay you!"

T'Mero leaped toward Lhar, but Lhar realized T'Mero's intent well before that. With the supple ease of a drifsen, Lhar evaded the knife. Before T'Mero could spring again, he made an odd strangling noise and sprawled across the stones. Lhar looked at the orange eyes lit with helpless hatred; deliberately he crushed the crystal knife underneath his boot.

"Enough, Syza," said Lhar tonelessly. "Let him breathe."

With a hoarse gasp, breath returned to T'Mero. Wisely, he did not try to get up. Diri said nothing, though hatred licked out from her like black flames.

"Stalemate, Diri," Lhar said. "Do you hear me, you silly glass god?" His tone narrowed to a ripping lash. "Without Syza's song you now would be nothing more than scraps of bloody silver smeared across stone."

Diri said nothing.

"If any harm comes to us or our native friends," continued Lhar, "I will break you as easily as I broke T'Mero's knife."

To reinforce his promise, he reached into her mind . . . twisted it. Diri reeled and cried out. When she could speak again her voice shook with hatred.

"Not stalemate. The natives will stay here, where they belong, worshiping their Dancing God." She laughed coldly. "You may leave. And Syza. And that child Nevin. You are not of My people."

"The Tal-Lithens are not yours," said Syza. "They have their own destiny."

"They belong to the planet Lythe. My ancestor discovered them, danced for them, possessed them. And

243

then Sidara-mi's treacherous lovers dragged her screaming from this planet."

"That's a piece of history your race never shared with the Concord," said Lhar skeptically.

"Why should we share our secrets with awkward children? Lythens lived and died in lightships when your ancestors squatted in their own dung. You could never understand the grandeur of our traditions."

"Try me," said Lhar, his calculated indifference a direct challenge.

Diri's gas-blue eyes glared at him as though by will alone she could know what he was thinking. But she could not. With an imperious gesture she accepted his challenge.

"Long ago, so long ago that even we have forgotten the time, Lythens developed the art of dance, of life, to its highest perfection. Each year the best dancer was sent out into the unknown galaxy. We called these dancers Lith. Where they found intelligent life, they danced. They were worshiped, for they were the essence of all souls.

"Until my birth, Sidara-mi was the greatest dancer Lythe had ever produced. To her was given the greatest challenge: to dance so that a whole race of people would die perfectly. For she had discovered Tal in the shadow of a nova. Sidara-mi's lightship outran the exploding star. Less than a year of life was left to this planet.

"She danced for them. Through the racing days she danced and her movements opened all the rivers of life to them. They worshiped her." Diri's husky voice dropped to a dreamy whisper as she relived the legend of Sidara-mi. "She loved them as no god ever loved its worshipers. She could not leave them to die alone and afraid. She created a dance for them, Lith's dance, and each move whispered to their souls about death and love.

"She planned a final dance, its end timed for the arrival of the nova's holocaust. She would die with her worshipers in an ecstacy of perfection.

"But Sidara-mi's lovers betrayed her."

Diri's husky voice became harsh as she told of Lith's abduction.

"Her lovers lied about the nova's time. She danced one day too soon. She danced for her people—and then her lovers dragged her to the shuttle. The natives fought, but not well enough. Tal faced the nova alone.

"Sidara-mi fought her lovers on board the lightship. She killed all but one of them, Yanin-dy. He was locked in the control room beyond her reach. When the lightship returned to Lythe, Sidara-mi was dead. Yanin-dy killed himself, but it was not enough to erase Lythe's shame. Our greatest dancer, our soul, died imperfectly, alone and unworshiped among enemies; a race died without its God."

Silence and darkness seemed to gather around the stone amphitheater. Unnoticed, the last light had faded while Diri talked. She shivered in the cutting chill; T'Mero got to his feet under Syza's watchful eyes and brought Diri the heavy silver-blue cape. Hardly aware that she did so, Diri drew the rich furs around her body.

"Now you understand," she said with unnatural quietness.

Lhar paused for a long moment before answering, waiting for the spell of Sidara-mi's legend to dissipate into the cold air.

"I understand," he said carefully, "that Sidara-mi loved Tal's people enough to die with them. It was the most she could do; there was no means of saving their lives. That was long ago, Skandiri-li. This time Lith can save her worshipers. This time—"

"No!"

Diri's near-scream shattered the aura of dignity and rationality that had transformed her as she retold the legend. Her lips writhed and her eyes burned with an unsettling light. Barely coherent obscenities tumbled out of her mouth; then she spoke a final sentence that Lhar understood only too well.

"We will die as we should have died three thousand years ago!"

Suddenly she swayed, dazed with emotion and exhaustion. T'Mero gently lifted her into his arms. With a long sigh she slipped into sleep. As T'Mero turned to leave, Lhar spoke softly.

"You know she is insane, T'Mero."

"You're a fool," said T'Mero indifferently, all his rage burned out by his aborted attempt on Lhar's life. "Diri understands the beauty of the right death at the right time. We will die perfectly, and you will only live." T'Mero turned away and walked into the darkness. His matter-of-fact voice floated back to them. "Don't expect off-planet help. I destroyed your psitran."

Automatically Lhar's hand went to his belt; his fingers touched smooth leather. Too late he realized that he had left his soiled fiber belt in the talmare with his old clothes. The belt could be replaced, but the resilient hairlike wires concealed within the fibers could not. With a horrible falling feeling he realized that they were cut off from the rest of the galaxy, alone and lost on a doomed planet.

Lhar?

Syza's concern forced him to control the animal panic that thrashed at the edges of his mind.

I need time to think, he responded. He knew that overtones of desperation colored his mindspeech to the point of distortion, but he did not care.

Syza knew better than to try to cheer him with optimism. Her carefully neutral thought moved him as no platitude could have. *Come with me to the talmare. We'll need food before we can think.*

Although the idea of food was repugnant to Lhar, he did not resist her. They walked through the deepening night, the only sound that of occasional pebbles crunching beneath their feet. The khaner compound was unnaturally dark and silent. Though they both noticed it, neither one commented. When they entered the sleeping room they found Nevin squat-

ting over a brazier, deftly grilling meat and grain cakes. Wordlessly he handed them steaming bowls of drif broth.

"Thank you," said Syza. At Nevin's startled look, Syza added distinctly. "I'll talk when I please. Diri can suck zarfs."

Nevin smiled fleetingly. "Just don't let a native hear you. Urari's men killed seven people that I know of. One victim's only sin was to groan aloud when he cut his hand on a rock." Nevin chewed a cake slowly. "I really underestimated that silver disaster. The no-talking command was brilliant. She won't let the women become pregnant until everyone is perfect, and everyone can't be perfect because speech is as natural as breathing. So nothing changes and her godhood is reinforced. Brilliant."

"She isn't," said Lhar, surveying his broth with distaste. "That must have been T'Mero's contribution. Not only does it reinforce her spiritual authority; it makes opposition impossible. How can we tell the natives the truth when they are forbidden to talk to us? And our song . . . " He swore and set the bowl aside.

"They're listening to it still," she said softly. "It sings in their silences."

"The ban could work against her," said Nevin. "People have to start talking sooner or later, or the city services will fall apart and the people will starve. When they talk and nothing happens, maybe they'll realize that Diri is no more God than they are."

"I doubt it," said Lhar grimly. "T'Mero knows almost as much as you do about how societies work. After a few days he'll tell Diri to lift the taboo for basics like trade. She'll be safe then; hysteria burns out quickly."

"Do you see any way to defeat her?"

"None that are fast enough. We're entering the indeterminate zone."

Nevin looked confused.

"The sun," snapped Lhar. "Remember? Contact's

figures were off by three years. Not much, considering the limited time they had to study Tal-Lith's sun. Too much, considering the mess I've made of this assignment."

"You mean," said Nevin tightly, "that the burn-off could come at any time?"

"Of course that's what I mean!"

"Then you'd better put a call through to the Access and ecstasan boys," said Nevin with feigned lightness.

Lhar swore savagely, shocking Nevin.

"T'Mero destroyed Lhar's psitran," said Syza.

"How—" Nevin stopped himself abruptly. How it had happened was unimportant; the accomplished fact was overwhelming. "When you don't make contact won't they know something is wrong and come in anyway?"

"There's a less than two percent chance of that. You forget that Contact's emergency section is probably working on not less than four hundred problems right now. There is an eighty percent chance that they don't even know how close we are to burn-off. The only monitoring station still working is on the middle moon. I don't know what its data-release interval is. Probably no more than every half-cycle."

"What about the shuttle?" asked Nevin in a strained voice.

"If the sun heats up slowly enough, the shuttle will land automatically at the edge of the city just before burn-off. If we get to the shuttle in time, and if the shuttle gets to the moon Access in time, we can watch in safety while the natives fry."

"I can't believe," said Nevin, "that Contact won't try to get the natives off even if you don't report in."

"What you can or can't believe doesn't matter," said Lhar brutally. "Contact will never intervene while there is the least probability that the team is alive. Their philosophy is simple: the mission is like a ball sent rolling along a groove chosen for having the greatest mathematical probability of success. The

248

team's job is to see that the ball doesn't jump the groove at the first rough spot. If we can't hold the ball in the groove we yell for help. But we can't yell for help and the ball is bounding out of control. Understand? Good. Now will you shut up and let me think?"

Nevin flinched and was silent. Syza touched his cheek, wordlessly telling him that he had not earned Lhar's rough anger. She sat close to Nevin and shared the meal he had prepared. Nearby, Lhar sat in motionless tension, pouring energy into his mind while he weighed possible alternatives and the percentages of their success. Numbers and plans raced through his consciousness. Sweat made his body clammy in the chilly room. Brazier fires flared and died and flared again, tended by Syza while Nevin slept. Lhar sensed her vaguely, distantly, except for the times when she made a lightning survey of his thoughts.

Finally fatigue and futility congealed in Lhar's mind. Further effort was useless, yet he refused to give up.

You're wasting yourself.

Syza's thought burned through his exhaustion. He sensed her condensing in his mind, a clear green presence, sure and swift. Before he could frame an answer she sent him into sleep.

XI

ON THE SECOND DAY OF LITH'S REIGN LHAR AND SYZA slipped through the secret stone gate and silently moved into the mid-morning darkness. A pale twilight stained the sky, dividing the world into shades of black. At the sound of approaching footsteps Lhar and Syza sank down to the ground and pulled their black robes over their faces. Unless they were touched by torchlight, they were effectively invisible.

Five.

Urari's, added Syza. *Their minds are filled with fear and hate and death.*

The five natives passed in a group. Before their footsteps faded there came the sound of one person running, then sounds of pursuit. The sounds merged, ended with a prolonged scream. Lhar sensed Syza's shudder and knew she had felt the violent death.

She didn't talk. She hadn't talked since yesterday. She was hungry and looking for food and they killed her just because she was within their reach.

Lhar accepted the agony and anger conveyed by Syza's thought and gave her what comfort he could. Before they could rise they heard more footsteps.

Eight.

The same.

They were not the same group but Lhar did not argue; the intent of the second group was the same as the first. As he had feared, Urari's terrorists had effectively taken over the streets.

We have to go back.

But the river, objected Syza.

No good knowing about the river if we die finding out. I'll try again to get the information out of a water caller's mind.

Reluctantly Syza agreed. *Firn and Daal? Kaffi?*

We'll have to use mindspeech.

They don't have the training for coherent two-way contact.

Lhar knew that Syza was not objecting; she was merely stating the truth. He silently cursed Diri and T'Mero with a rage that Syza felt like a blow.

Sorry. But I could quite happily feed them to a lary of zarfs.

The image that Lhar sent with his thoughts was both amusing and brutal.

Ready?

Wait, answered Syza.

He sensed her fading from contact and realized that she was attempting to search the immediate area for hostile groups. It was a technique he had been thoroughly trained in. It was also useless at this moment; the natives were in too much turmoil for Lhar and Syza to effectively read them. Lhar sensed that enormous fatigue hampered Syza's search as much as lack of training. With a sudden flash of fear he realized what yesterday's song had cost her.

Save your energy, he advised gently. *Most of the population is seething with the same kind of feelings Urari's terrorists have. If we assume that everyone out on the streets is a murderer we won't be too far off the mark.*

When they were sure no one was close to them they moved soundlessly back to the stone gate. Once inside they hurried to their room.

"What went wrong?" said Nevin at their unexpected arrival.

"Urari's murderers own the city," said Syza softly, but bitterly. "We couldn't get more than a short distance from the compound."

"Kaffi?" he asked worriedly.

"Still with Firn and Daal as far as we know," said

251

Lhar, reaching for a grain cake and chewing it absently.

"That breaks the river plan," said Nevin.

"Maybe not," said Lhar between bites. "Let's assume that Syza was right, that there was an ice fall and the river is at least partially blocked somewhere in the mountains and that its level has continued to drop steadily. The weather isn't cold yet," he continued, ignoring Nevin's unspoken objections. "I doubt if even individual pools have frozen—which means that there is Xantha's own lake piling up behind the dam. Sooner or later that lake will come down the mountains."

Lhar waited for comments but there were none.

"Firn and Daal will explain this to the khaner and guild people once Diri lifts the ban. Then the first three khaners, plus any volunteers, will cross the river with us."

"What about Diri?" said Nevin, his brown eyes unreadable in the muted orange light from the brazier.

"We'll explain it to Diri and get her consent," said Lhar grimly. "Even if we have to bend her mind into a four-dimensional spiral to do it. Once across the river and away from Diri, Urari, and all the rest of the killers, we'll try to make contact with . . . " His voice faded; contacting Centrex was the weakest part of their plan.

"What's your mimax?" said Syza, her voice a whisper of fatigue.

Lhar stroked the brazier without looking at her. "A mimax is useful only in weighing alternatives," he said finally. "We don't have an alternative."

"Kill Diri," Nevin said succinctly.

"That would guarantee a cultural disaster. You know it. I know it. The people drift near the edges of Unity . . . terrible."

"Unity?"

"A massive psi linkage," said Lhar.

"But they're not trained. And not all of them have psi," said Nevin.

"Enough do." Lhar hesitated, searching for a way to make Nevin understand. "We have knowledge of a race that attained Unity. Controlled Unity."

"The Lavistari?"

"No. They rarely link. The people I'm talking about were called Singers."

"I thought they were a legend."

Lhar smiled bleakly. "It would have been better for them if they were. But they could control their own Unity. It's an awesome power to have. Tal-Lith can't do it. Remember the Dyrnsta?"

"I'd rather not. The only survivors had less mind left than a stone."

"That's what uncontrolled Unity can do."

"But why?"

"It's the ultimate survival reflex. A race flowing together, thinking with one mind, Unity, trying to batter through extinction. It's an uncontrolled will to survive that turns into violent destruction if no way to survive can be found."

"But Tal-Lithens don't know they're going to die."

"They do," Lhar said in a gentle voice. "Believe me. They know that Lith is a God of death. Some of them welcome it. Urari's terrorists are just the beginning."

"What good are dead worshipers to Diri? She doesn't want them dead yet."

"She doesn't know what could happen. There's an eighty-three percent probability that Diri will lose control within the next tenth-cycle even if the natives never reach Unity. With luck, and if T'Mero realizes what is happening, she'll stretch it to two tenth-cycles. If she's very lucky, burn-off will come before the population explodes."

"Then tell her before it's too late!"

Lhar's body moved in silent, bitter laughter. He looked bleakly at Nevin, wishing that he, too, could be young and ignorant enough to hope. "The only thing that could deflect the natives is the certainty of a reason for living. A future. Children. So you go explain to Diri. Tell her the natives won't live to share her perfect death. And don't turn your back on T'Mero while you do it."

"You can't control her mind?" said Nevin without any real hope.

Lhar turned back to the brazier, methodically stoking it with braids of straw.

"No, Nevin," said Syza, her voice barely a whisper. "We can kill her but we can't cure her insanity. Or T'Mero's. And perhaps they aren't insane after all. Perfect death, perfect release."

"You can't mean that," said Nevin.

Syza did not answer. Lhar touched her mind swiftly; all the colors of life were dulled by a clinging gray exhaustion. The clarity and subtle music of mindtouch that he had come to expect from her were totally absent.

Sleep, Syza.

No.

Syza's response was flattened by fatigue but he immediately sensed the nightmare stalking at the edges of her control, waiting for exhaustion to reduce her to helplessness.

Sleep. Zomal is dead; he can't touch you anymore.

Zomal is alive. We heard him walking tonight. Bjmsk again. Her thought fractured into separate words lit by lurid fragments of memory. *Laughter.* and pale-skinned pale-eyed people, mouths black circles of mirth surrounded by scarlet *Screaming* and *Zomal.* hideous in torture, bleeding purple in blue light, countless circular cuts echoing laughter in sluggish blood, frantic efforts to heal at a distance forcing her deeper and deeper into his mind, knowledge *Hatred.* scraping her raw and frantic, blood purple, black circles mocking her (I can't heal you) purple congealing into *Laughter.* (don't) and he's telling me (no) telling (NO) tell (NO!) *I won't hear him!* (listen to) *I won't know know no NO I WON'T (but it's such a grand joke you stupid child) I WON'T NO*

Lhar's imperative cut through the clamorous dialog of memory and fear and Syza and Zomal. Manic laughter subsided into gray silence.

"Do you understand your memories?" he asked softly, not wanting to risk breaking the fragile, quiet balance by using mindspeech.

"Not memories," she answered, her voice slurred with fatigue. "Nightmare."

"Memories distorted by past emotion and present fear," said Lhar calmly. "The seven people had classic Bjmsk phenotypes for the middle continent where Zomal's group worked in secret. They were the Seven Equals. I recognized at least three of them. Qzlt, Mnzn and Sbnl. And Zomal, of course."

Syza said nothing, felt nothing, thought nothing.

"I wonder why they were torturing him," he mused, but Syza ignored the bait. "A hard way to die."

"He didn't feel much of it," said Syza tonelessly. "I blocked the pain for . . . a long . . . until."

"Until?" said Lhar softly, more echo than question.

". . . days . . . sleep." She shuddered and breathed shallowly.

Lhar waited, carefully concealing his passion to know. She was—they were—so close, so close. If she could just remember. Let herself remember. Carefully. Slowly. If he prompted her again she would flee.

"I woke up screaming . . . he was screaming, they were laughing . . ." Her dull eyes looked around, seeing a different room, a different world. "He told them . . . Centrex, Contact, the Concord . . . everything. He was dying and they heard the truth in his voice. Now he's laughing. They aren't. I . . . called . . . to the group in the other city and they heard me and they fled and I stayed. He needed me, love . . . I tried but they were so cruel and he, he goaded. Laughing at them while I held the pain. And."

Just before her eyes and mind became opaque, a grotesque picture/memory/emotion leaked out: Zomal and the Seven Equals writhing in erotic ecstasy as they tortured a faceless victim.

"I've remembered enough," said Syza with toneless finality. She stretched out on the robes and fell into a sleep so heavy it was like a coma.

Lhar covered her and turned back to the fire.

"Is she all right?" said Nevin, his voice low, frightened.

"I don't know."

"What happened?"

"When she's strong she can blot out Bjmsk. When she's exhausted she can't. Earlier tonight she felt a woman sliced to death for no better excuse than blood lust. It triggered a buried memory of Zomal's death. He was tortured for several days before he died. With knives."

"Horrible."

"Only for Syza. Zomal apparently enjoyed it." Lhar measured Nevin's disbelief with a grim smile. "Let me tell you about Zomal and the Seven Equals of Bjmsk. The Equals had absolute control over sixty-three percent of the population and nearly all of the planet's wealth. Hereditary control. They were naturally long-lived. Two centuries was common, even for those who were less than Equals. The cultural taboos were extensive and unusually irrational."

Lhar's expression conveyed disgust. "The Seven were taught that any use of the mind was degrading, as were all physical efforts. Except sex, their specialty. Only their siblings were allowed to have children; sex was viewed as a pastime, not a means to an end for the Equals. But even sex gets dull if that's all you're allowed to do."

Nevin started to speak, said nothing. Lhar glanced at Syza and resumed talking.

"The Seven, like other Sevens before them, had tasted the Sixty-six Ecstasies before they were fifty years old. They turned to Transcendence. That was their name for it; the rest of the galaxy called it sadism. They—" Lhar paused and his face became totally expressionless. "I'll just say that they were unusually ingenious sadists, even for Equals. Their pursuit of blood and sexual climax shocked even the Labalites at Centrex."

Nevin tried to conceive of an activity which would shock the militant pan-morality of a Labalite. He couldn't imagine one.

"Zomal—" Lhar broke off to check that Syza was indeed asleep. "Zomal was a sadist long before he met his Equals. Centrex knew it, used it; several cultures which sickened other agents were perfectly accepta-ble to Zomal. In these cultures he functioned as an integrated, very valuable agent. His personal life was a matter of indifference to Centrex so long as it didn't interfere with his work."

"But Syza wouldn't—"

"Exactly. I'm guessing now, but I'd bet my life on my accuracy—I already have. Despite her early training as a victim, she refused the role to a great extent. Zomal wasn't stupid. He kept his treatment of her within the boundaries of conventional cruelty; he needed her talents as a healer. She kept her part of the tacit bargain by staying out of his mind.

"But one day on Bjmsk she had to enter his mind or let him die. She loved him, believed he loved her. She entered. And then her carefully constructed emotional world exploded into a thousand cutting pieces. Zomal must have laughed then, the same laugh that lives in her nightmares."

Lhar sat very still, his face lined with unspoken emotions.

"I don't know if you can understand what she saw and felt and what it did to her," he said after a long time. "I don't even know if I can understand. I tried, and would have gone insane if she hadn't shoved me out of her mind."

"I almost remember a day on Miran Ridge. You took that memory away, didn't you?" said Nevin, his brown eyes haunted by sliding shadows. "And now Syza remembers all of it."

"She remembers only up to the moment she entered his mind. She doesn't remember the instant when she discovered that everything she believed in and loved was a lie, when she met her careful blindness and called it complicity, when she flowed into her lover's mind and found a sickening morass and he degraded her desperate love with his perversions."

Syza moaned and turned fitfully beneath the robes. With a stricken look at her Lhar closed his mind completely and stared at his clenched hands. He opened his fists slowly, turning his hands over and examining them as though they belonged to a stranger. "Why was I denied the pleasure of killing Zomal," he said musingly, his voice resonant with an emotion that frightened Nevin. "It would have been quick and clean and that would have been it. But Syza killed him and so it's not finished."

Nevin blindly tossed a straw braid into the brazier. Sparks burst forth and burned quickly to ash. "What are we going to do?" he asked hopelessly. "What can we do?"

"What Syza did. Sleep. When she wakes up we'll go to work on Firn and Daal."

"The river plan."

"The river plan," agreed Lhar.

"Is she strong enough?"

"No. If I could, I'd Access her off-planet so fast she'd think Tal-Lith was just another painful dream."

"Too much like Bjmsk?"

"Understatement," said Lhar, rolling onto his sleeping hides and closing his eyes to the outer world. With surprising speed he found relief in sleep.

On the third day of Lith's reign Lhar walked quietly into the room where Syza was sleeping. Nevin was braiding dyn straw. The straws squeaked between Nevin's fingers. Lhar sat next to him and grabbed a fistful of dyn. Though Lhar knew how desperately Syza needed rest, he was impatient to begin implementing their plan; he sensed that time was slipping from his grasp.

"Can't you contact Firn and Daal without Syza?" said Nevin.

"Easily. But if I tried to stop their bodies from reacting, they wouldn't wake up before burn-off. I don't have Syza's intimate finesse with nervous systems."

"And one startled squeak could be a death sentence." With a dispirited curse Nevin tossed his finished braid onto a nearby pile of gleaming straw. "And how was the great God Lith this morning? Still stiff and tired?"

"Recovering. Called me several unpleasant names and demanded that Syza attend her divine aches."

Nevin looked up in alarm.

"I told her about several unpleasant facts," continued Lhar, twisting straw with vicious satisfaction, "including Urari's terrorists."

"What did she say?"

"Nothing useful. T'Mero understood, though. He asked me when burn-off was due and I told him, not soon enough for their purposes." Lhar drew in his breath quickly and straw dropped unnoticed from his hands.

"What's wrong?"

"Notice anything different?" said Lhar in a strained voice.

Nevin glanced quickly around the room, then back at Lhar. "No."

"Breathe out and tell me what you see."

Nevin exhaled, made a startled sound. He stood quickly and walked away from the open brazier. When he was well back from any heat source he exhaled again.

"I can't see my breath," Nevin said, struggling to control the fear which surged through him. He failed. Panic thinned his voice.

"It's not actually burn-off," said Lhar, his tone

strangely indifferent. "We can expect several fluctuations before the main event."

Nevin sighed and his body visibly relaxed. Then he snapped erect as though pulled up by strings. "The river," he said hoarsely. He turned and crossed the room with urgent strides and bent over Lhar, demanding. "How much warmer is it? How long will it stay like this? Will it get any worse?"

Panic made Nevin's voice rise and fall, but Lhar heard it as at great distance, like the ululations of a mountain wind. "Too long," he said softly. "Too warm." He felt himself stretching, humming.

"We've got to cross the river now!" yelled Nevin. "Now!"

He turned and yanked at Syza before Lhar could stop him.

Nevin.

Lhar's seemingly gentle call swept through Nevin's mind like a knife. The younger man clapped his hands uselessly over his ears and moaned. Lhar maintained his hold until the initial explosion of panic began to ebb from Nevin's mind. When he was released Nevin slumped to the floor, shaken but unhurt. Lhar murmured a wordless apology in his mind and would have helped him further but he suddenly sensed T'Mero in the room. A quick desire to reach out and destroy things surged in Lhar. Even as he spun to face the hunter, he sent a harsh command to Syza: do not interfere.

"You lied to me about burn-off," hissed T'Mero. Fingers spread, he advanced on Lhar.

"Have it your way, assassin," smiled Lhar, contempt sharpening every word as he crouched to meet T'Mero's cautious stalking. "Go shake Diri out of her hides and tell her perfect-death time is near. She can dance until she drops. The sun won't care. And neither will I."

T'Mero halted, poised on the balls of his feet, undecided.

"Do you want to help your stupid glass god?"

taunted Lhar, violence in his voice and in his body.
"Then get out and beat the drum and tell the people
they can talk. Even a real Lith couldn't keep their
mouths shut about the sudden warmth."

"They'll plot against her."

"I devoutly hope so," said Lhar. "I hope they skin
her for a rug."

T'Mero did not know whether to kill Lhar or to
acknowledge the truth that was as clear as the violence in his voice. Sweat gleamed on T'Mero's dark
face and reaching hands. With a sigh that was almost
a groan, T'Mero stepped back and his hands dropped.
"You have a plan." It was a statement, not a question.

Lhar waited while the silence grew and T'Mero's
unspoken capitulation hung in the air. Reluctantly,
Lhar controlled the violence that burned in his body
and made his mind as cold as river ice.

"Yes," said Lhar, turning his back on T'Mero, "I
have a plan. I can help your pitiful attempts to control Tal-Lith." He bent over the brazier and poured
himself a bowl of ssan. Every movement, every gesture reinforced the contempt that made his voice
metallic. "I wonder if it's worth it?" he said as though
to himself. "I should let them tear you to scraps a
taman would spurn."

"Why don't you?"

"That's not the way I choose to die."

"So you'll keep everything going until the shuttle
gets here."

"The shuttle?" Lhar finished his ssan in a long
swallow and tossed the bowl aside. "There's a zero-six
mimax for escaping in the shuttle. With those odds,
all that's left is dying the way I want to."

T'Mero's body relaxed; that was a sentiment he
could understand. "So?"

"I choose to die on the other side of the river.
Among friends."

T'Mero's laughter was as unpleasant as the orange
light reflected in his unblinking eyes. "And how does
that help Lith?"

"It doesn't. It will help Diri, though."

T'Mero stopped laughing abruptly, and anger narrowed his eyes.

Indifferently Lhar outlined the plan for the river crossing, omitting only their ridiculous hope of contacting Centrex. He waited while T'Mero weighed the plan. The waiting was easy, for the plan no longer mattered. Nothing mattered in the too-warm room on a planet lit by an unstable sun.

"You hope that all the natives will cross with you," said T'Mero. "I know you."

"I don't give a zarf's reeking ass what you know."

"Only the God-haters will cross. You're welcome to them."

With uncanny speed and silence, T'Mero left the room. Nevin let out his breath in a long rush.

"You pushed him too hard," said Syza, no trace of sleep in her voice. "He almost jumped you."

"I was hoping he would. He's a dead man walking. And our treacherous Lith is a dead God dancing."

The sound of his knife sliding out of its sheath was as sharp as a cry. With the speed and strength of panic, Nevin surged to his feet and rushed at Lhar.

"If she dies we'll all die!"

Lhar delivered a single swift blow that left Nevin gasping, helpless. He caught Nevin's sagging body with one hand and eased it onto the cool stone floor.

"We're already dead," said Lhar gently.

"The—river—Centrex," gasped Nevin.

"Feel the warmth," Lhar said, his gentle tone more terrible than a shout. "Feel warmth and ice melting, time melting, gone. Feel death."

The tapestry hissed across the stone walls and Kaffi stood in the doorway, horror on her face. Lhar glanced at her, then returned his attention to Nevin, whose body was rigid with unthinking fear. He loosened Nevin's robes to ease his breathing.

"The first time you face the reality of death is always the worst," he continued calmly, ignoring Kaffi. "Accept death. You have too little life remaining to squander it on fear. Can you understand that?" Lhar reinforced his words with healing mindtouch.

Panic drained slowly from Nevin's rigid face. He drew several shuddering breaths and swallowed convulsively. "I'm all right now," he said raggedly. "All right." He smiled wanly. "I'll even help you. I'll hold her while you cut her lying throat." He laughed, choked, began to breathe steadily. "No. Too easy for her. Even the acid vats are too easy." He laughed again, a full laugh. "And I thought you were crazy!"

"I am. A sane man would kill Diri. But I'll try the river first."

Lhar looked up at Syza. A strange smile drifted over her beautiful lips. She understood how slender their chances were and she smiled. She had met death before.

"Join us, Kaffi," Lhar said casually. "Is that your own blood on your hands?"

Kaffi looked at her hands and then at his laughing gray eyes. She laughed with them. "Not mine. Theirs." Her hands clenched suddenly. "I'm mad. I came here to kill you and you say you're already dead, and I smile and laugh and listen to you talk of death as though it were merely another wind blowing in our direction." Kaffi visibly struggled to collect her volatile emotions. "Is she—" she stammered, "is Diri—"

"No."

Kaffi laughed and they heard hysteria in her voice.

Lhar eased into her helpless mind; the shock Nevin had sustained was nothing to what Kaffi had been through since Diri danced. Simple words would not help her. With gentle care he built a barrier between her uncontrolled emotions and her reeling rationality. The barrier was not difficult to build—she had unknowingly tried to build it herself—but such a division could be dangerous. For the moment, it was more dangerous to be without it.

"Aahhh," sighed Kaffi deep in her throat. "Thank you."

"It's only temporary," warned Lhar, "just to give

your mind a chance to channel your emotions. Temporary."

"So is life." Kaffi laughed again, but now there was no hysteria lurking in her tone. "Tell me," she said simply.

"First," said Syza, "we should contact Firn and Daal. We don't have time to go through it twice."

Kaffi's objections died unspoken as Lhar and Syza reached out to include her in their mesh. They felt her wonder as Syza lightly controlled the g'miran's bodies until she knew they were safe from observation. Syza held the mesh while Lhar showed Firn and Daal how to receive thoughts without effort. Very shortly a simple link was set up, with Lhar acting as relay.

Let go, Syza. They can sustain it now.

All of them sensed his silent worry about the limits to her strength.

Now, Lhar began, part of his mind monitoring the g'mirans, and part of it bringing Nevin into the mesh. *What you hear will be strange and frightening. I'm sorry. It's too late to soften the truth. Diri is not Lith. She does not have godlike powers. She can't give you children. She can't give you crops. She can't know your secret thoughts.* Lhar felt the g'mirans' relief at his last statement. *Diri can dance. She is one of the greatest dancers in the galaxy. She is also one of the greatest fools.*

Kaffi's eyes burned yellow in her dark face.

"Question, Kaffi?" he asked softly.

"Not yet. Finish."

Lhar wondered if their emotions could stand knowing the truth of the first Lith. He hesitated, then decided it was necessary to undermine whatever hold Diri still had on them.

Out in that night sky you call kylith, there are many, many planets that support life. One of those planets is called Lythe. The people of that planet are famous for their flexible bodies, their dedication to dance, and their enormous arrogance.

In the past, Lythen dancers used to ride out in— Lhar groped for a native analog to lightship but found nothing. He used the galactic word without explanation. *—lightships. They sought unknown planets where they could dance and be worshiped as gods for their skill. They found many planets. One of them was Tal, now called Tal-Lith.*

Emotions leaped from the g'mirans to Lhar. His face lined with pain, he waited for them to subside before he continued.

*Tal was tragically unique. A nearby star had exploded. A deadly . . . wind . . . swept out toward Tal. The Lythen lightship outran the wind. A Lythen dancer came to dance. She knew that many, perhaps all, of Tal's people would die in the deadly wind. She could not save them. She could only explain their tragedy in dance.

*In her own way she loved Tal's people; she wanted to die with them. She knew the time of the wind's arrival. She planned a dance, Lith's dance. The dance would raise its watchers to ecstasy. They would die fulfilled and she would die perfectly.

*The people who came with her did not want her to die. They forced her to leave. The lightship outran the storm once again. Tal could not.

The survivors of the storm remembered the alien dancer. They made her God and blamed themselves for the catastrophe.

Lhar paused in his deliberately simple narrative but the g'mirans sent no emotions to him. They were dazed, their feelings suspended. They could not deny the truth of the story spoken so simply in their minds. Nor could they wholly comprehend it.

Deep inside himself, hidden from all but Syza, Lhar gathered his strength. Lith's story was the least of what he had to tell them.

As terrible as the catastrophe was, its legacy was far more cruel. Tal-Lith's own sun became . . . diseased. The layer of air surrounding Tal-Lith was thinned. The result was slow death for Tal-Lith's people.

Lhar thought of trying to explain radiation damage, accelerated mutations, broken genes, and the vastly subtle animal instinct that recognized its own slow extinction and responded by causing infertility. There were no concepts, no words in the native tongue for him to use, yet the three Tal-Lithens moaned, and he knew his own emotions had seeped through to them.

Fewer children were born in each cycle, but not because of past sins or a stolen God. If the dancer had died here it would have been no different. Lith did not cause your slow extinction. Diri cannot cure it.

"Why did you bring us a useless God?" said Kaffi.

Lhar felt Kaffi's pain as if it were his own. The g'mirans also heard and felt; her question was like a stone flung into the still pool of their suspended emotions.

I thought that Diri would help you.

"How could she help us if she is not a God?"

*I've told you that there are many planets in kylith, the galaxy. There are also many races of man. All of us are from separate planets. Just as your i'khaners are part of the First Khaner, the planets are part of the Concord. The five of us work for the Concord. At least, three of us do; now Diri and T'Mero work only for themselves.

*One of the things our Concord does is to study unusual stars. Though the star near Tal-Lith exploded long ago, it left signs. Our people followed those signs and found Tal-Lith. Usually when a new race is discovered the Concord spends hundreds of cycles learning about the culture before they tell the new race that they are not alone in the galaxy. Usually the new race is not informed at all until Concord is certain that the dominant culture will be able to absorb Contact without being destroyed.

*But nothing concerning Tal-Lith was usual. Concord rushed the studies, rushed our training, rushed us here. Because there was no time for subtlety, they bribed Diri to dance for you. She fit your god myths; you could accept her without destroying your culture and yourselves. Because she was your God you would follow where she led, even into kylith.

You would follow her to a new planet, a planet where children would be born, a planet where your unique race would grow in numbers and knowledge, a planet where your unique culture would evolve until it had the resilience and complexity to benefit from Contact. With his simple words Lhar sent lightning images of a galaxy gravid with potential

of suns in all their radiance pouring every color of life over teeming planets, of restless singing oceans and the haunting silence between the stars, of racing clouds that were faces from his own past, barely glimpsed, wholly cherished, forever lost because

Diri had her own god myths. Instead of leading her worshipers into life she condemned them to death so that she could die perfectly with Tal-Lith as her funeral pyre.

Lhar stopped the painful narrative and waited; he found only an expectant silence. With an inward rage he realized that he would have to hurt them still more. They did not understand.

No one on this planet will live to see sunrise. The sun will flicker and leap and the river will turn to steam, and we will burn like drifcakes in a khaner fire!

The emotional storm that Lhar had expected did not come. They understood. And felt nothing. Too late he knew that he had destroyed their God, their planet, their future and their dreams. Nothing remained. And they did not hate him. He had guaranteed their annihilation, and they did not turn away in loathing. There was nothing left.

But Kaffi whispering about the jeweled colors of the stars, "water moving under different suns. Your memories are so beautiful, Lhar. You have lost so much . . ."

Mingled grief and rage tore through him. With an effort that left him trembling he gathered the shreds of his will and faced Kaffi's compassion for the galaxy and friends he had lost.

"I'm not alone in my loss," he said harshly. "I've failed your people."

A melancholy smile brushed her lips. "We would have died anyway."

A low, far-off rumble pervaded their bodies, a sound as much felt as heard. The stone floor vibrated just below the threshold of awareness, a deep hum that ached in their bones while an explosion of ice and water and rock smashed through dark canyons toward the land below. Like a curse from a savage god, the crest of the flood burst down the mountains.

When the talmare lurched in response to the battered earth, Lhar's survival reflexes overrode all emotion. He found himself in deep rapport with Syza, one mind, one body, their hands dragging Nevin and Kaffi out of the room, pushing them through the stone gate into the high fields as ancient walls crumbled and the world was subsumed in a primal roar of destruction.

They ran blindly through the darkness, seeking higher ground with the sure instinct of animals, running until the blood thundering in their ears matched the pounding of ice and rock and water. Then the fusion that was Lhar/Syza shattered as pain poured through it, twisting agonies of violent death, bodies broken, lungs filled with icy water, splintered bones, and crushed flesh shrieking . . .

Silence.

Lhar tasted sand and dirt on his tongue, felt blood hot on his raw hands, felt stones sharp against his cheek and heaving chest, and knew he was alive. In the long shadows of the racing moon he saw the city and the cold gleaming flood. He stared, unbelieving, at the distant water, remembering how it had seemed to close his throat and lungs, the water that he had not tasted, the bones he had not broken, his body whole and the city below, black stone shapes beyond the reach water. He and the city were alive.

He looked to his left, at Nevin and Kaffi huddled together. To his right lay Syza, a shadow with dulled eyes reflecting the heedless moon, a face overwhelmed by pain, a face that had known inhuman agony. Separate. Even as he reached out to her mind he realized what had happened. The maimed and dying flesh he had felt was real; the deaths were real; the relentless pain was what a healer felt when defenses were forgotten.

Syza.

There was no response. Hesitantly he established minimal contact, braced for a tearing resurgence of pain. There was none. He felt a deep relief that her defenses were working again and that he would not have to try to separate Syza's mind from the terrible influx of pain and death.

Syza.

Hear his laughter?

I hear ice grinding over rocks.

He's down there torturing them. I reversed Decline and he is whole and strong. So strong. Hear them screaming. He should have died . . . I saved him. For this?

She rose slowly and seemed to drift away from him, gliding down to the city where nightmare and reality fused in a primal cry of pain.

Syza.

She was gone as though pulled by the racing moon. He staggered to his feet, pursuing her, a darker black slipping through changing densities of midnight, losing her.

Syza!

Pain convulsed him, threw him to the ground with careless strength as the taste of blood and dirt spread through his mouth. From the blackness ahead he heard Syza's agonized moan. He breathed shallowly, tensed against another onslaught of pain. Pebbles clicked; Syza was walking. He did not reach out to

269

her, did not tear again the fragile veil that kept his mind and Tal-Lith's pain separate from her. Such pain could kill.

Numbly he rose and followed her toward the city. Behind him came stumbling sounds, Nevin and Kaffi helping each other through the darkness. He did not wait for them.

Compound walls rose black above the dry ground. He saw Syza in the flickering light of a single torch. Silently he ran to her, stopped when he was just behind her. She did not notice him. Her pace did not change as she skirted the walls, unerringly choosing the shortest path slanting down toward the pool of night where all torches were quenched and screams eddied across rapidly falling floodwater.

The river was no longer two days distant. Lhar tried to calculate the mass of water that had raced down the shallow bowl of the valley. He could not. He could only be grateful that most of Tal-Senet was on high ground. The area below, the granaries and fields and river gardens, were gone beneath the flood's sullen mercury gleam. As fast as the water could batter through the narrow Gate, the next lower plateau would be innundated, and the next and the next, until the flood finally thinned and expired on the plains of Namaylith.

Lhar wrenched his mind back to the darkness where the living wept and cursed and screamed at an impotent God to end their suffering. Syza turned suddenly, her robes blooming over the rubble of a house. He saw the pale form of a leg, a hand. He bent and began heaving aside slabs of broken stone. The bruised outline of a woman was revealed. Syza knelt and touched her; he sensed a soundless fall of power from Syza and the woman rose, whole.

Syza turned away, drawn irresistably to the darkness where no torches glowed. Lhar followed her. Behind him walked Nevin and Kaffi and the woman Syza had healed.

They walked beyond the khaner walls, beyond the

270

maze of paths connecting tiny straw and stone huts to market streets. People moved aimlessly around the streets, unhurt but for the fear that clawed in their minds. Syza walked through the doorway of a building where candles guttered over stunned faces, and a bleeding woman cursed Lith as she held her broken lover in her arms.

Power flowed, lingered. The woman looked up in time to see a flash of green eyes, a swirl of bronze hair; then her lover spoke her name. Lhar stood aside as Syza returned to the streets. When he moved to follow her, the people in the crowded room silently moved after him.

From moonlight to torchlight to blackness she went, pain leading her to the people in greatest need. She stopped often in the oozing streets and in buildings, touching, healing, her tears silver and orange in the changing light, the dark drawn lines of pain on her face, unchanging. The silent crowd moved with her step for step, swelling with each healing, each life saved. Its members removed rubble that barricaded her progress, comforted those whose injuries were minor, followed their healer with gentle, silent tenacity.

Lhar sensed the undercurrents of awe that flowed among minds, unifying them, currents that swelled in power with each new person, each new silence. The people followed Syza through buried streets and dripping buildings, followed her until she reached the swollen edge of the river and turned back to thread through another part of the city. Only Lhar noticed that she walked more slowly now; only he noticed that her body trembled like grass in a wind. With all the delicacy his mind could command he reached out to her.

. . . Syza . . . ?

*I'll find him please don't scream I'll find him findhim . . . I'll kill him kill him killhim. Noooooo I'll heal, I'll heal *heal.**

He called out to her, but she was far away in an

alien room talking to a man who was dead. He held
the link, undemanding, and swung like a pendant between Bjmsk and Tal-Lith, Zomal and the flood,
dying and healing, with Syza's agony the only constant in the two worlds, her waning strength the only
measure of passing time.

*Can't stop the pain any longer. Zomal . . . can't.
Unless.*

(why are you laughing?)

(Come into my mind. I have something to)

(No.)

(tell you.)

I am a healer.

Lhar watched a dazed man stare up at the eyes
and face of the woman whose hands had taken pain
from him as the sun takes darkness from the sky.
Arms reached out from the throng behind Syza and
plucked the healed man out of the rubble; the man
and his friends blended without hesitation into the
rippling mass of silent people. Currents leaped,
twined, unity and power growing and Syza's strength
fading inevitably until she had less life than some of
those she healed, but still she walked and touched
and gave life, driven by her own need and a dead
man and the silent massive presence of those who
followed.

Lhar felt the unthinking power of the quiet people
filling the streets, minds brushing in partial links, as
undisciplined as sheet lightning and far more powerful. Even now they began to focus, currents of their
power reached through Tal-Senet, awakening . . .

"You're killing her!"

No one answered his shout, for no one had heard;
only he saw death waiting in Tal-Senet's darkness,
waiting for an exhausted healer. He turned toward
the crowd that overflowed the streets and filled door-
ways and alleys and paths like a rising tide suspended in the moment before it broke over the shore.

Help her!

Lhar felt a flash of strength, familiar; Firn/Daal/

Kaffi grappling, trying to respond, trying to answer him.

The throng parted, and flowed around him. Syza walked on and he ran to her beyond the edge of the people, but still their power flexed like a thing alive . . . filaments of potency were reflected in her staring green eyes.

She staggered and he touched her and the frail link between them blossomed suddenly, resonant with unexpected power.

He's close. Hear him?

Zomal is dead.

No. I hear him laughing. He has something he wants to tell me.

He told you a long time ago.

He did? Then why is he still bothering me?

Syza's questions held a child's plaintive confusion.

You're very tired, Syza. You've worked very hard. You can rest now.

No. Zomal needs me. I can't let him feel pain and the Equals are so cruel. He told me that if he doesn't hurt he won't answer their questions.

What are they asking him?

The 'locubes. He never should have brought them but he did and the Equals found them. He smashed the 'locubes and they got mad.

Holocubes? Off-planet holocubes?

Yes. Impatience. *Weren't you listening, Quirl?*

Lhar kept the knowledge that he was not Quirl from disrupting the contact. *Sorry.*

But I can't . . . hold him much longer.

Let go, Syza. He felt sorrow and pity. *Let go.*

Contact thinned. He had told her something so at odds with her memory that it had shaken her. He must strengthen the contact . . . and then he knew what the unknown agent Quirl must have told Syza to do.

Kill him.

No!

Zomal isn't worth a planet. Kill him!

"I am a *healer!*"

Syza sagged against him, her green eyes blindly searching the city ahead as though she had the power to see through stone. With a shuddering sigh she straightened and walked on. The link was still there, but like Syza it was changed, distant. Tal-Lith was stretching her inexorably, stretching her beyond resilience, thinning her down to a core of survival stripped of hope and love and song. Only the past remained, a sore oozing pestilence.

The tidal crowd lapped gently at his unmoving body. If he resisted them they would flow around him, and Syza would be alone with her past. He caught up with her and again took her hand. Contact bloomed. Zomal's screams echoed in his mind and she was screaming

> (You told them!)

> she had to stop the pain
before it killed both of them she had to go into his mind

and she fell to her knees and the tide pressed softly against them, discreetly urging, irresistible. Something waited ahead in a lake of torches, where black and silver and orange were mingling. Go on, nudged the tide. Go and see T'Mero crouched over the silver form of Lith. Go and help us decide as you remember . . .

T'Mero looked up and saw them standing together.

"Heal her!" cried T'Mero, his voice twisting like the light. "Heal her or I'll let them kill you too!"

Syza swayed in the storm of his demands, their demands, the past. Lhar measured the surge of people gathered around Diri, felt the immense currents stirring in the faceless mass behind him; he sweated in sudden fear that the two forces would explode in an orgy of death.

T'Mero screamed at Syza again.

"She can't hear you," said Lhar. "She can't hear anything but a dead man screaming."

Diri moaned as pain shot through her wounded

body. T'Mero looked away from Syza's frightening eyes and talked softly, as though sound could hurt the bleeding woman at his feet.

"She wanted to walk in the streets and hear the silence of worship. They didn't know it was Lith. I killed them . . . all of them, but I could not put blood back in Her body. She knew. She shook the Ramparts and sent death."

"Urari's terrorists," said Lhar, voice hoarse with too many emotions . . . and pity for the graceless huddle of flesh that was Diri.

The people surrounding Diri moaned confirmation and whispered prayers for Lith's forgiveness, prayed that death would rise and dance for them again.

"They know that Diri is a god of death . . ." His whisper fell between the silence behind him and the prayers ahead of him, until Syza's climbing scream drowned silence and prayer in spreading waves of fear and hate and he held her as she screamed, and knew that it was too late—it had always been too late— past and present fused in screaming as they all descended into Zomal's

mind seething ghastly faces gruesome death
(They know.)
(Yes. Now let me tell you)
(No I don't want to know no)
dry laughter blowing from his face
(Pain is the only friend)
(No)
(Agony is the only lover)
(NO)
(Death is the only consummation)
naked and desiccated and laughing, curling and crackling
(Just one more thing to tell you a grand joke Syza)
curling and rustling and cracking laughter
(A healer helped me kill a planet—unique race will die—healed unto death.)

> laughter cracking and spewing deadly dry
spores spreading
> (thank you little healer you were a faithful tool)
> his laughter
> quiet and deadly
> growing in me
> drying
> me
> (I can heal all of you all of you I WILL
HEAL YOU)
> and cracking
> them

Lhar closed his eyes as her horrified litany seared through minds and her body shook against his as she felt the blows of eight deaths, seven Equals, and Zomal.

I wanted to heal you; why wouldn't you let me.

Syza . . . Syza. You didn't know that forced healing would kill.

Meant to heal.

Yes.

Wouldn't let me.

Yes.

*Forced . . . *

Lhar whispered against her hair, felt it fall, cool, across his fingers. He knew he should care whether she had forced Diri's healing, killed as she had killed on Bjmsk, but he cared only that Syza would return and call his name.

An exhalation like a soft wind stirred Diri's followers. Lhar opened his eyes reluctantly . . . saw Diri standing in all her silver grace. He hoped that she was sane, healed in mind as well as body, but the silvery smile had lost none of its arrogance, none of its cruelty. Diri had accepted healing only as a necessity for the perfect death she desired. She pirouetted before them, torchlight flowing like liquid fire over her sleek strength in a foretaste of the final sunrise.

Lhar closed his eyes, sickened at what he had

276

brought to Tal-Lith. A whisper that could have been his name slowly seeped into his numbed mind. He looked and saw Diri's lips moving, but he could hear nothing except the tidal wave stirring behind him, its moment of suspension past, as unknown links condensed and locked him into seamless Unity while a voice spoke in his mind calling his name—Syza's call—and he knew he must find her among the links or both of them would vanish in the linking of the massed minds.

Lhar/Syza huddled in fusion while all the futility of Tal-Lith swept through them, a dark sea of rage breaking on the shores of grief, each wave a separate cry for life; two minds fused in a survival reflex stronger than the remorseless sea of Unity. There was a shattering instant of silence before the inexorable waves took up a new rhythm, pounding, beating at the two fused minds that were a bubble defying Unity. There was no escape short of death, but Lhar/Syza wanted death no more than did the raging Unity.

Escape.

Access.

YES.

In desperation Lhar sent the coded thought out to the stars, but without his psitran the thought expired far short of its goal. He tried again and again, strength diminishing, Syza slipping away, and he held onto her and himself and poured strength into the coded call to a monitor gone deaf. Unreachable, like the stars. No psitran, no focus, no strength. Nothing but failure, waves breaking, calling, breaking and calling his name in a rolling swell of sound: use us—*use us* —USE US.

Lhar reeled with the monstrous call, the tolling resonant will to live, and Syza's haunting song

(use them as I used them).

Slowly, with infinite caution, Lhar eased the barriers he and Syza had erected against the seething Unity. Its strength poured through, overpowering him.

He fought against it; too much too much he needed a drink and they were drowning him; the power increased and a terrible question belled in his mind. Shock-waves of power pealed through him, questioning, searching for the singer/healer who had used a fragment of the awesome Unity, used it unknowingly to control when her own strength was spent, and to heal when she had no strength, and then she was with him, flashing and burning as they fought to channel uncontrolled Unity

NOW

The coded pulse of thought/energy tripped monitors to Centrex and beyond. A babble of galactic minds demanded to know the emergency. Out of chaos, linkages condensed, and all but one mesh faded. Twelve minds worked as one to meet the torrential power of Unity, asking *What are you?*

LINK WITH US

Lhar/Syza struggled desperately to ride a tidal wave of potency gone mad until they felt the trained mesh of the galactics touch them. Lhar/Syza snatched at the contact and dragged themselves out of the maelstrom of Unity. Lhar absorbed the sensuous beauty of the most superbly balanced group mesh he had ever experienced; Syza's joyous song shimmered through the linked minds. Surprise and pleasure radiated as the galactics recognized the Chanteuse.

Lhar tried to give the mesh all that had happened, all that Tal-Lith needed, tragedy and hope and death and Unity, but it was too much, inchoate. He adjusted the linkage between Syza and himself until they flowed evenly through the mesh; they would have to explain slowly.

Are any of you Contact?

The desperate urgency of Lhar's question relayed far more than simple mindspeech.

Not yet. Tell us what you need.

Accesses. They're already set up. We're on Tal-Lith, sector G12-6y. An emergency Contact. I miscalculated a pivotal factor. Syza's protest swept

278

through the mesh. He overrode her. *Unless we get through to Contact a race will die.*

The balance of the mesh shifted, condensed along new lines. Another mind flowed in, a mind Lhar recognized. Yarle, Contact Supervisor. Lhar did not pause to greet his friend.

The sun is worse than we calculated. Diri blew on us. Ram the Accesses through at the northeast edge of the city as planned.

Lhar sensed the rapid relay of orders even as Yarle asked questions. Lhar answered the pouring questions curtly.

All we need are continuous flow Accesses.

Not enough power.

Tap the sun.

It will nova.

Lhar performed rapid calculations that the mesh followed with wordless respect.

*Acceptable risk. Tap it. Get these people off *now!**

With his demand Lhar relayed the sensory storm of an undisciplined mass mesh. The galactic mesh shuddered, and there were no more suggestions; accidental Unity was a force more feared than nova.

You're in contact with this Unity?

Their choice, not mine.

The first Access just went through. Relay to Unity: disperse or your individuals will be destroyed.

The galactic mesh gathered itself and Lhar/Syza were on the crest of the tidal wave again, screaming to a force that might or might not comprehend. In the instant before their minds would break, the galactic mesh recalled them, examined them, soothed them, released them.

Reluctantly Lhar/Syza fell away from the mesh, braced for the tearing onslaught of Unity. But nothing came. Unity was there; they could sense its restive power. Silence.

They opened their eyes and saw Diri finish her pirouette and knew that their long struggle with Unity had taken only an instant.

Diri leaped, silver, and the nearby hills were limned in the blue glow of a huge Access. She leaped again, her fluid fingers speaking to the yellow moon, and another Access bloomed, then another and another until they made a blue arc around the edge of Tal-Senet.

Don't they know? thought Lhar, raggedly. *Do we have to touch that seething . . .*

No. Listen.

With a long rustling sigh Unity dissolved. He could still sense the currents of awe and the indomitable urge to life that was deeply burned into the individual minds. But the geometrical increase of power that came with mesh was gone. Where Unity had seethed, thousands of people now awoke as from a deep dream.

Singly and by twos and threes the people of Tal-Lith sifted past Diri's leaping silver dance. Lhar watched them and thought of all that must be done, of supplies and tools to be gathered, the ill or injured or exhausted to be helped, the herds which had survived that must be driven through an Access, and so much more . . . and he did not even have the strength to move his tongue in his mouth.

You don't have to, Lhar. Their Unity went beyond Tal-Senet. It saw and comprehended and disposed. They don't need us any longer. We're a catalyst after the reaction is complete. We're free.

They stood close together while people walked slowly through the darkness toward the blue dawn pouring down from the hills. Many of the people paused, touching Syza or Lhar fleetingly, then walked on to the beckoning glow. Only a few of them glanced at Diri's lithe spins; fewer still noticed the motionless thousands that still ringed her dance.

So many. Anger and sadness and failure were woven together in his mind. *I can't leave them here to die.*

Then they will die unwilling on Seytal. You can't . . . force.

280

Zomal's laughter hung between them, an echo that had lost its awful power. He was dead.

Pure blue radiance washed over Tal-Senet as Accesses hummed to full power. Lhar and Syza watched dark rivers flow uphill and spill into blue light, felt time turn slowly around them, turning and transcendent blue light spinning, liquid dancer leaping to welcome death while life flowed by, ignored.

At last Syza and Lhar let the gentle touch of passing people draw them away from Lith's impervious grace. They walked through Tal-Senet's dying echoes, through fields where sand whispered with the passage of men and animals. Dust motes burned blue sparks around them as they stepped into an Access's potent blaze. Space lanced through them, falling without motion until a new world condensed beneath their feet, a world nine thousand light years removed from Tal-Lith.

Together they looked back, saw only blue radiance dividing two worlds, wondered if any would remember and mourn Skandiri-Li, torchlight caressing her leaping silver body, torchlight sinuous over dark worshipers' ecstasy . . .

torchlight devoured as naked incandescence answered the prayer of a dead God dancing.

SCIENCE FICTION AND FANTASY
FROM AVON ◭ BOOKS

☐ All My Sins Remembered Joe Haldeman	39321	$1.95
☐ All Flesh Is Grass Clifford D. Simak	39933	$1.75
☐ Behold the Man Michael Moorcock	39982	$1.50
☐ Cities In Flight James Blish	41616	$2.50
☐ Cryptozoic Brian Aldiss	33415	$1.25
☐ Forgotten Beasts of Eld Patricia McKillip	42523	$1.75
☐ The Investigation Stanislaw Lem	29314	$1.50
☐ The Lathe of Heaven Ursula K. LeGuin	38299	$1.50
☐ Lord of Light Roger Zelazny	33985	$1.75
☐ Macroscope Piers Anthony	45690	$2.25
☐ Memoirs Found In A Bathtub Stanislaw Lem	29959	$1.50
☐ Mindbridge Joe Haldeman	33605	$1.95
☐ Mind of My Mind Octavia E. Butler	40972	$1.75
☐ Moon Pool A. Merritt	39370	$1.75
☐ Omnivore Piers Anthony	40527	$1.75
☐ Orn Piers Anthony	40964	$1.75
☐ Ox Piers Anthony	41392	$1.75
☐ Pilgrimage Zenna Henderson	36681	$1.50
☐ Rogue Moon Algis Budrys	38950	$1.50
☐ Song for Lya and Other Stories George R. Martin	27581	$1.25
☐ Starship Brian W. Aldiss	22588	$1.25
☐ Sword of the Demon Richard A. Lupoff	37911	$1.75
☐ 334 Thomas M. Disch	42630	$2.25

Available at better bookstores everywhere, or order direct from the publisher.

AVON BOOKS, Mail Order Dept., 224 W. 57th St., New York, N.Y. 10019

Please send me the books checked above. I enclose $_____ (please include 50¢ per copy for postage and handling). Please use check or money order—sorry, no cash or C.O.D.'s. Allow 4-6 weeks for delivery.

Mr/Mrs/Miss _____

Address _____

City _____ State/Zip _____

SSF 6-79